Village People

(by)

Harold McGlumpher

This is a work of fiction. Any resemblance to actual persons, living or dead, or to real events is purely coincidental — except in cases where it is entirely intentional.

For the residents of Al Hamra Village

Friday 13th June

Chapter 1

Robbie O'Malley

Detective Sergeant Robbie O'Malley stood bleary-eyed and half-naked on the second-floor balcony of his rented Airbnb, staring out over the Persian Gulf. Below, a teenager shouted for a dog that had slipped its collar, while poolside, a skinny blonde in her early twenties rubbed sun lotion into her aging husband's flabby, sunburnt back.

The morning call to prayer had woken him — hungover, head pounding — at 5.30. Now, at 8.30, it was almost forty degrees, and the piledrivers had taken over from the preacher. The humidity, pushing ninety percent, made it feel even hotter. By midday, it was expected to hit fifty. Robbie wondered why anyone in their right mind would be out walking a dog — let alone sunbathing.

He retreated quickly to the shade of his umbrella and the artificial breeze of the swamp cooler, which offered some small measure of relief. It was an older model, and the drone of the fan and water pump made listening to his favourite radio station, Galway Bay FM, almost impossible. When he finally checked his phone, he saw six missed calls from an unknown number.

'Oh, fuck off,' he muttered. He'd come here to escape — from texts and emails, midnight phone calls, unwanted knocks at his door… from life in general, and work in particular.

'What a marvellous little invention,' he mused, lifting the cold bottle from the beer condom he'd brought back from Bangkok earlier that year. His thoughts drifted to that unforgettable trip — the haze of weed, cheap beer, and Nong.

He had honestly believed — albeit briefly — that he'd been given another chance at true love. Maybe his final chance. But now he wondered: had he really? Was it his fault it had ended? Had he squandered it again with his drinking, gambling, and gallivanting? Or had she simply been playing him? A meal ticket, perhaps. A bit of harmless fun.
It might have been harmless to her — but he hadn't escaped unscathed.

As he slugged from the bottle, he fumbled with his other hand, trying to fish a cigarette from the packet of Chesterfields on the glass table. With his thirst temporarily quenched and the cigarette lit; he picked up his phone again.

He would normally block unknown numbers, but he was on holiday. What if it was the Airbnb host? Though they'd probably contact him through the app. Maybe it was the tour guide he'd booked for the desert safari, or the taxi driver meant to take him back to the airport in two weeks. He was sure he'd saved all their numbers — and if he had, surely their names would show up.

Then he noticed the small message icon at the top of the screen.

'Strange,' he mumbled. 'Who the fuck sends texts anymore?'

His fingerprint, damp from beer and humidity, wouldn't unlock the phone, so he entered the four-digit PIN — 1111. The message, sent at 1.45 a.m., read:

ANSWER YOUR PHONE

This time, the sender's identity was clear — Har de Luc.

Chapter 2

The Waldorf Astoria

Robbie stared at the phone. What was this? Some sort of prank? *Who the fuck was Har de Luc?* And where the fuck had he been last night? It was all pretty hazy — always a sign of a good scoop. Sure, wasn't he half-cut getting off the plane? He'd been in some swanky hotel bar... What the fuck was its name? Bits and pieces were coming back. Some golfers. Some expats. Happy hour. That was it! He'd met a few expats who'd promised to take him for a round of golf. Could Har de Luc have been one of them?

Having spent years working for the Fraud Investigation Unit, he was well aware of the rising number of fraudulent calls and scams that targeted innocent, unsuspecting people every day. The 'call-back' scam was the latest, where returning a call connected you to a high-premium number, resulting in exorbitant fees. He also knew that scammers had become sophisticated enough to include bogus names with their phishing texts. He was not about to be scammed!

Something in the back of his mind, however, told him this was no prank, no scam. His instincts told him that something more sinister was at play. He hesitated. He usually trusted his gut, at least when it came to work. It wasn't quite so black and white when it came to women. Should he trust this sense of unease? Should he act at once, risk being scammed and looking foolish, or wait, and do some digging?

Robbie never wore a watch — he hated this new trend of smartwatches. What possible good could come from counting your steps and calories?

Though his own waistline had been expanding recently, he despised fat people even more. 'Lazy bastards,' he'd mutter. 'Just go for a walk and eat less,' was his typical advice.

Alexa informed him that it was now nine-thirty. He could go to the local police, but he was reeking of drink, and what on earth would they make of his intoxicated demeanour? This was supposedly a dry country, after all. Then there was the language issue: he spoke no Arabic beyond 'As-salamu alaykum' and the occasional 'shukran,' which would hardly be enough to convey his concerns.

He'd only been in that hotel, so he had to start there — the scene of the crime — crimes against the liver at least. What was it again? *Walton? Walrus? Walmer?* Robbie had been getting more forgetful lately. He liked to blame the drink, but in his darker moments, he prayed that it wasn't something more sinister. There was some family history. *Fuck it.*

'Alexa, fancy hotels in Al Hamra, Ras Al Khaimah.'

From the list she provided he recognised the Waldorf Astoria — a five-star hotel overlooking Al Hamra golf club.

He downed what little was left of his beer and jumped in the shower, hoping the cool water might sober him up a little and bring some clarity to the situation. But even on a cold setting, the water was roasting. It was all he could do to quickly scrub his face and bits and bobs, and he was sweating again by the time he fetched his towel from the horse on the balcony!

Fumbling through his hand luggage, which he had yet to unpack, he found the wrinkled white cotton shirt that he picked up in duty-free before leaving Dublin airport yesterday. The heat would surely iron it out over the course of the day. He pulled it on over a pair of khaki shorts, slipped into his YSL sandals, grabbed his phone, keys, Chesterfields, and matching YSL sunglasses, and headed downstairs to hail a taxi.

Taxis weren't as easy to find as he'd expected. After waiting a short while in the air-conditioned lobby, the security guard gave him a number to call. Five minutes later, he was on his way to the Waldorf Astoria, hoping to jog his memory and, if luck was on his side, meet his new acquaintances from the previous evening.

He hadn't realized just how grandiose the hotel had been last night. Perhaps it was the jetlag, or the ten miniature Jack Daniels he had consumed on the flight, but wow, this place was impressive. The lobby was spacious, blending Arabian opulence with contemporary design elements. The high ceilings, adorned with intricate chandeliers, gave a feeling of space and airiness, and he could nearly see his reflection in the polished marble floors.

For all its luxury, however, this was not Robbie's kind of place. He felt uncomfortable in these kinds of surroundings. Somewhere in the recesses of his mind his low self-esteem and Catholic guilt whispered that he didn't deserve such indulgences. Dark, dingy watering holes were more to his liking. He could get away with more in the shadows—nobody noticed his drunken antics, his blotchy red face — or so he told himself.

A sharp left turn took him down to the Lexington Bar & Grill, where he'd indulged in happy hour — and beyond — the previous evening. *Grill?* He hadn't noticed any evidence of one. Last night, the place had been buzzing, but now, at this hour, it was dead. Where was the early morning club, he wondered — the pissheads, the jakies, the real drinkers?

'Can I help you, sir?' enquired the suited and booted waiter.

Looking rather displeased, Robbie asked 'Where is everyone? It was packed last night!'

'Last night was Gentleman's night, sir. It's always busy on a Thursday night, but we don't have much of a day trade here. Is there someone you're looking for?'

'I was hoping to catch up with some of the guests from last night. Do you know where I might find them, Gilbert? Robbie asked, squinting to read the name on the mandatory badge pinned to the waiter's waistcoat.

'Is your eye okay, sir? Maybe you got some dust in it?' replied Gilbert.

Jesus, here we go, thought Robbie. *Another fuckin' one.*

'Guests, Gilbert?'

'Sorry, sir. Those men usually drink in the Bay,' Gilbert replied, his tone a mix of embarrassment, apology, and curiosity.

'The beach bar?' a miffed Robbie replied. They hadn't looked like men who would wear budgie smugglers — more like smugglers of far more lucrative contraband. 'This bloody language is doing my head in,' he muttered under his breath.

'No, sir, the Bay bar is in the golf club. It's a five-minute walk, but I can arrange for one of our porters to take you in a buggy,' Gilbert offered helpfully.

Two minutes later, Robbie was climbing the steep steps to the golf club.

Thursday 12th June

Chapter 3

The Village

Har de Luc was, quite literally, down on his luck. He had been hammered eight-nil by the giant Finn Gerino the previous evening in a first-to-five encounter on the potholed, beer-stained cloth of the free pool table at his local hostelry. Har was a sore loser and had never liked Finn; he was a perennial thorn in his side. To compound this, Finn — or Finnian — was English, and there was no one Har hated losing to more than an Englishman, particularly that 'English cunt.' Angry words had been exchanged; security had been called and Har had stormed off without paying his bill again.

Of his many excuses would be the annoying little brats that now frequented the place since the closure of the yacht club. The place was more like a creche than a boozer these days, and that pissed Har off, as it did many of the loyal patrons who had long frequented the place. The newcomers from across the water had ruined it. They'd swan in with their fancy four-by-four prams, order half a Guinness, and dump their kids on whomever might care. Har de Luc did not! Not one fucking iota did he care. 'Never have, never will' was one of his favourite maxims… especially after a thumping like that.

The eight-nil scoreline was testament to de Luc's thrawn nature. He could never accept defeat and always convinced himself that he could, and would, turn things around — if only his luck would change. But change it rarely did, and it certainly hadn't last night. He was on a downward spiral alright. He knew it, his friends knew it, Finn knew it... hell the whole damn village knew it.

That was another thing that pissed de Luc off: the "village"! He'd grown up in a village — a real village — with real people who had real problems — not one of these man-made excuses for a village. Where was the football pitch, the park, the chipper, the butcher, the post office, the betting shop? What the fuck were they thinking when they contrived to build this godforsaken hellhole? This shithole. Where was a kid supposed to do his drinking, his smoking, his shagging? Eh! Where?

'Fucking kip of a joint,' and he didn't mind telling anyone who would listen.

Fewer and fewer of those people remained, however. The well was running dry, and so was his throat when he finally hauled his sorry carcass off the couch late that morning.

Coffee just seemed to be too much trouble and, given no one was around, there was no need to keep up the pretence that he always started his day like most normal people. Kicking empty cans out of his way, and fumbling his way past the half-eaten, half-empty tinfoil containers that retained the remnants of last night's delivery, he made a beeline for the fridge.

Har hadn't spent much money furnishing his apartment, but his fridge was a stylish thirty-six-inch French door smart-fridge with high shelves to avoid the need for stooping, wine drawers, self-filling top-shelf ice buckets, deep shelves ready-designed to hold pizza boxes, and a lockable fourth drawer with an adjustable temperature control to store and protect his beloved cheese collection.

He grabbed a cold can of stout, rinsed the pint glass he had stolen from the pub the previous evening, and with one steady pour delivered a near-perfect pint. If there was anything that Har was good at, it was mixology and tending bar.

'Priorities,' as he often reminded himself.

He repeated this routine multiple times before, eventually making his way down the pier to catch the ferry to the local.

'This used to be a nice pier,' he mused to himself.

Now, it lay in a pile of rubble. In days not so long gone, there had been a chipper, a burger joint, an ice cream parlour, a café, and a wine bar. How he missed that little wine bar — the cheap booze, the lovely cheese. He even let out a rare wee giggle thinking of the crazy landlady, 'Mad' Mavis.

He would sit out on the pier on a cool winter's evening, beer in hand, smoking cheap cigarettes, watching rich people get off their superyachts and tourists line up to be taken on deep-sea fishing trips. The boats were laden with crates of beer — crates that would return empty, if they returned at all. Many ended up wrapped around the neck of some poor turtle or another unfortunate sea creature native to the Persian Gulf.

Fuckin' tourists!

To Har's delight, there wasn't a tourist in sight. This was no crisp winter evening — it was a blistering summer afternoon, and the streets were dead. Sweat was pissing out of him by the time he reached the last jetty on the pier — yet another thing that fucked him off.

The ferry used to run from the first jetty, right across from the card-operated metal gate meant to keep undesirables out of the gated community he'd called home for the past five years. Not that it ever worked. The card sensor rarely read anything, and the gate was usually wedged open with a rock or whatever else people could find. Failing that, any half-wit could stroll in through the barriered car entrance.

After they tore down the yacht club, the powers that be moved the ferry to the furthest jetty. The move made no sense — but then, common sense was always in short supply, whether in the running of the village or the pub.

Upon boarding, only his trusty companion, Top Shelf Terry, was there, waiting for departure. Terry was retired, having been a Headmaster in St. Mary's, the local Catholic school. These days, he earned his beer money as a part-time private investigator — trivial stuff, mostly: lost cats, cheating wives, unpaid loans, and the like.

Both men always took the afternoon three forty-five ferry to ensure they'd make the four o'clock happy hour kickoff — unless they were rolling over from the previous night or hadn't been to bed at all. In those cases, living in this cashless hellhole, they'd order a Careem taxi, since the ferry didn't start running until three p.m. That had arguably been Har's first of many mistakes yesterday.

People generally drove to their establishment of choice, as police checks in this part of the country were almost non-existent. Instead, authorities relied on visible signs of intoxication or anonymous tip-offs to catch offenders. As a result, drink-driving was rampant.

However, it was the need to call the police after an accident that proved the downfall of both Har and Top Shelf. Not that either had made the call themselves. Har even tried to flee the scene on foot but was so inebriated that he ran in circles, ending up right back where he started — five police cars waiting.

As the small monohull ferry made its short trip from the marina to the golf club, a gentle breeze lifted the relative coolness of the water, and for a few brief minutes, the worries of the world seemed to drift away from both men.

'This is the life, eh?' exclaimed Har. He had been lost in a daydream, but his thoughts somehow found their way into words. The ferry crossing always reminded him of proposing to his wife — ex-wife — on the Rhine back in happier times.

Before the mooring lines had even been secured, they hopped over the fender gap onto the small wooden pier and back into the stifling heat. The captain shook his head.

'One day, I'm telling you, one day,' he muttered, just loud enough for both men to hear — referring to the very real possibility, nay, probability, that someone was bound to fall in — especially given the state of some passengers, particularly on the return leg of the journey.

Although it was five minutes early, the staff knew the two well enough to offer them happy hour prices.

Pint in hand, Har wandered out to join the boys at the round table on the golf club's patio, where the pub was tucked away — typically hidden, like all places selling alcohol in the Gulf. Hotels, resorts, private clubs — no shortage of them. Locals knew exactly where to find the cheap deals: happy hours, buy-one-get-one offers, ladies' nights, gents' nights, or cheese and wine evenings.

Ah! The cheese and wine night. Har had completely done the dog on it again last night, and everyone knew it. A lot of damage could be done with a cheese platter and two hours of unlimited grape!

The boys used to sit on a low, sunken beer bench but had recently moved to the round table, where they could control the numbers and keep the riff-raff out — not that they'd ever admit this. For all his faults, Har was always afforded a seat at the round table.

There was no one here today, but it was early, and the golfers usually timed their rounds to finish just as happy hour kicked off. Double-handed, to prevent the shakes which had now set in from spilling his pint, he took a large slug of his Guinness and waited for their impending arrival, which, it is fair to say, he was not particularly looking forward to.

Chapter 4

The cheese & wine

Big Tam Pieman was the first to hit the eighteenth green, smashing a stoater of a fairway wood from 250 yards out. He was also the first to appear in the clubhouse, rosy-cheeked after knocking back eight cans of cider during the round. Tam had cut his drinking teeth in the pubs and clubs of Glasgow and was a hardy man. At six foot three, eight cans were barely a drop in the ocean for him.

'Ye were at it again, H,' said Tappie, as he was sometimes known.

'At what?' retorted a somewhat annoyed Har de Luc.

'The fuckin' cheese 'n' wine — or should I say the wine 'n' wine?' chortled Tappie. 'You couldnae hit a fuckin' baw. Big Finn thumped you eight-nil.'

'Did he fuck,' snapped Har. 'And it wis first tae five anyways. He wis fuckin' lucky an aw. Ma cue baw kept going doon.'

'Lucky me erse,' guffawed Tappie.

Slowly, the rest of the boys trickled in, one by one. Auld Davie — never one to shower after a game — was next, followed by Dick and Mick. Each, in turn, took their wee digs at de Luc for his antics the previous evening.

"It was those wee fuckin' brats," was the best Har could muster.

'Why do you drink that shite?' enquired Tappie.

'You know why.'

'Naw, I dinnae. Tell us again.'

'For fuck's sake… when I wis growing up in France —'

Har was cut short as the whole table erupted into fits of laughter.

'Shut the fuck up, the lot o' ye,' barked Har. 'I need another fuckin' pint. Where is that useless cunt when you need him?'

At that precise moment, Rej — the Pakistani waiter — appeared, wearing his customary white slacks that rode halfway up his shins. It may have been a fashion statement, but the common consensus was that he had drawn the short straw (and the short trousers) when staff uniforms were being issued.

'Pint, Rej,' asserted Har, waving his near-empty glass in the air.

'Aye, I'll have one tae,' Tam chimed in, quickly followed by a chorus of, 'Aye, me too,' 'Same here,' and 'Och, go on then, Rej,' from the others.

'Certainly gentlemen,' replied the ever-courteous Rej. 'But Mr. Harry, you have an outstanding bill from last night. Would you like to pay it now?'

'What?' snapped Har. 'I always pay my bill.'

Mick nearly choked on his pint.

'I'm afraid you didn't last night, sir. You left in a rather angry mood after your game of billiards without paying,' explained Rej.

'How much?' screeched a clearly annoyed Har, trying hard not to let his face redden with embarrassment.

Rej opened the small leather wallet he was carrying, revealing the receipt: thirteen hundred and forty-five dirhams.

'Are you fuckin' serious?' slurred Har, now looking extremely serious himself. 'Jesus!'

'You were here since nine a.m. Mr. Harry.' explained Rej, trying to justify the size of the bill.

Har squinted his eyes to read the bill:

- 12 x Guinness (non-happy hour)
- 8 x Guinness (happy hour)
- 16 x Jack Daniels (happy hour)

'Sixteen Jack Daniels?' Har, his face now red from anger rather than embarrassment, screamed. 'I don't fucking think so.'

'You were drinking doubles, sir. I can show you the CCTV footage of you wish. I'll need you to settle this in cash, sir, as it will be taken from our wages if you don't.'

'Who the fuck carries that kind of cash?' Har exclaimed to Rej and the wider audience, which was growing by the minute. 'I certainly don't.'

'Dinnae worry, H, I'll sort you oot,' offered Tappie, trying to defuse the situation. 'You can square me up the mora.'

'Fukin' daylight fuckin' robbery. Cheers Tappie, Aye I'll sort you out tomorrow,' Har muttered, in a slightly sheepish tone as he expressed his gratitude.

With that, Tappie paid the bill, and Rej trotted off to finally pour the men's pints.

'What were you saying about cheese again, Har?' Tappie teased, a mischievous grin spreading across his face.

Chapter 5

The lads

Har de Luc had long claimed that he was of French descent. His Grandfather had moved from a commune, Le Luc, in the Provence-Alpes-Côte d'Azur region of southern France to ply his trade as a musician in the theaters, opera houses and cabarets of Paris around the turn of the twentieth century.

Har's father had followed in his own father's footsteps. He'd been a promiscuous talent before being conscripted into the army during the Second World War where he had played a pivotal role in the Liberation of France. A gifted player of stringed instruments, he was also called upon to perform emergency first aid — starting with simple stitching, but quickly advancing to amputations, shrapnel removal, and even thoracotomy. Har — allegedly — had inherited all of his father's gifts, and was now himself a talented musician, marksman and stitcher.

After the war, France experienced a cultural renaissance in literature, film, and philosophy. Thinkers like Jean-Paul Sartre, Simone de Beauvoir and Har's father, Urbain de Luc — occasionally called simply 'U' or 'Oo' — contributed to post-war existentialism. While this brought 'Oo' much kudos, especially amongst his peers, it did little to put french loaves on the table.

Consequently, due in part to his allegiance to the Auld Alliance between Scotland and France, and Scotland's growing need for doctors and medical practitioners, the family relocated to Scotland in the 1960s. There, his father became Surgeon-in-Chief at the Western Infirmary in Glasgow, the largest hospital in the country at the time, where young Har was born in 1971.

Now, Tappie knew Glasgow well, and nobody had ever heard of Oo de Luc. He had also seen Har eating cheesie single toasties in the early hours of the morning, so he, along with the others, was highly skeptical of the veracity of this story — something that also pissed Har off!

Richard 'Dick' Butler was not one to suffer fools. Born in the South of Ireland, he an Auld Davie FitzGerald didn't always see eye to eye, but they agreed on this one — it was, according to Davie, 'pure pish.'

The Butlers, once one of the most powerful families in Ireland, no longer wielded the power or influence of old but they were still a wealthy family. Dick had been ostracized at an early age for his inclination to over-imbibe, his reputation as a philanderer, and his proclivity for marijuana, which often led to minor run-ins with law enforcement. Fortunately, the family still had some connections and were able to pay off the local Gardaí. He was sent away never to return.

Davie was a harmless old soul, a true gentleman, and it was a wonder at times that he tolerated the disheveled company that he now found himself part of. He had no family — or none that he spoke of — and had left Ireland decades ago in search of a better life. Aside from the company he now kept, it seemed he had found what he was looking for.

'Mild' Mick Quinn — an ironic nickname if ever there was one — was a different kettle of fish altogether. Skinny and wiry, he had the kind of sharp, calculating look in his eye that spoke of someone who'd made a life out of looking for trouble. From Limerick, Mick was a man whose every move was measured, malice lurking just beneath the surface.

His diminutive size belied the strength he possessed and, he spent his days hanging from a rope… quite literally. His official title was *rope access technician*, but he preferred to call himself a 'rope monkey.'

These men played a vital role in maintaining, inspecting and repairing the countless oil rigs scattered across the Gulf. They were handsomely rewarded for their work, though you'd never guess from Mick's tight-fisted antics.

The boys liked having him around; his hostile attitude was perfect for keeping strangers at bay. Few things annoyed them more than some new kid in town trying to make small talk while they were plowing through their endless happy hour pints.

'Last orders' cried Rej. It was seven forty-five in the evening. The bar would stay open until midnight at least, but this was the last opportunity to take advantage of happy hour prices.

'I'll have four.'

'Same, Rej.'

'Three'll do me.'

'I'll just have two, I'm working tomorrow.'

The patrons calculated and planned their next moves. It was either home or down the road to the Frisky Fox after this. Fuck paying full price!

'Isn't it Gentleman's night in the Waldorf?' Mick, rummaging through what was left of the day's brain cells, wondered.

By nine-thirty the place was dead.

Friday 13th June

Chapter 6

The Bay

When Robbie finally reached the top of the steps, he was sweating and out of breath. 'Must get fitter this year,' he wheezed. He made a mental note to use the disabled ramp on his way out—the steps looked like an accident, or worse, just waiting to happen. Maybe one already had. Not that anyone would have heard about it; freedom of the press wasn't exactly a hallmark of Gulf countries.

Once inside, the cool, air-conditioned air gave him a chill. *There was cool and there was fuckin' freezing,* he thought, keeping the complaint to himself for once. He passed a shop selling overpriced clubs, fancy designer-label garments, golf balls, and the usual knick-knacks you might expect; a real estate office promoting new, off-plan developments in the area; and finally the reception, where he was greeted with a friendly smile and a 'Hello, sir.'

'The bar?' Robbie asked.

'Straight ahead, sir,' responded the cheery Magnolia, her name once again displayed on her staff-issued uniform.

Though a little sterile and bright, this was more to Robbie's liking. It was quiet, as one might expect at this hour, but among the few patrons, some were playing darts, others were at the pool table, and a few were puffing away on their ever-more-popular vapes. A couple of pints were in sight, and someone was digging into a full Irish breakfast, complete with what smelled like pork sausages. Robbie knew pork was haram here — he'd done his research — and he was slightly perplexed.

'You just need a pork licence and a separate kitchen, sir,' explained Princess, the barmaid, noticing the confused look on Robbie's face. 'Don't tell anybody I told you this, but those chicken sausages are horrible,' she whispered with a wink, glancing around nervously in case anyone overheard.

She's a beauty, thought Robbie, suddenly and unexpectedly feeling quite horny. 'Do you know a man named Har de Luc?' he enquired.

'Of course, sir. May I know who is asking?' replied Princess.

'Oh, my name is Robbie, Robbie O'Malley, and I think I may have met him last night,' Robbie explained. 'He texted me this morning as well,' he added.

'My shift finished at seven, but he was here last night. Everyone left around nine-thirty, I believe,' Princess confirmed.

'They may have gone to the Frisky,' she added, more hopeful than certain. 'He'll be in later for Happy Hour, I'm sure. He always is!' This time, her tone was more confident. 'OK, I'll call back later,' Robbie said with a thankful smile. 'Sure, I might as well have a pint while I'm here.'

'Certainly, sir. Take a seat anywhere and I'll bring it over to you. Guinness, I'm guessing, by the accent?' replied a perceptive Princess.

Robbie spent the rest of the morning joking, drinking Guinness and chatting up the beautiful Princess, who reminded him a bit of Nong. Maybe it was just the beer goggles. Around noon, he ordered a Careem from the app Princess had installed for him and trudged off down the disabled ramp, heading home for a siesta — to sleep off the grog and dodge the afternoon heat.

He didn't even have the energy to ask Alexa to set the alarm. He collapsed, fully dressed, onto the bed and conked out instantly.

Chapter 7

The sniff test

Robbie drifted off into a deep slumber, his mind slipping away into the realms of dreams. He found himself standing in an ornate Temple, its walls adorned with intricate carvings that seemed to glow in the soft, golden light. A monk chanted in a strange, lilting language, his voice reverberating like a gentle lullaby.

Beside Robbie stood Nong — or was it Princess? Whoever she was, she wore the most beautiful, vibrantly coloured dress he had ever seen, her presence radiant, almost otherworldly. Around them, people gathered, pouring water over their hands in a delicate blessing ritual.

Robbie felt a deep, inexplicable happiness that seemed foreign and yet utterly familiar. The rhythmic beat of the *Klong Khaek*, a traditional double-headed Thai drum, filled the air, punctuating the moment with a celebratory cadence. Strangely, he knew its name without ever learning it. How?

Then, the vision shattered. Robbie jolted awake, drenched in sweat, his fleeting bliss replaced by the relentless, ear-splitting pounding of a pile driver outside his balcony window.

His head was pounding now, too — maybe from the noise or the morning pints he had so thoroughly enjoyed. He hadn't meant to drink so many, but he had been so mesmerized by the beautiful Princess, and with having her — almost entirely — to himself, he found it difficult to say no to her repeated 'another one, sir?' offers.

Sliding open the small drawer in the bedside locker, he fumbled around until he found the packet of Panadol Extra, the only item he had unpacked from his hand luggage. He slugged two down with the customary glass of water he had placed beside him before going to bed.

'Alexa, what time is it?'

'Good afternoon, Robbie. It's two forty-five p.m.,' replied the ever-courteous Alexa.

'Perfect,' said Robbie, thinking out loud without realizing it. First, he sniffed the armpits of his new cotton shirt. 'Fuckin' hell, that's rank,' he muttered, again out loud. Next, he sniffed his own armpits. 'Oof.' Lastly came the worst part of the *sniff* test — the crotch. 'Not too bad, I'll get another day or two out of these,' he thought to himself, feeling quite chuffed.

How anyone could choose to live in this climate was beyond him. Had he known it would be this hot and humid, he would have opted for his beloved Majorca. But the recent spate of anti-tourism marches had deterred him. And, what with the climate changing, the Balearic Islands could also be prohibitively hot at this time of year.

Maybe Ireland wasn't so bad after all, he pondered.

'Alexa, what's the temperature?'

'Mm, I'm not sure.'

'What the fuck does that mean?'

'Sorry, I don't know the answer to that.'

'For fuck's sake.' Robbie caught himself. 'It's a bloody machine,' he mumbled, almost incomprehensibly. *Save your energy for the human arseholes.* He was sure he'd find plenty of those later today.

It was forty-nine degrees, with humidity rising!

Pointless though it was, Robbie threw himself under the hot shower, dried off the already-formed sweat, and pulled on a new set of clothes, khaki shorts aside. Looking in the mirror, he realised that he had grabbed his favourite Motörhead T-shirt. Robbie loved

Motorhead. Their lead singer, Lemmy, had died on his wedding day, but rather than casting a shadow over the celebrations, the dance floor had ignited to the sound of *"Ace of Spades."*

But this T-shirt, with its flipped bird emblem, was almost certain to cause offence here. With some reluctance, he pulled it off inside-out and tossed it on the floor before swapping it for his AC/DC T-shirt. 'That's more like it,' he said, giving himself an approving glance in the mirror.

Not that he was looking forward to the task of meeting Har de Luc — or socializing at all, for that matter — but he was looking forward to a pint. With a bit of spring back in his step, he bounded down the boardwalk toward the ferry, only to find the gate locked and no ferry.

'You must call the captain,' said a voice behind him in a posh accent he couldn't quite place. It was Top Shelf Terrence.

'He'll be over at the golf club,' he motioned, pointing across the water.

I'll call him now, though he's probably already on his way — he knows I always take the three forty-five ferry. You must be new to the area?' asked a helpful but slightly nosy Top Shelf. 'Heading over for happy hour yourself?'

'I'm Terrence.'

'Robbie. Pleased to meet you. Yes, thought I'd pop over for a look,' lied Robbie, not wanting to give much — if anything — away. *Nothing worse than getting someone's life story the minute you meet them*, he thought to himself.

'I don't suppose you know a Har de Luc, do you, Terrence?' said Robbie trying to act indifferent.

'Everyone knows Har de Luc — unfortunately,' joked Top Shelf. 'I'm surprised he's not here, to be honest. He usually takes this ferry — unless he's already on the beer, that is.' But Robbie knew that wasn't the case, at least not at the golf club — he'd been the one drinking there.

'You might see him over there,' Top Shelf continued, full of chat.

'Thanks,' Robbie replied. 'Is he a friend of yours?' He pressed further, wanting to learn as much as he could about this Har de Luc before meeting him.

Why had he sent that message? Was he the one behind the six missed calls? If so, why was the number different? Did he have two phones? Robbie was always suspicious of anyone with more than one. A second phone — any extra phone, really — was usually a burner. But he didn't think they sold those here. Not legitimately, anyway.

'It's a small village, Robbie. Everyone knows everyone. Calling him a friend might be pushing it, but yeah, I know him well enough. We usually take this ferry together, and he helps me out with work now and then,'" replied Top Shelf.

'Oh? What is it you do, if you don't mind me asking?'

'I'm retired now, but you might say I'm a problem solver. I find things, help people — that sort of thing.'

What kind of a fuckin' answer is that? Robbie thought, resisting the urge to say it out loud.

'That's rather cryptic Terrence,' was all he could manage.

'A private detective, Robbie.'

Robbie found it hard to keep a straight face. *A private detective?* Was this guy for real? A private dick, more like.

'Really?' Robbie half-spoke, half-laughed. 'Maybe you can help me out then?'

'If I can, I will,' replied an eager and intrigued Top Shelf.

Just then, the captain moored the ferry alongside the pier, and following Top Shelf's lead, Robbie made his way up the rear entrance to the golf club.

'I always use this entrance, Robbie,' Top Shelf said, unprompted. 'That way, I can see who's here before they see me.'

Maybe this guy's not as daft as he looks, thought Robbie.

Chapter 8

Finn Gerino

There was no one there; the place was dead. Robbie was starting to wonder if it was always like this. Well, nearly dead. A solitary figure sat at the bar, poking around on a small laptop or tablet — or *whatever the fuck they're calling them these days*, Robbie thought, inexplicably irritated.

He cut no ordinary figure, though; this guy was huge.

Top Shelf approached him. They shook hands, exchanged pleasantries, and then Top Shelf made the introductions. 'Finn, Robbie. Robbie, Finn.'

'Finn's a tech wizard,' continued Top Shelf, piquing Robbie's interest further. 'Hacker-for-hire, you might say.'

Robbie couldn't tell if he was joking or not.

The two strangers shook hands, Finn's massive hand easily dwarfing Robbie's.

Finnian Gerino, Finn to his friends, was a complex character. At six foot ten, he towered over everyone in the village. He wasn't small in girth either — hands like shovels, feet like paddles, ears like

Dumbo, eyes like saucers, thighs like tree trunks, head like a cue ball and missing two front teeth. He was, quite literally, unmissable.

I wouldn't like to mess with him, thought Robbie.

To believe Finn's tale meant believing that he was more than one man — something that, given his size, wasn't particularly far-fetched. Born and raised in England but half Apache, quarter Canadian, quarter Italian, quarter Irish, one eighth Russian…

The story goes something like this: his great-great-great Grandfather, Anson, or 'An,' was born into the Bedonkohe band of the Apache tribe, which was part of the larger Apache group in present-day Arizona and New Mexico. There, he fought alongside the great warrior Geronimo until Geronimo's final surrender in 1886. Keen to avoid the same incarceration as the mighty leader — and sharp enough to do so — 'An' threaded his family through the United States he so reviled, eventually reaching the safety of the Canadian prairie provinces, where he settled in Saskatchewan.

There, the family — all of whom were giant in stature — found work on the railways, contributing to the expansion and improvement of the Canadian Pacific Railway. It was rumoured that An's Grandson and Finn's great Grandfather, Dan, could lift three railway sleepers under each arm.

The economic troubles of the early-mid 1910s, coupled with growing racial tensions and discrimination against native Americans, forced the family to flee to the relative safety of post-war Europe. Packing all they could carry, the family embarked on a twelve-day voyage from the Prince Rupert port in British Columbia across the Atlantic Ocean to the shores of Naples, Southern Italy. It was here that the family adopted the surname Gerino.

The family found work in the booming shipbuilding and steel industries, but the Gerinos were far from simple labourers. Their great-great-great-grandfather had been a talented percussionist with the Apache tribe, and the apples hadn't fallen far from the tree. Generation after generation produced a stunning array of musicians, artists, and poets.

Running parallel to the growing socialist and anarchist movements was the increasing introduction of women into the workforce. The Gerino men were well known for their eye for the ladies, and it was during this time that Finn's father met the love of his life, Maria, who worked as a welder in the Cantiere Navale di Napoli (Napoli Shipyard).

Maria's family had fled Ireland during the Great Famine of 1847, and, like many Irish families, they were naturally quite musical. This match made in heaven eventually produced young Finn, who was born shortly after the family relocated to England.

The economic boom of the 1950s and 60s had come to an end in Italy. Amid political instability and rising inflation, the time had come for the Gerinos to once again up sticks. They headed north, only to find the situation in England much the same, with shipyards and mines closing all around them.

Work was scarce — and the Gerinos felt it, just as much as everyone else. However, the 1970s also coincided with a golden era for music in England. It was here that young Finn found his niche as a piano player. By the age of twelve he was a well-known name in the working men's pubs and clubs of Sunderland and the surrounding Tyneside area.

Sunderland in the 1980s was a tough place, and knowing how to hold your own in a fight could be a valuable skill. The giant Finn had no problem with that. Whether there was any truth in his story or not, he was hard as nails — never backed down from a fight and never lost. Never! A giant with a fuse as short as a firecracker's wick wasn't someone people wanted to mess with, but that never stopped Finn from provoking trouble.

Unfortunately, Har de Luc had lit that fuse last night with his insults, bigotry, and general anti-English sentiment.

Although Robbie found Finn *a bit odd*, they found common ground in their shared love of alcohol and music. When they had exhausted both topics, Finn suggested, 'A game of pool?' Robbie was only too happy to accept. He'd always enjoyed a game of pool, though his ever-deteriorating eyesight hadn't been doing him any favours lately — especially after he'd had a few, which he had by now.

'What are the house rules, Finn?' enquired Robbie, keen to avoid any unnecessary arguments later.

'Two shots don't carry, white ball anywhere behind the line, black ball any pocket, and no pints on the table.'

The last rule hadn't been strictly adhered to, judging by the state of the table, Robbie thought.

The game went back and forth, both men missing shots they shouldn't, expletives flying, the occasional complimentary tap on the table, until the itch for nicotine got the better of Robbie. Finn was fine sneaking his vape behind the giant plant pot next to the table, but the 'real' smokers were all outside, gathered around a round table.

Before stepping outside, feeling he had bided his time well, Robbie threw in, 'I don't suppose you know Har de Luc?'

'Don't get me started on that fuckin' racist arsehole,' Finn replied, clearly angered. Robbie had touched a nerve.

'Oh!' Robbie made his excuses and wandered outside.

Chapter 9

The mince pie

'Anyone got a light, lads?' Robbie called out in the direction of the only occupied table.

An outstretched arm handed him a lighter, no words exchanged. The gale from the swamp cooler made it almost impossible to light his cigarette. He cupped his hands, turned his back, stuck the lighter under his T-shirt, then disappeared around the corner. When he finally returned, he handed the lighter back to the waiting arm.

'Thought it would be easier than that,' joked Robbie, trying to break the ice. A few chuckles suggested it had worked.

'Mind if I join you?' Robbie asked, spotting a vacant chair.

'Aye, sit yourself doon, pal,' Tappie said, easing the chair out to welcome the stranger.

'Cheers,' Robbie said, raising his glass to no one in particular. 'Robbie,' he added, introducing himself.

'Were you in the Waldorf last night?' asked an inquisitive Tappie.

'Yes.'

'Aye, I thought I recognised the face. Were you talking to Har de Luc?'

Robbie, pleased to have this confirmed, lied. 'I'm not sure, to be honest.'

Tappie let it go.

The pints were going down well — *too well*, thought Robbie — but tongues were beginning to loosen. Being Irish, he had plenty in common with the table, and they seemed to accept, even enjoy, his company. The feeling was mutual.

Then, from nowhere,

'Come to think of it, has anyone seen de Luc today?' asked Tappie. Robbie couldn't believe his luck.

'No, and Top Shelf said he wasn't on the ferry either,' replied Auld Davie.

'Princess hasn't seen him either,' chipped in Dick.

'Fuckin' slimy bastard. Cunt owes me fourteen hun'er Ds,' a wound-up Tappie shouted, banging his fist on the table. His outburst was just loud enough to grab the attention of a couple of tourists who had just ordered today's special — mushroom soup.

'Mind your own fuckin' business,' roared Mick across the patio. 'Away back to your mushroom fuckin' soup.'

The obviously upset and startled tourists grabbed their plates of soup and scurried inside as fast as they could, hot soup spilling down the white trouser leg of the now, not-so-cocky lothario — much to Mick's amusement.

It was strange though, where was Har de Luc?

'Fingers,' Mick called Finn that. 'You seen de Luc today?'

'No, he's barred, and I hope I never see the cunt again' replied Finn, wiping tomato paste from his chin. He loved his pizza. His size demanded it, and it gave him an excuse to 'wash it down' with another ten pints of Peroni.

'Barred? You sure? He was with us last night. Was he not in the Waldorf with us?'

'Aye, I was here when they barred him. I think you lads had just left.'

'I knew he was barred from the Hilton. Where's he drinking now? The Frisky?'

'No, he's barred out of there as well,' a delighted Finn crowed.

'How the fuck did he get himself barred from here?' a puzzled Tappie added.

'I heard he tried to steal a mince pie,' chortled Finn, 'and that idiot Rej wasn't having it.'

'A mince pie? How the fuck do you get barred for stealing a mince pie? pitched in Dick. 'And why the fuck are they even selling mince pies in June. Does Rej think he's the second coming of Christ or something?'

Tappie interrupted the fits of laughter. 'Oh shite, that might have been ma fault. You ken Chef Andy?'

'That miserable Polish bollock?' Mick probed.

'Indeed!' concurred Tappie. 'Well, you know that specials board oot there?'

'The one with the stupid mushroom soup?'

'Aye,' Tappie added, nodding in approval. 'Well, they have a pie-and-a-pint deal on it, and I was asking Andy one night why they didn't have any Scotch pies on it. He had no idea what I wis talking aboot, so I explained it wis a pie wi a hole in the lid, filled with mincemeat.'

'Fuckin' love those things,' interrupted Robbie.

'He never went and baked a rake of Christmas mince pies. did he?' quizzed an eyes-wide-open Davie.

'Fuckin' idiot did, and they cannae give them away, let alone sell them. So, I dinnae ken why they're getting so upset with de Luc robbing one,' Tappie continued, before concluding, 'I wis robbin' them aw last week and naebody said tap!'

'It wasn't the pie,' came a voice from inside. With ears the size of Finn's, it was sometimes hard not to eavesdrop, and he was dialed into this one. 'Har lost it — like really lost it. He was calling Rej all kinds of names, and you know what Rej is like when it comes to bad language. He threatened to call the Police on me one night for saying the "bad" word.'

'What was the bad word?' enquired a humoured Auld Davie, also a man heavily against the use of bad language. *Totally unnecessary,* he would often tell the table.

'I donno, I called him so many,' roared Finn, setting off laughter around the table. 'And Har was using them all last night. The more offended Rej got, the worse Har's language got. The whole place was looking at him. They had no choice but to bar him,' Finn explained, without a shred of empathy for his archrival.

'How the fuck did we miss that?' asked Tappie, clearly annoyed to have missed the action.

'Fuck knows,' replied Mick. 'But come to think of it, he wasn't on the buggy when we went to the Waldorf. He appeared later. I thought he must've been trying his luck with Princess again.'

At that point, Stu Smith wobbled his way over to the table. Stu knew everything... about everything and everyone — or so he thought.

In fairness, he did know a lot, especially about his beloved Aberdeen Football Club. But he never let his absence of knowledge get in the way of a good yarn. He'd lick his lips, wobble his head, and start rolling his eyeballs around in his skull as he'd bamboozle you with either his knowledge or his imagination. It wasn't always easy to tell the difference.

Having obviously overheard the last part of the conversation, he stated emphatically, 'He's away up to the Thirsty Horse,' as if there were no other possibility.

'Where the fuck is that?' a slightly dubious Mick enquired. He loved it when "Rudolph," — so nicknamed for his spindly legs and often-red nose — was wrong.

'Up in the free zone. Beside the Catholic Church. All the Indians drink there. It's nine dirham a pint or two for a tenner,' imparted the ever-sure-of-himself Rudolph.

'Is de Luc that skint?' enquired a concerned Tappie, wondering how on earth he was going to get his fourteen hundred dirham back.

'Donno, but the staff accommodation is over the Thirsty Horse. The Bay staff, that is,' added Rudolph. 'And you know who lives up there?'

The table fell silent. The boys all looked at one another. Robbie wasn't sure what was going on. Who was going to say it first? In the end they all said it almost simultaneously:

'Fuck, Rej!'

Princess appeared at that moment with her little notebook to take last orders. The usual scattering of pints was ordered, and Davie took the opportunity to ask, 'Is Rej working tonight, Princess?'

Robbie was looking at her like a lost puppy — something not lost on the boys — when she replied, 'He was supposed to be on at seven, but he hasn't showed up, and we can't reach him on his mobile. He's left us short-staffed for a Friday night. It'll be busy tonight. Fingers and Saxy are playing later.'

With that, she skipped away, leaving Robbie and the rest of the crew to admire her tight little arse.

Chapter 10

The Thirsty Horse

As usual, the men had drained the last of their happy hour pints by nine-thirty, creatures of habit that they were. During that time, Eugene had joined the table. A mild-mannered Scotsman, though the accent was hard to detect after so many years working in insurance in the Gulf. Thirsty and slightly annoyed to have missed happy hour, he didn't want to return to his empty studio or pay inflated non-happy hour prices. What happened next would be called a *"once-in-a-hundred-year event"* in the insurance industry.

Some jaws hit the floor; others, too shocked to speak, simply looked aghast. Auld Davie glanced towards the heavens. Cool-headed Mick, unshaken, merely said, 'Say that again.'

'The Thirsty Horse,' Eugene repeated. 'C'mon, we'll see if Har is up there and find out the craic.' Auld Davie had never ventured anywhere but the golf club. He'd be like a fish out of water up there — most of them would. They weren't just creatures of habit; they were prisoners of it. Robbie smiled to himself, once again unable to believe his luck.

Robbie was a well-travelled man. He had explored the wonders of South America, driven the 'Mother Road' — 'Route 66,' as it's better known — from Chicago to Santa Monica, seen the Eiffel Tower, the Mona Lisa, the Colosseum, and even run with the bulls in the Encierro. Here, he had marvelled at the fake opulence of Dubai, with its spotless streets and bright lights.

Now, in Ras Al Khaimah, he was witnessing the luxury of floating palaces. *This was the playground of the rich*, he thought to himself.

So, he was absolutely gobsmacked when Dick Butler turned his Toyota Land Cruiser off the main road and into the industrial zone.

It was barely a road — rubbish everywhere, no streetlights. People cycling rickety old bicycles with no lights, wearing dark overalls, going the wrong way down the street. Men sat under trees, drinking cheap super beers — rocket fuel. Dead rats lay on the street, while live rats jumped in and out of overflowing rubbish bins. A putrid smell permeated the humid air.

This was worse than anything he'd seen in the most poverty-stricken regions of Asia. *Where have they been hiding this*? he thought. *Was Dubai like this? Had the world been misled by the polished images in the censored media?*

The two cars continued in convoy. Robbie made a mental note as they passed St. Anthony's Catholic Church. He hadn't been to mass since his Mother's death. What was it? *Must be two years now*, he thought, unexpectedly feeling quite emotional. *Get a grip Robbie*, he told himself, *get a grip*.

Suddenly, bright lights appeared — restaurants, off-licences, food trucks. Yet, the stench still filled the air, rats still scurried about, and men still sat under trees. The only difference was the atmosphere. It was buzzing. This was obviously where the other half lived. And there it was, in all its glory — the Thirsty Horse.

Tappie had actually been there before, for Har de Luc's fifty-first birthday — covid having robbed him of his fiftieth celebrations — so he led the way.

However, as they approached the entrance, a burly security guard stood in front of the all-too-familiar, yellow and black tape — **CRIME SCENE DO NOT CROSS** — familiar to Robbie, at least.

Top Shelf stepped forward. 'Alaykum as-salam!' he offered. The Nepalese security guard, said nothing, simply staring blankly back.

Robbie, blowing his cover, interjected, 'My name is Robbie O'Malley. I'm an officer of the law.'

Again, the security guard said nothing, merely staring blankly back.

'For fuck's sake,' roared Mick. 'What the fuck is going on?'

'Sorry, sir, I can't tell you anything until the police arrive,' the security guard replied. Robbie and Top Shelf exchanged a look of dismay.

'The fuckin' filth,' Tappie uttered in disgust. 'You kept that one quiet, ya cunt!'

'Listen, boys,' Robbie tried to explain.

'Shut it,' Tappie snapped, his rage intensifying.

This was not good. Robbie had had ample time to tell them the truth, but he had prioritized rapport over trust, and now it had come back to bite him on the arse.

'I'm sorry, boys,' offered Robbie, well aware that his words were woefully insufficient. 'Can we leave that till later? This is what I do; it's my bread and butter and if Har is in any sort of trouble, maybe I can help.'

'I dinnae trust the cunt.'

'Lying bastard.'

'Slimy fucker.'

The boys were not happy.

Top Shelf, the voice of reason, stepped in to calm things down. 'Lads, this isn't getting us anywhere. Let's see if he can help, and we'll deal with the lying scumbag later.'

The night was now filled with the sounds of police cars, ambulances and fire brigades. No one remained sitting under the trees. Security guards were doing their best to prevent the growing crowd from getting any closer to the scene. The police would surely establish a more secure and significant perimeter upon arrival if this turned out to be a serious crime.

A serious-looking man, dressed impeccably in his pristine kandura, exited a brand-new Lexus.

'That'll be Mohammed Alshahari, the Chief Investigator from the CID,' said Top Shelf.

'Is that not a bit OTT?' Robbie whispered in Top Shelf's ear.

'Not really. He probably just wants to get out of the office. They don't have much to do around here. I probably solve more cases than they do,' Top Shelf said, a hint of pride in his voice.

Top Shelf nodded and threw in the occasional 'Salam' as a steady stream of Patrol officers, plainclothes detectives, scene-of-the crime officers and forensic experts followed Investigator Alshahari, past security and into the building.

With the perimeter now secured, the boys found themselves, somewhat in no man's land, caught between the security guard and the baying crowd. A Patrol officer was heading their way.

'Good evening, Terrence,' he nodded as he acknowledged Top Shelf. 'I'm afraid I'll have to ask you boys to move away from the entrance. This is a crime scene now. Please move back behind the perimeter.'

Despite his apparent familiarity with Top Shelf, there was no trace of friendliness in his request. Three of his colleagues were quickly on the scene to usher the reluctant group back to the madness of the agitated crowd.

Top Shelf explained that, despite the region's reputation for safety, crime was more common than one might think — especially for those unfamiliar with it. Injured or dead ex-pat construction workers rarely made the papers. Many of these workers were here illegally, their visas long expired. Who's going to miss them? They didn't even exist in the eyes of the law.

The problem is, the community they live in — the chaotic world of labour camps, cheap liquor, and drink-driving — knows this. They might not miss them, but they certainly notice when they're gone.

There's honour among them, bound by the injustice of it all. Many — if not most — have nothing to lose, no reason to keep quiet, and every reason to shout, stand up, and fight. And now, this crowd was visibly and audibly angry at the thought of one of their own being the victim of a serious crime.

The boys, of course, were worried for different reasons. Had Har attacked, or done something worse, to Rej? Had something happened to Har himself? He still wasn't answering his phone.

'Well, we're no gonna get a fuckin' drink here,' a thirsty Tappie broke the moment. 'The Red Chilli's only up the road, it's pretty cheap tae.'

'Right, c'mon,' said Dick, 'I could do with a drink.' The others nodded and fought their way through the crowd, back to the Land Cruisers.

Chapter 11

The Red Chilli

The Red Chilli was little more than a ramshackle prefab, tucked away behind yet another off-licence. *They're everywhere,* thought Robbie. Having initially assumed this a dry country; he was rapidly changing his opinion. Outside, a dilapidated bus provided construction workers with a place to drink their sixteen percent cans of *Red Horse*, offering some shelter from the scorching heat. During the summer months, the ageing fan did little more than circulate the heat. Take your pick: scorching sun or baking tin can??

'Spit it oot then,' ordered Tappie, staring down Robbie O'Malley. 'You've got some explaining tae do.'

A sheepish Robbie explained how he had come here, on vacation, to escape the stress of his job, the rigours of life, and the pouring rain in the West of Ireland — something the Irish and Scottish lads could relate to, even if they couldn't relate to his deceit.

'It's not something I advertise, as it makes people uncomfortable,' Robbie continued. 'And you would never have known, had it not been for this.' He pulled his phone from his pocket and showed the boys the missed calls and *that* message.

One by one, they wrestled with the phone, as if each believed they alone might uncover the meaning of the meaningless. They couldn't. No one could. This wasn't Har's style. He wasn't good at communication. He usually left his phone at home, had the blue ticks turned off on his WhatsApp messages, and rarely had credit to call or text. He certainly wouldn't call six times, and, as far as they knew, he didn't have two phones.

'That's not Har,' pointed out Mick.

The atmosphere thawed with every bucket of unordered Heineken — communication seemingly no issue here.

Dick then made a small gesture with his forefinger and thumb. The waiter mimicked this but repeatedly moved his forefinger up and down — clearly, this was how they communicated. Mick, apparently comfortable interpreting this sign language, mimicked the waiter's raised forefinger. Nods followed all around, and a round of double Jack Daniels soon arrived.

Robbie spoke of his work with the Garda Síochána and how he was looking forward to retirement, Top Shelf shared stories of his time as

Headmaster, remarking that the best thing he ever did was taking early retirement. Davie extolled of the blissful merits of retirement itself, while Mick regaled everyone with tales of his antics on the rope.

Dick described his underwater adventures, and running a welding business with a scuba diving sideline. He also had a team installing CCTV and security systems.

Rudolph, however, launched into a ten-minute, head-wobbling, eye-rolling, lip-licking rant about his work, leaving everyone none the wiser by the end.

The banter flowed long into the evening. Gambling, fighting, women, music, Celtic F.C., binary, non-binary, prostitution, racing — horse racing, dog racing, motor racing — drinking, smoking — cigarettes, weed, hash — the price of a pint, food, chip-shops, brown sauce, political correctness, politics, Scottish independence, religion, boxing, snooker, darts... they had exhausted every subject imaginable by the time they began pulling down the shutters.

Feeling pretty steamed by the point, Robbie said 'I think I'll call it a night lads. Anyone want to share a Careem?'

'For fuck's sake, Robbie,' Tappie joked, though he was serious. 'I thought you were a Guard? Come on, we'll finish this bucket, and I'll drive us down the road.'

'Aye, I'll take mine too,' added Dick. 'No problem.'

Robbie couldn't believe his eyes or his ears. Sure, he'd spent some time working as a Traffic Officer in his early years on the force and had seen his fair share of drunk drivers. Back in the early days of the "*don't drink more than four*" campaign, they'd just wave people on, telling them to "*drive slowly and take care*." How things had changed, he thought. But these boys were on a whole different level. They could barely talk, let alone walk.

'Let's meet tomorrow, boys,' Top Shelf slurred. 'We'll not find anything out tonight. These lazy bastards,' he said, referring to the local Police, 'are thick as thieves, so it'll be difficult finding anything out at all. I have some contacts, though, who might be able to help.'

Robbie was impressed at how lucid his thought process was, even if his enunciation made him almost incomprehensible.

'Aye, okay. Shall we say ten a.m. in the club?' added Tappie.

'We're playing golf at nine,' said Dick, waving his finger between himself, Mick and Auld Davie.

'GOLF?' shouted Tappie, with his customary bang on the table. 'Har could be dead, or a murderer, and you three want to play golf?'

'Fair point.' 'Oh, alright.' 'I suppose so…' the trio reluctantly agreed.

They split that tab eight ways. Jesus, Robbie thought, paying his share of what he considered a very reasonable bill. 'They don't half fuck us in Ireland, do they?' he blurted out without even thinking.

No one disagreed as they stumbled out, single file, into the hot, humid night. Top Shelf cranked up "*The men behind the wire*" at full blast, much to Robbie's delight, and tore off down the road, with a wired Tappie, hot in pursuit, blaring "*A Nation once again.*"

Saturday 14th June

Chapter 12

The flying rats

Alexa woke a groggy Robbie at 8.45 a.m. He had been in and out of sleep since the 'screecher' woke him at five-thirty.

'Alexa, what's the local radio station called?' Robbie demanded.

'Good morning Robbie,' an irritatingly chirpy Alexa replied. 'The local radio station in Ras Al Khaimah is RAK Radio, would you like me to play it now?'

'Yes'— nothing played.

'Alexa, yes,' repeated Robbie, only louder.

'According to the dictionary, yes is an affirmative response or agreement...'

'Alexa, STOP,' roared Robbie.

He Googled RAK Radio and connected his phone to his JBL Flip 5, a Bluetooth speaker that had travelled the world with him. *Another marvelous little invention*, he told himself.

To his surprise, it was an English-language station, offering a mix of music from the 1970s to the present, along with local news and events. He was just in time to enjoy "*Walking on sunshine*." *Who was that again?* he asked himself. *The Bangles? Atomic Kitten?* He was embarrassed he even knew these names.

'And a very good morning to you all,' came a voice from the radio, with a slightly American'ish accent. 'That was *Katrina and the Waves*, from all the way back in 1983.'

'Fuck,' said Robbie, suddenly feeling his age.

'And now it's time for the nine o'clock news,' the host continued.

Traffic updates, weather reports, an update on the progress of the proposed new casino development, information about upcoming festivals, and a report about a delivery driver knocked off his motorcycle — all peppered with the usual annoying adverts. But nothing about an incident at *the Thirsty Horse*.

Was that good news, or bad? Robbie pondered, now pacing the room, wondering whether a coffee or a beer would be the better option; no milk settling that internal conflict pretty quickly. In fact, the fridge was empty bar three cans of Guinness.

'Oh well,' he smirked as he heard the all-too-familiar "psst" of a can opening.

He turned off the radio and put on "*Brothers in Arms.*" After texting Mild Mick to arrange a lift to the club, he jumped in the shower, performed the *sniff* test, drank the remaining two cans, smoked five Chesterfields, and sauntered down to the lobby, ready to face the day.

Mick collected Robbie, and then Top Shelf from the neighbouring apartment block. As they pulled out of the carpark, he let down the window to say hello to an older lady feeding pigeons.

'You're late today,' he joked.

'Yeah, ladies' night Mick,' she replied, as if he'd know exactly what she meant. He did.

Her face was a little weathered and battle-hardened, but she had the figure of a teenager and had clearly been a looker in her day.

'That's Rhianna,' Mick offered freely, noticing the inquisitive look on Robbie's face. 'She's the crazy cat lady.'

Robbie's expression searched for more.

'She's normally out there first thing feeding those flying fuckin' rats. Must've had a few too many last night. Used to be an air hostess with British Airways back in the day — quite the heartbreaker, they say, and pretty high up too. Her son still works in the industry — Emirates? Or is it Etihad?' He was beginning to waffle.

'She's in real estate now but seems to spend most of her time feeding pigeons and rescuing stray and lost cats. She must have about twenty in her place. She knows every ladies' night in town. I'd wager she's broke.'

Mick closed the window, gave her two quick honks of the horn and sped out of the carpark — ignoring the 25 km/h sign.

To Robbie's surprise, the others were already there when they arrived, milling about the bar, chatting with waiters, chefs, receptionists, maintenance staff and other guests. No one looked too concerned about the whereabouts of Har de Luc.

Princess was working so Robbie made a beeline for her.

'Good morning Mr. Robbie, sir' she beamed. Robbie blushed. He quietly whispered, 'Please call me Robbie, I'm no sir.'

'I'll try sir… eh… Robbie,' replied Princess, herself now blushing.

'Could you bring a round out to the table, please, Princess, and put it on my tab,' instructed Robbie. He knew it was too hot to sit outside, but he didn't want any unwanted ears overhearing their conversation. The blaring swamp cooler would make doubly sure of that.

'Of course, Robbie,' replied Princess, beaming again.

'So, where are we at, lads?' enquired Robbie without so much as a good morning. 'Any news, Terrence?' He still wasn't quite comfortable calling him Top Shelf, especially when sober.

'No,' replied Top Shelf.

'I presume you've all tried calling him?' Robbie knew it was a stupid question.

'What do you fuckin' think?' Mick was in no mood for unnecessary pish.

'His work? Actually, what does Har do? I don't think you've told me that,' continued Robbie.

The boys all looked at each other, a little perplexed. Robbie thought this would be an easy one.

'He used to be a teacher — computers, IT, that kind of stuff. He's pretty smart,' began Dick. Nods of agreement followed.

'But he got sacked. He says his contract wasn't renewed due to some administrative balls-up, but everyone knows he got the sack.'

'For what?' asked a captivated Robbie.

'Drink, basically,' Rudolph butted in. 'We all drink, but he was doing the dog on it. And, on the job — before, during and after.'

'During?' Who does that?' Robbie's puzzled brain was struggling to keep up.

'In his car, in the toilet, in his water bottle. Anywhere and everywhere. He was hammered in there.

'Jesus!' exclaimed Robbie. 'Did he fall out with anyone? Was he disciplined?'

'Don't think so. They just let him go. Now he just does bits and pieces. He helps out old Top Shelf there, does a bit of consultancy work with IT, 3D printing, and all that shite, but basically, he does as little as his drinking habit allows him to do,' added Tappie.

'Okay. Let's ask up in his school if anyone has seen him. What about his friends, his family?'

'We *are* his fuckin' friends,' snarled Mick, his aggression quickly returning.

'Hospitals? Morgues?' Robbie asked sheepishly.

'Look,' an increasingly irritated Mick continued, his temper rising — Robbie could see he was close to losing it — 'we might not be fuckin' detectives, but do you seriously think this is the first time any of us has gone missing? We know how to look for someone.'

Robbie shut up.

Top Shelf continued, 'I contacted my source — a retired police chief — that I know from my teaching days. I tutored his son, and he owes me a few favours… more than a few actually,' he digressed. 'He knows something went on last night but couldn't — or wouldn't — give me any more than that.'

'Well, that's no good to us,' stated Robbie. 'Is there any CCTV up in that dump?' He thought he probably knew the answer to that as well.

'Yes, the industrial zone has CCTV. The warehouses and self-storage units need it. I used to store some of my diving gear up there,' said Dick.

'What about the Thirsty Horse itself?'

'Very doubtful,' said a somber Top Shelf. 'They don't really want people knowing what goes on in there.'

'ATM cams?'

'Yes, there's a RAKBANK across the road. That'll have a camera, and the Al Ansari money exchange right next door should also have one,' continued Top Shelf.

'Great.' Robbie felt a sense of progress, knowing this could help them move forward. 'Can we get access to any of those? Dick, do you still know anyone up there?'

'Pfff, maybe, I'll make some calls,' pondered Dick, not sounding too hopeful.

'Can we get up there and start asking questions? See if anyone has seen him, or saw him last night? Ask the workers, the boys under the trees.' Robbie was slipping back into his DS role without knowing it. 'Can we see if Har has used his bank cards? Withdrawn any money?'

'And phone records. Can we get our hands on those?

'The banks won't give out that kind of information,' quipped Eugene, showing his knowledge of financial institutions. 'Nor will the phone companies—data security, confidentiality, and all that.' It all made sense; *this was the case worldwide*, thought Robbie.

'No, but can we somehow get into his mobile banking?' Robbie suggested.

'I've got his account number,' Tappie, quieter than usual until now, chimed in. 'I had to wire him some money a while back. Come to think of it, did the bastard ever pay that back?' He rubbed his chin. 'His password cannae be that hard to guess. This is de Luc we're talking aboot!'

'I'm good at Wordle,' joked Rudolph. 'I'll have it in minutes,' he confidently stated, licking his lips.

'Right, Dick, you and Eugene head up to the industrial estate. Eugene, with your background, you might convince the bank or money exchange to let you see their CCTV? Dick, ask around the warehouses — see if anyone's willing to let you have a look.'

No one disagreed, so Robbie continued, 'Mick, Tappie, you two head up there as well. Stir things up, see if you can get someone to talk. Those googly-eyed Indians are always staring — maybe they saw something. Put the hammers on them if they won't talk. Threaten them with anything you can — true, or not. Try and track down that security guard as well. He was on the scene, he fuckin' knows something, I'm sure of it.'

'Rudol… em..Stu, try to crack that password and get into his bank account. Terrence, get onto your contact. Someone must know something about last night?'

'Where does Har live? Can someone pop round to his place and take a look? Anyone got a key?

'Aye, we'll go round before we head up tae the Indians,' offered Tappie. 'He's in the same building as you, Robbie — ME. He never locks his door — no one does. The only thing he locks is that stupid cheese drawer. You'd swear he had the crown jewels in there. Fuckin' cheese.' Tappie's humour was a welcome break from Robbie's militarism.

'Sound,' said Robbie. 'Do you know that cat lady as well? What's her name…?'

'Rhianna. Of course. Everyone does. She'll not be much help. She's for the birds, that one,' chortled Tappie.

'Aye, but if she's out there every morning, she might just have seen something.'

'Davie, you're coming with me. I need someone that knows the lay of the land. We'll go to the police, and I'll introduce myself. Maybe someone will talk to us off the record. I'll make some calls before we go — maybe someone in Dublin can help us or put us in touch with someone over here. Doubtful, I know, but worth a go. We'll have to take your car. I didn't think I'd need one.' Robbie was now in full DS mode.

'I don't have one Robbie. All I've got is a golf cart and I'm not supposed to take that on the road. It'd take us all day anyway,' said a joking Davie. The others quietly joined in the laughter.

They're taking the piss, thought Robbie. But they weren't.

'Take mine,' offered Dick. 'I'll ride with Eugene.'

'What about the insurance?' an unsure Robbie asked.

'The car is insured here, not the driver, so you'll be fine. You okay driving on the right?' continued Dick. 'It's automatic.'

'How hard can it be?' Robbie replied confidently.

'Right, keep your phones on. I've set up a WhatsApp group and added you all. We'll meet back here at four p.m.' Robbie was learning: crime or no crime, happy hour was not to be missed.

The groups splintered off and went about their respective tasks.

Chapter 13

The police station

Robbie dialled Mill Street Station in Galway, where he had the number on speed dial. The front desk officer answered.

'Sean, is that you?'

'Aye, is that you Robbie? They told me you were on holiday?' Sean replied, sounding slightly puzzled.

'Look, Sean, I don't have time to explain, but I need you to find out if we have anyone — even loosely — connected to the UAE or the Gulf. See if we've got any Arabic speakers on the team. Surely we must by now. Check the Garda Reserve as well.'

He vaguely recalled that the Garda, lacking any active officers proficient in Arabic, had launched a recruitment drive a few years ago to attract Arabic-speaking individuals, particularly from the growing Irish Muslim community.

'Aye, sure, boss…' Sean began, but Robbie cut him off.

'Be discreet Sean. This is all off the record. I'm in a place called Ras Al Khaimah,' Robbie said. His voice racing. 'If you find someone — anyone — see if they can get me a contact here. I've got to run. Cheers, Seanie. I owe you one.'

'Mind if we stop for a coffee, Davie? Want one?' Robbie asked, seeing a Starbucks drive-through.

'Never touch the stuff,' replied Davie. 'Silent killer.'

Undeterred, Robbie pulled into the drive-through lane. Just before he reached the collection point, his phone pinged — the WhatsApp group. A picture? Rudolph, taking a selfie, pint in hand, grinning at the golf club. The accompanying text simply read:

Cracked it lads.

He always was a backwards clown

'Jesus, that was fast!' a delighted and pleasantly surprised Robbie blurted out loud. 'Text him back Davie and ask him to trawl through the statements, deposits and withdrawals, and look for anything unusual.'

'On it, Boss,' Davie smirked. He was beginning to come out of his shell, Robbie thought.

'Very droll, Davie,' Robbie responded. 'Right navigator — point the way.'

'Right at the roundabout and straight all the way,' Davie said, motioning with an outstretched hand.

The road was quiet — at least compared to Galway or Dublin. Robbie was hugging the right side a little too tightly at first, overcompensating to avoid drifting into oncoming traffic — but far too close for comfort to a cyclist coming the wrong way.

'Fuckin' hell, Robbie,' Davie stammered, ashen-faced and breathless. He never swore, so Robbie knew he needed to get his act together.

'Sorry, Davie.'

They passed the mall on the left as they headed north on Sheikh Mohammed Bin Salem Road (E11), towards the city centre. Robbie was keen to stick to the speed limits — not entirely convinced he was properly insured to drive the car. Still, he wasn't crawling either. Yet almost every other car on the road flew past him.

'What's the story with the speed limit, Davie?' Robbie asked, passing an 80 km/h sign while doing 78, as two cars tore by. 'Do they not care about speeding tickets?'

He'd heard rumours — that the government paid locals' fines, even periodically cleared their credit card bills. Could that be true? he wondered.

Davie chuckled, his shoulders rising and falling in rhythm with the motion of the car.

'They give you the first twenty free,' he explained, as if that vindicated everything. But from Robbie's face, he could tell he'd have to elaborate.

'You're allowed to drive 20 km/h over the limit — unless you're in Abu Dhabi. They've got their own laws. This is an 80 zone, so you can drive 100 here,' he added.

'Why don't they just make the speed limit 100, make everyone stay under that, and then everyone would know what speed to drive at?' said Robbie, genuinely puzzled.

'That would require a modicum of common sense.' Davie raised his eyes before continuing. 'And they wouldn't be able to pretend they're doing us a favour. It's all a show out here Robbie.'

Robbie was beginning to realise that.

They continued past a row of shops, car washes, and restaurants — punctuated by barbers offering a shave and a haircut for twenty dirhams. He'd always enjoyed a hot towel shave, but at that price, he couldn't help wondering how clean those places really were. The area, though bustling, was decidedly run-down.

Now playing the role of tour guide, Davie shared his local knowledge.

'That's Al Jazirat — the old town, before they built that kip of a village you're staying in. The name means "The Red Island." They were pearl fishermen once. It was a thriving community, but pretty much abandoned in the sixties after they found oil. Only poor expats live there now — the lucky ones, anyway. The unfortunate ones end up in labour camps.'

'Labour camps?' Robbie had heard the term before.

'Yes, most of the migrant workers live in them. Think battery chickens — overcrowded, poor living conditions, no personal space. Leave your dignity at the door.' Davie painted a vivid, disturbing picture. 'You don't see that on the news, Robbie.'

Picking up the pace now, mindful of the speeding regulations and almost centred in his lane, Robbie continued straight, as instructed, passing the Road and Traffic Department and the Forensic Laboratory, until they reached the main police headquarters.

'Pull into the right here,' Davie instructed. 'Got any I.D.? You'll need it just to get past the front desk.'

Fumbling in his pocket, Robbie pulled out a passport and an I.D. card, both as worn as anything Davie could remember.

The men were greeted with the customary, 'As-salamu alaykum,' to which Davie confidently replied, 'Wa alaykum as-salam.'

He continued, as if fluent, 'Hal tatakallam al-Ingleeziya?'

Robbie was impressed.

'A little,' the Duty Officer replied, sounding like he knew more than that. A good start, Robbie thought. 'Can I help you?'

'My name's Robbie O'Malley, and I'm a police officer with the Garda Síochána — in Ireland,' Robbie said, realising they probably wouldn't be familiar with the Irish term.

'Do you have any I.D., sir?'

Robbie produced his passport and Garda ID. The Duty Officer studied them closely.

'Mr. Robert...'

'Mr. O'Malley,' Robbie interrupted.

'That's what they say around here, Robbie,' Davie interjected with a wink.

'Really? Oh, okay. Yes, sir, that's me.'

'How can we help you today, Mr. Robert?'

'We are looking for information about a friend, Har de Luc, and a possible incident at a bar called the Thirsty Horse,' Robbie said, trying to speak slowly and deliberately without sounding "*special*" — just to make sure he was understood.

The officer stared at him, more shocked that Robbie knew about it than by the news itself. Without a word, he pulled his phone from his pocket and made a call.

'Please follow me,' the Duty Officer said.

Robbie and Davie exchanged a glance before turning back to the officer.

'Only you, Mr. Robert,' the officer asserted.

'On you go. I'll wait here,' Davie said, irritated but graciously conceding.

The officer led Robbie past the reception, the public service counters, and administrative areas towards a small windowless room at the back of the building. The walk seemed to take forever. Robbie couldn't remember ever moving so slowly.

'Wait here,' the officer said sharply, shutting the door behind him. Robbie was left alone with nothing but the four bare walls and his own thoughts for company.

He pulled out his phone and searched the local news. Nothing about the Thirsty Horse. Strange, he thought.

Though it felt like an age, only a few minutes had passed when a civilian — maybe security — entered pushing a trolley.

'Would you like some tea or coffee, sir? Perhaps some dates?'

You don't get this in Pearse Street, Robbie reflected, thinking back to his early days on the streets of Dublin.

'Coffee and dates would be nice, thanks.'

Mohammed — as the name tag once again suggested — poured Robbie a thimble of coffee: no milk, no sugar. It looked more like tea than coffee.

'What's this?' Robbie asked, disappointed.

'Arabic coffee, sir.'

Noticing the packet of Chesterfields Robbie had placed on the table, Mohammed added, 'Would you like an ashtray, sir?'

Fuckin' hell, Robbie thought. *This place was more like a restaurant than a police station.*

'Yes please. And a light?' Robbie beamed; the earlier disappointment long gone.

The ashtray was half-full, and the unventilated room reeked of smoke by the time the door opened again. A man in his late forties, Robbie guessed, entered wearing a dark green blazer adorned with golden shoulder epaulettes — which Robbie took to indicate high rank — matching trousers, polished black boots, a green beret, and a belt with a holster, the firearm clearly on display.

Jesus! thought Robbie. *What have I gotten myself into?*

He looked familiar — neither tall nor particularly strong-looking, but familiar all the same. Robbie couldn't quite place him. Had he seen him in the pub? He'd been surprised at the number of locals in the bars, but this guy would have stood out. He pushed the thought to the back of his mind. *Focus Robbie, focus.*

'Good day, Mr. Robbie. My name is Mohammed Alshahari,' the man introduced himself, though Robbie had already seen the name on the badge embellishing his well-decorated chest. 'I am the Major here, responsible for criminal investigations.'

He spoke in a squeaky, almost irritating voice, but his English was impeccable, and he carried himself with authority — which only made Robbie feel even more anxious.

Then it hit him. This was the same man who'd been up at the Thirsty Horse the other night. The one Top Shelf had pointed out. Head of CID, or something.

What the fuck was he doing here?

'Am I in some kind of trouble?' Robbie asked, hearing the quiver in his own voice.

'Not at all. My sister called me. She works as a translator with the Garda Síochána in Dublin and mentioned there was a man who needed some help. So, how may I assist you?'

Saying a silent prayer, Robbie breathed a sigh of relief. *God bless you, Seanie.*

'Cigarette?' offered Mohammed.

Robbie began to explain…

'Okay, Mr. Robbie, I think we have everything we need for now,' Mohammed declared, helpfully. 'Let me make some calls. Leave me your number, and I'll get back to you as soon as I know anything.'

What a godsend, thought Robbie, as he scrawled his number onto the office stationery. He made a mental note to text Sean and thank him.

After they shook hands, Robbie thanked Mohammed for his time. Mohammed then walked him back to reception, where Auld Davie was sipping a cappuccino and tucking into a plateful of chicken biryani.

Lucky bastard, a hungry Robbie thought with envy, uncertain if he had said it out loud.

Chapter 14

The broken nose – part I

As Robbie and Auld Davie ambled up the ramp leading to the rear entrance of the golf club, they were met with the thump of loud music, the clinking of glasses, raised voices, random bursts of song, and riotous laughter from within.

'Go on..' 'Sláinte!' 'Ya useless bastard' '*Low lies the fields of Athenry...*'

Someone was having a party — and it sounded suspiciously like the men that Robbie thought he had put to *work* earlier that day.

They wandered out to the patio to find the round table in full flight. Robbie — the policeman — lost it.

'For fuck's sake. What is going on here? Did I not tell you to ...'

He didn't get to finish.

Mick slammed his fist onto the table and rose with such force that his knees rattled the table top, sending drinks flying in every direction.

'Who the fuck do you think you are?' he roared.

'Easy, Mick,' said Rudolph, reaching out to grab his arm.

'Get the fuck off me,' Mick snarled, swinging his arm free with such force that his elbow cracked Rudolph square in the face, splitting his nose wide open. Blood sprayed everywhere — into pints, across the table, all over Mick's back.

'Fuck this.'

Mick lifted the table and flipped it clean over, smashing every single glass and drenching everyone in a disgusting cocktail of drink, cigarette ash and blood.

'You don't get to come in here and tell us what to fuckin' do,' Mick raged, his fury locked on a petrified Robbie.

Robbie had heard the stories — Mick's temper, the chaos — but witnessing it firsthand, and being on the wrong end of it, was terrifying.

'I was only...'

'Well, don't!'

Robbie, shaken, backed away and made for the relative safety of the bar, where a pale-faced Princess was waiting for him, her concern evident.

'Is everything alright?' she asked, though she already knew the answer.

'You don't have to explain,' she said softly.

'Mick's not right. He hasn't been for a while.'

Robbie exhaled.

Still trembling, he ordered a pint, but kept his eyes firmly fixed on the door, scared stiff of whom — or what — might appear next.

He breathed a sigh of relief when Auld Davie's head popped around the corner.

'Jesus, Davie, what was that? I'm trying to help those guys.'

'They don't see it that way Robbie,' Davie replied calmly. 'They see a stranger, coming into their midst and ordering them about. Nothing ever happens around here — and that's the way they like it. Work, golf, beer, and home — rinse and repeat. They don't need this.'

'Don't they care about their friend?' Robbie asked, frustration creeping into his voice.

'Of course they do,' Davie said with a nod. 'But they'll be here long after you've gone, Robbie — with or without Har. You need to be more diplomatic. These men are too long in the tooth and have worked too hard to take orders from anyone. They are all bosses in their own right, and they don't answer to anyone.'

Robbie nodded, reluctantly accepting the flaws in his controlling approach.

'What should I do? What can I do?' he asked, almost pleading.

'Nothing. We'll get some Vaseline and a rag for Rudolph's nose and give them a few minutes to calm down. Once Princess has cleaned up the mess, send out a round. Nothing clears the air better than a free pint.'

Davie paused, a hint of mischief flickering in his eyes.

'If you really want to get back in Mick's good books, take him a clean shirt. The golf guys will give you a club T-shirt. Oh, and maybe a Jack Daniels,' he added, ever the pragmatist.

Literally unbelievable, thought a somewhat reassured Robbie, acknowledging Davie's advice.

'Pint for Davie please, Princess.'

He enjoyed the calmness of relatively mundane chit-chat with Davie. Back in England, when he was younger, Davie had worked as a welder and fabricator, though his real passions had been tiddlywinks, ballroom dancing, and golf. After retiring, he started his own landscaping business — that's where he made his money, working for some pretty wealthy clients in the Gulf. These days, given the lack of ballrooms and the dearth of credible tiddlywinks opposition, he mostly just *pottered around* — to use his own words — and was happy playing golf every day. He used to be pretty handy too, apparently.

'C'mon, we'll go out,' said Davie, seeing that Princess had restored the battle scene to its former glory. He drained his pint and ordered two more — it was happy hour after all.

The table was calm and quiet — eerily so — when Davie and Robbie rejoined. Nods replaced words, until a meek Robbie offered a quiet, 'Sorry lads.' Another round of nods implied it had been accepted.

Princess arrived with a tray of pints; Robbie passed Mick his Jack Daniels; and Magnolia, the receptionist, produced a pristine new golf shirt. The men shook hands — all forgiven, it seemed, for now at least.

Maybe it was Robbie's failing eyesight, but he could swear Tappie was trying to suppress a laugh, staring straight at the two bit of cotton wool dangling from Rudolph's nostrils.

Trying a change of tack, Robbie offered, 'Right, who wants to start?'

Chapter 15

Freedom

Tappie led the way, with Mick still reeling internally — his forgiveness more a gesture than heartfelt.

'We popped round to Har's place. The door was open as usual,' he stated categorically. 'But someone had been in, and not Har. Har was almost OCD about some things — straightened the labels on his cans and jars, always washing his hands...that kind of stuff.'

Robbie wondered where this was going.

'Someone tried to make it look like they hadn't been in, but the cushions on the couch weren't straight, the underpants in his drawers weren't folded, and there were blue pens mixed in with the black ones on his desk. Someone had rummaged through everything — and tried to cover their tracks.'

'Okay, great work. So, Har had something to hide or had something that someone wanted. What was it? Did they get what they were looking for? Was there anything missing?' Robbie probed, re-assuming his lead role but trying to use some diplomacy.

'No, nothing. Nothing was missing I mean,' Tappie added. 'Nothing material anyway. He didn't have much to take mind you, but his laptop was there, his TV, his car keys — cash even… it wasn't a burglary.

'But' he paused, 'all his ID was gone. No passport, no driving licence, no Emirates ID.'

'Could he have those on him? Aren't you obliged to carry those?'

'You're supposed to, but few people do. Some people keep their driving licence in the glove box, and some might have their ID in their wallet — but Har didnae have a wallet. No one, no one,' reiterated Tappie, 'carries their passport around. They've either taken that, or Har has it stashed somewhere very safe. I had a good root around. Nothing.'

'Okay, we need to find them. Can we check his car and anywhere else he might hide something? What about his phone?' asked Robbie.

The mention of phones gave Robbie a jolt. He'd meant to text Sean to thank him for putting him in touch with Mohammed — the police major.

'Sorry, lads. One minute…'

He fired off a quick WhatsApp message:

YOU'RE A STAR SEANIE. MOHAMMED WAS VERY HELPFUL. I OWE YOU ONE

'Right, sorry about that. Phone?' continued Robbie.

'No, that wis also gone, but he might've had that himself,' suggested Tappie.

'Okay. We need to find out what they took — if anything — or what they were looking for. Go back to his apartment. Turn it inside out and upside down. Check the ceiling cavities, the ductwork, everywhere he might have hidden something, or they might not have looked.'

'Did you have joy with the Indians? Did anyone see anything?'

'They're pretty angry. They say something, possibly a body bag, was loaded into an unmarked van long after the crowd had dispersed. They reckon it was one of their own, but no one will tell them anything. Funny thing, though — they all know Har de Luc. He's up there all the time, apparently. They just thought he was there for the cheap drink.'

'Hmm. Okay. Noted.'

Robbie lit a cigarette and, deep in thought, unconsciously offered the packet to the rest of the table. It was half-empty by the time it came back.

'Dick, Eugene… any luck with the CCTV. Any evidence to corroborate the Indians' story?'

'Yes,' responded an eager Eugene, as if he had been waiting for his cue. 'We managed to get the CCTV from the bank and the money exchange.'

'Brilliant. And??'

'There was a lot of activity up there last night. It's odd though,' Eugene continued enthusiastically. 'We can see all these people going in — Har included — but half of them never come out.'

'What time was that?'

'Seven forty-three p.m.'

'Well, they're hardly still in there, so there must be another way in and out,' deduced a rhetorical Robbie.

'All of those places have back doors for deliveries,' chipped in Dick. 'Half of them aren't locked either. Anyone could come or go. But why you would go in through the front and leave out the back?'

Indeed, thought Robbie. There weren't many genuine reasons, if any at all.

'Okay, good work. So, we need to find out where he was before that,' said Robbie, to no one in particular. 'Anything else?'

'Yes,' Eugene continued, 'we clearly see the body bag — or what looks like one; we can't be sure it's a body — being brought out and loaded into an unmarked van at two twenty-two, long after the crowd and police vehicles are gone.'

'Right. Well, if it's not a body, what is it?' the new diplomat continued.

'Stu, you cracked that password pretty quickly. Did you find anything unusual in his bank records?' Robbie intentionally refrained from asking how he'd cracked the password.

Never one to miss an opportunity to boast, Rudolph launched into one... 'I tried all the usual combinations — birthdays, family members' names, favourite football teams...'

'Aye, aye, aye... get on with it, Red Nose,' an agitated Mick interrupted. 'Or I'll give you another punch in the nose.'

'No need for that, Mick,' Rudolph replied, clearly offended.

'No — well done, Rudolph,' said Robbie, stepping in to mediate. 'Great job, but time's no friend of ours. Remember, the first forty-eight hours are crucial. Eugene, what time did you say Har was seen entering the Thirsty Horse?'

'Seven forty-three p.m.'

'Okay, so it's been nearly twenty-four hours. What have you got for us Rudolph?' Robbie pressed.

'This is good,' said Rudolph, his tone suddenly deadly serious — no rolling of the eyes or lip-licking.

'There are regular, large deposits going in every month. Always the same amount: forty-two thousand dirhams. The ledger statement lists it as "SALARY," but Har didn't have a regular job. This has been happening for over two years. Then, every five months, he withdraws the lot — on the second Thursday of the month. And before you ask — yes, he withdrew two hundred and ten thousand on Thursday.'

'Fuck, no wonder no one's seen him. I'd be gone too,' joked Tappie, rather inappropriately.

Rudolph cleared his throat to remind the boys to focus before continuing.

'Other random, smaller amounts are being deposited too. Could be from his consultancy work, but the statement doesn't give any details. And here's the strange part — no one's cashing any rent cheques. He always pays his credit cards on time, though.'

'That doesn't sound right,' said Tappie, more serious now. 'He's skint all the time, so who's paying his rent if no one's cashing the cheques?'

'And where is that money coming from? What's he doing with it? Rudolph continued. 'It's not like he's been buying anything, has he?'

Shakes of the heads followed muttered 'nos.'

'Okay, keep on that.' said Robbie. 'Eugene, can you help him? Your financial background might come in handy.'

Moving round the table and turning his attention to Top Shelf, he asked 'any luck with your contact Sherlock?'

The humour was a welcome relief. Robbie was still conscious of *bossing* the situation.

'Not really, to be honest,' replied a somewhat disconsolate and disappointed Top Shelf. 'He's usually on the money — very helpful — but it's almost as though someone's got to him, told him to say nothing. He's clammed up.'

Robbie's phone suddenly chimed, the glass tabletop exaggerating the buzzing. He ignored it. It chimed again. Then again.

'For fuck's sake, PC Plod, you going to check that?' asked an irritated, scowling Mick.

Robbie's face turned as white as a ghost...

Sean: **Sorry Robbie I meant to call**

Sean: **I couldn't find anyone**

Sean: **Who the FK is Mohammed?**

Ignoring the inquisitive and worried looks, Robbie typed back:

Robbie: **The translator's brother**

Sean: **What translator?**

Having only known Robbie a short time, the boys knew him well enough to sense that something wasn't right. Auld Davie broke the silence —

'What is it, Robbie?'

Robbie explained the events of the police station: how they seemed to be expecting him, they knew his name — or did they? He now wondered, remembering handing over his I.D at reception. They had asked him to explain in detail everything he knew, but had offered nothing in return — only the promise of a phone call.

Were they just fishing to see exactly what he knew? They must have known about the incident at the Thirsty Horse. Someone must have told them people had been asking questions. They must have also known about the body bag. Surely, they had checked the CCTV and realised that not everyone who entered the premises left — at least not through the front door.

Hell, they knew everything that Robbie and his crew knew — and probably a whole lot more.

How had they pulled off this 'translator' stunt? Had they been in touch with the Irish police?

What were they hiding, or trying to cover up? It didn't take a detective to see something fishy was going on. It was hardly a coincidence: Robbie had six missed calls from an unknown number, a midnight text from Har de Luc, and now both Har and Rej were missing. A body bag had been removed from the premises—the same premises Har had entered but never left. Large, unexplained deposits had been made into Har's bank account. His apartment had been ransacked. Top Shelf's contact was saying nothing. And the police? They were playing them for information they clearly already had.

'This fuckin' stinks,' Robbie said to the table, disgusted. 'I need to make some calls, lads. See what the fuck's going on. Find out how they knew I was coming. I could be a few minutes — alright?'

Robbie was already dialing, nearly out the door, as the table nodded and grunted their approval.

'Thank fuck for that,' an exasperated and thirsty Mick spat out. 'You'd nearly be hungover listening to the fuck. Who's working anyway?'

'I think it's Rej,' someone muttered.

The table erupted into laughter. Tappie, ever reliable for lightening the mood, stood and raised his glass. 'C'mon, let's scoop up before he comes back. That Robbie can take our lives, but he'll never take our FREEDOM!' he roared in his best *Braveheart* accent — not that far off from his own.

In fits of laughter, the boys all raised their glasses — 'Forty-eight hours, my arse,' boomed Mick, spilling half his drink all over poor Rudolph.

Chapter 16

Har's place

Sean explained to Robbie that he had made some enquiries, but nothing more. Yes, he'd called Dublin, but he hadn't shared any particulars — Robbie hadn't given him any. He was as bewildered as Robbie about how the Emirati police had gotten wind of it, though they both agreed they must have. The only logical explanation they could come up with was that someone had made a call to the UAE — perhaps trying to help — asking if they knew of any Emiratis working in Ireland. Why that would raise suspicion was beyond them.

Had the Emirati police managed to piece together what little information they had? Robbie had let slip that night in the Thirsty Horse that he was a police officer — but had he also told them he was Irish? He couldn't remember, he'd been pretty drunk. Had Sean mentioned that it was Robbie O'Malley who needed help? Had his name set off alarm bells when he handed over his I.D.? After all, there had been a considerable delay between showing his identification and being escorted to that room.

Were the Emiratis complicit in this? Whatever *this* was.

Two things were certain: Har de Luc was at the centre of this, and until they knew more, they couldn't trust the local police. There was something about that police Major — Mohammed what's-his-face — that Robbie couldn't quite put his finger on. Whatever it was though, he couldn't afford to let it show.

They'd have to play along and act dumb — something Robbie figured might come easily to some of his new acquaintances.

Robbie knew pursuing anything — even remotely related to this case — tonight with those new acquaintances would only incur their wrath, so he decided to leave them at it.

He called the captain of the ferry, and five minutes later was ambling up the ramp onto the pier.

What a fuckin' state, he thought, passing the ever-growing mounds of rubble and litter — presumably the remnants of the workers' lunches.

Davie's comment echoed in his mind: *You don't see that on the news.*

It was freezing when Robbie entered his apartment. The air-conditioning would take a while to figure out. Thankfully, he and Davie had stopped by the off-licence on their way back from the police station, and Robbie had re-stocked the fridge. He cracked open a cold Guinness and checked his phone.

Nothing. For the first time in hours, he could finally relax.

Of the few dubious perks of working with — or was it *for*? — the Garda Síochána, the fuel allowance and the free phone with unlimited local and international calls were the standouts. He dialed his brother, Donal.

They must have spoken for hours because Robbie woke to the sound of extremely loud music, sitting bolt upright on the sofa, still fully clothed, with half a pint of Guinness locked in his hand. Several empty cans littered the table, ash was scattered everywhere, and a cigarette butt had been stubbed out in half a pizza lying on the floor. He checked his phone — it was 4.45 a.m. Two new messages had appeared in the WhatsApp group:

> Tappie: **COME ON UP. WE'RE IN**
>
> Tappie: **304**

'What the fuck,' Robbie groaned. 'What are these cunts up to now?'

He was still half asleep, or half-cut, or both, and needed this like a hole in the head. What number was he again? 203? He vaguely remembered Tappie mentioning Har living in the same building. He wasn't sure if he'd said the apartment number or not. But it seemed highly coincidental that a party was going on, in his apartment block. The noise was coming from above, and they were blaring Irish Rebel songs — "*Come Out Ye Black and Tans"* the most recent of them.

There was no point in showering for this lot, he thought. *Fuck them.* He may have been half-cut, but he was still far too sober to deal with their drunken antics, so he poured himself a generous *home-pour* of Micil — a peated whiskey, produced by Galway's first legal distillery in over a century. He allowed himself a moment to savour the aroma. He'd brought it with him from Ireland, knowing that duty-free wouldn't cater to such a sophisticated palate.

Robbie grew up in a small Irish village in Connemara, where his fascination with the peat bogs and the family tales of illicit poitín distilling sparked a lifelong love for spirits. That thirst carried him through university, where he studied chemistry, before joining the Gardaí. His scientific expertise led him to the Forensic Unit, where he made a name for himself analyzing substances — and occasionally sampling them too. Eventually, his talent earned him a promotion to detective — a role he sometimes wished he didn't have.

This was one of those occasions.

He decided to take the stairs, rather than the lift that everyone seemed to use. The levels of obesity here reminded him of his days in Boston, where he'd briefly given lectures on drug enforcement to new recruits. *God, how he'd love a Taco Bell now... and a Kane's Boston cream donut.* The thought was so vivid that he nearly lost his footing, caught in a delirious haze of hunger and nostalgia.

Gathering his thoughts and putting his cravings to the back of his mind, he opened the door to the third floor — and his ears nearly exploded. There was no doubt it was *them*. The door to 304 was wide open, and the unmistakable whiff of hashish filled the hallway. *First alcohol, now hash? Where the hell had they gotten that?*

Robbie shook his head, marveling at how the UAE had so easily duped the West into buying their puritanical facade. Nothing here seemed illegal — or maybe everything was just quietly tolerated. And yet, despite the debauchery, it still felt safe. It was a bizarre contradiction.

His mind drifted again, this time to the recently deceased Kris Kristofferson and his lyric: "*partly truth and partly fiction.*" R.I.P, he thought, glancing upwards in quiet respect.

Sunday 15th June

Chapter 17

The passports

If Robbie thought he had woken up to a mess, this place was a full-blown bombsite. Everything — and everyone — was scattered in absolute chaos. Tiles were missing from the ceiling, duct grids lay on the carpet, not unscrewed but ripped straight from the walls, and the cistern lid lay cracked on the bathroom floor. The kitchen resembled a makeshift workshop. Tools were strewn everywhere — hammers, screwdrivers, crowbars — and the fridge was in tatters, its door barely clinging to its hinges.

Had they found it like this? If not, this was a demolition. He had told them to 'turn it inside out and upside down,' but Jesus.

Tappie stood in the middle of the chaos, wearing a Green Bay Packers baseball cap backward over his bald head, waving a packet of Kraft Singles in the air like a trophy. The Eurythmics blasted through the speaker as he belted out, *"Sweet dreams are made of cheese!"* Everyone, including those already on the floor, burst into laughter, rolling around as if it were the funniest thing they'd ever heard.

'Morning, Boss,' Mick smirked, exhaling a heavy cloud from the joint dangling from his lips.

This is not going to be a good day, thought Robbie, doing his best to keep his face from betraying his emotions.

He really didn't know how to start, the memory of yesterday's disastrous, heavy-handed approach still fresh in his mind. So, using all his diplomacy, he offered 'Cigarette anyone?'

'Fuck cigarettes,' Mick announced, already rolling another joint.

'Whisky?' Robbie offered, waving his prized bottle of Micil.

For a moment, it was as though time stood still. He had their attention now. *Mental note to self,* Robbie thought. *I must remember that. Pricier than cigarettes, but that trick is worth repeating.*

Robbie poured a generous measure into vessels of various shapes and sizes, took a drag of the joint Mick kept wafting in his face, then raised his own glass with a, 'Sláinte mhaith.' Finding an empty, dry spot to sit, he settled down and began. 'Okay, you have something, I take it?'

The boys were never sure if it was the drink, the drugs, or just his naturally wobbly legs, but

Rudolph was far from steady as he staggered in from the kitchen, bottle in one hand, and five passports clutched in the other.

Mick motioned to Rudolph to set the passports on the table he'd just wiped clean with the sleeve of his shirt, taking care not to lose any hash. Rudolph, taking his cue, obliged — before casually placing an enormous wad of cash beside them.

Robbie's jaw dropped.

'The crafty cunt had them stashed in his cheese drawer,' an exaggerated Rudolph chirped, clearly delighted with himself. 'And for my next trick,' — pulling a bundle of credit cards from his back pocket — 'ta-da.'

'And you had to destroy the place to find that out did you?' Robbie asked, a mix of rhetoric, delight and disbelief in his voice.

'Well, I wis gonnae call the locksmith...' chortled Tappie, his usual humour in full swing.

'What more do you fuckin' want, ya miserable fuck? Did we find it, or did we find it?' Mick added, full of sarcasm.

'Are you going to hog that all day, Mick?' asked Dick, who hadn't taken his eyes off the joint since Mick had finally managed to squint a roach into it. Mick took a hit before passing it over.

Robbie managed to slip in, 'Where are you getting that from?' mimicking a smoking action — partly out of curiosity, but well aware of the repercussions should anyone complain or alert the authorities. It was something this crew seemed blissfully unaware of — or unconcerned about.

'Har gets it from time to time,' replied a bloodshot-eyed Mick, the weed seemingly calming him down at last. 'From some Pakistani or Nepalese dude. Never asked him the details.'

Meanwhile, Top Shelf, ever the voice of reason, had managed to clear a space on the table and found seven seats, all with four legs. Robbie had to admit that, for all their failings, they were just about the most functional bunch of reprobates he'd had the misfortune to come across.

Top Shelf actually seemed quite together as he began stating the obvious.

'Right, Har's got five passports, maybe more. At this point, we have to assume that at least four of the names are fake, but which four? Is his name really Har de Luc? Can we find that out? Enquire with the Scottish authorities, or the French, or wherever he claimed he was from?'

'I knew he was full of shite — French descent, my arse,' piped up Auld Davie, clearly feeling the night. He was a good bit older than the rest of them.

'Does he have any more? Is he even still in the country? Could he have travelled on another? That could explain why no one has seen him,' continued Top Shelf, relishing his moment in the spotlight.

'There's only one reason a man has multiple passports... and you have to be well-connected to get them. It's not easy. You need to flood the data banks with multiple addresses, dates, places of birth, bank accounts, national insurance numbers, and so on. It all has to be verified and consistent. After all that, you need an individual who is competent enough to retain all that information and reproduce it fluently upon request.'

'Either that,' Robbie interrupted, 'or you need someone pretty influential on side to arrange *relaxed* airport security protocols.'

'Yes,' continued Top Shelf, 'one way or another, he's in someone's pocket. It's either a well-organized criminal organization, or, given the way the police have been behaving, it could well be them — or both.'

'So, where do we go from here?' Robbie asked.

Never one to miss a trick, Tappie chimed in, 'the Bay opens at six,' resulting in more hoots of laughter from the relentless rabble.

'I'm serious,' he added, 'and I'm starvin,' and we've drunk the fridge dry.'

Robbie was not about to tell them that he had restocked his fridge, so he relented too and agreed to take the *meeting* over to the club. It would be cleaner — and quieter, at least.

Mick and Top Shelf rooted through the mess of hash, tobacco, rizla papers, roach material and empty cans for their car keys.

Robbie said a silent prayer: *Lord save us and protect us.*

A beaming Princess answered those prayers with a cheerful, 'Good morning, Robbie.'

'It is now,' Robbie beamed back.

Chapter 18

Moderation dearest Robert

A few diehards were sipping coffee prior to their early morning tee-off. The boys knew them all, exchanging "*good mornings*" and the usual bits of mundane chit-chat.

Robbie thought it was warm — twenty-five degrees. The high temperatures of the previous night had dropped slightly during the relatively cool morning hours, leaving the course damp with dew the morning sun was trying hard to burn off. Robbie couldn't believe the others found it cold.

To Robbie's dismay, but totally unsurprised, Princess arrived with a tray of pints that no one had ordered. 'There we go, gentlemen.'

Empty stacks don't stand, popped into Robbie's head, just as Tappie ordered, 'Seven breakfast baps please Princess.'

Tappie had quite the belly on him, thought Robbie, as he studied the company he had been so unexpectedly thrust into. Mick aside, he felt oddly comfortable with them. They weren't all that different from him, really.

Not that he regretted becoming a policeman, but he did wonder sometimes where he might have ended up had things taken a different turn.

'Any sign of Rej?' Rudolph asked, just as Princess turned to leave.

'No, sir. No one has seen him since he finished his shift on Thursday,' she replied, clearly concerned.

'Has anyone reported this?' Robbie asked.

'You would have to ask my manager, sir… eh… Mr… eh… Robbie… sir,' Princess said, now visibly flustered Princess.

'Anything we should know, *Sir* Robbie?' winked Tappie — which, if nothing else, broke the tension between the flirting couple.

'Is he here?' Robbie asked, ignoring Tappie's jibe.

'I think so. I'll ask him to come out.'

Pablo, the manager, appeared in a silver suit, well-polished shoes, and a pink tie. He looked the part, if slightly overweight — but what caught Robbie's eye was the distinctive monobrow and the thick Cork brogue, as Pablo greeted them with a simple, 'Morning, boys.'

Robbie closed his eyes briefly. He could have been back home in Galway. All around him was the chatter of Irish and Scottish accents. He was beginning to see why these boys felt so comfortable — so at home here.

'Pablo, this is Robbie O'Malley. Robbie, Pablo Botty.' Dick said making the introductions.

That can't be his real name, thought Robbie as they shook hands.

'How can I be of service to you Robbie?' Pablo was well-spoken — his accent thick yet posh. He was clearly no 'daw,' as Robbie might have said himself.

Robbie gave Pablo a brief synopsis of events, careful not to divulge too much. He was quickly learning that rumours spread like wildfire around the village — and he was no longer sure who he could trust. Only now was it dawning on him that someone within his own circle, one of the very men he had brought into his close company, might have alerted the local police to his movements.

'Princess tells us that no one has seen Rej since Thursday night. Is that correct? Robbie asked, trying to keep it casual.

'Yes, that's correct.'

'Would that be like him? Would he not usually contact you if he were sick or something had come up?'

'No, it's not like him at all. He's usually pretty anal about his timekeeping — about everything, really, to be honest. And he can't afford to lose a day's wages, let alone two. None of them can, not on the wages we pay them.'

'Have you alerted anyone? The police? That's more than forty-eight hours now.' Robbie's tone now less casual.

'No, and to be frank, I'm not sure there's much point. The police don't care about these guys — they're just numbers. Hundreds go missing every week. Some have had enough and just go home. Others get into trouble and 'disappear.' Some just go on a bender, then crawl back with their tails between their legs, looking for their job back.

Rej actually goes home fairly regularly — twice a year, outside of his annual leave — which is unusual. He doesn't know that I know this, as he always phones in sick, but I do, and I let it slide. It's important for these guys to see their family.

I assumed that was the case this time too. He always seems to go around the middle of the month.'

Robbie interrupted. 'When does he get paid?'

'The second Thursday of every month. But, as I say, he always phones in sick, and he hasn't this time, which is odd. At the end of the day, they're all easily replaceable. So, no, we haven't reported it. I'll tell you this though, and I'll tell you for nothing: he won't be getting his job back, should he deign to grace us with his presence any time soon.'

The second Thursday of every month. Hmm. Where had Robbie heard that before? His mind was racing. He also got paid on the second Thursday of the month — or was it the last Thursday? It was Thursday, anyway... he was drifting. Yes, that's it, he remembered — Har withdrew two hundred and ten thousand dirhams on Thursday — the second Thursday of June.

Before Robbie had a chance to respond, he was off. 'Sorry lads, lots to do. You know where to find me. It'll be easier than finding de Luc or Rej,' he said with a wink.

No one, Robbie excepted, was the least bit surprised — or interested — in what Pablo had said. The conversation quickly shifted back to jovial, meaningless banter as the men enjoyed their baps and pints.

Robbie took the opportunity to catch up on emails. Thankfully, he had remembered to activate his out-of-office message before leaving. He deleted the few he had received without even bothering to open them.

Another round appeared.

'What's going on lads? It's not happy hour is it?' joked Robbie. He hoped the real meaning behind his remark would go unnoticed — but these men, despite being up all night, were sharp as tacks.

'Wind it in, Plod,' muttered a thick Mick. Robbie was getting a little tired of the 'Plod' insult, but he let it go.

'We all get members' discount — thirty percent — so happy hour doesn't really make any difference to us,' remarked Dick.

Robbie, completely baffled by this revelation, couldn't help himself. 'Why the hell do you only drink during happy hour, then?'

'Moderation dearest Robert, moderation.' It could only be Tappie.

It was going to be another one of those days. Robbie's inward voice was already going into overdrive — he felt like he'd put in a day's work already, and it was only 7.30 a.m.

Chapter 19

The excuses

'Right,' Robbie began. 'Big Finn says Har was still here on Thursday night after you all left for the Waldorf at nine-thirty. He had a falling out with Rej over the mince pie, and Rej hasn't been seen since. What time did Har arrive there? Can we find that out? And what did he do between leaving here and arriving there?'

He continued, 'I received those six missed calls, all between twenty past one and one forty a.m. on Friday morning. The text from Har, if he was the one who sent it, arrived at one forty-five. What time did we all leave?'

'Hold on, I'll check my phone. I would've gotten a ping when I paid the bill.' replied Top Shelf, eager to get in on the action. 'One a.m. on the button.'

'Right, so who was Har with at the end of the night? That's another forty-five minutes we need to account for. We need to see their CCTV. Dick, Eugene?'

'Har also fell out with Finn on Wednesday night,' added Top Shelf. 'We assumed it was just their usual drunken antics, but apparently, Har was pretty upset. What if it was something more? We need to talk to Big Finn. Where is he, anyway? I haven't seen him since Friday — no one has.'

'Har then appears on CCTV, at seven forty-three on Friday evening, entering the Thirsty Horse. He doesn't come out — that's the last we see of him,' Robbie continued, keen to maintain control of the meeting.

'Where does he go after that? We then see something that looks like a body bag being removed and loaded into an unmarked van at two twenty-two a.m. Could that be Har or Rej? Do we have the reg number of that van, Eugene?'

'Yes, I think so. Let me check.'

'Get back on to the hospitals. See if any DOAs came in during the early hours of Saturday morning.'

'Rudolph, can you head back up to that industrial estate? See if you can figure out what's going on behind the Thirsty Horse. There's a little lane where you can park, so you won't need to be on your feet long. Why were they using the rear entrance? Was it just that night, or is there some sort of back-alley operation running up there? And if there is, who's involved? It's a CCTV blackspot, so you'll have to check it out firsthand. Tappie, you go with him in case there's any trouble.'

'We also now know that Har has multiple passports, bank cards, and a bundle of cash. Where did he get all that? Is he still here? Or has he already left the country using another fake passport?'

'If he has, he left in a hurry because he left all his cash behind,' added Top Shelf.

'Good point. Is there any way we can check that?' Robbie continued. 'Is there any point going to the police? They'll either tell us nothing, tell us what they want us to hear, or tell us what we want to hear, but it won't be the truth. We know that much.'

'What about Rhianna?' Mick offered, his voice lacking its usual malice. 'Doesn't her son still work at the airport? She used to be quite close with Har.'

'Brilliant idea Mick,' said Robbie, trying to keep on the right side of him. 'You seemed to get on with her the other morning. Could you ask her? She seemed pretty straight though, and this would need to be off the books, like.'

'Aye, no bother,' Mick replied, oddly nonchalant. 'She always looks like that, but she's far from straight.' This brought about clinking glasses and roars of belly laughter from the boys. Robbie didn't get the joke.

Eager to get out of there, Robbie quickly added, 'On second thoughts, we do need to go back to the police. Davie, it's you and me again.'

'Really? Why? There's only so much chicken biryani a man can eat, Robbie,' Davie said irritably, 'mind you, their cappuccinos aren't bad.'

'We need to play along, play their game. They're not going to tell us the truth, so maybe we can beat them at their own game. They've probably been puffing on that dokha all weekend, and half of them were likely in the Frisky last night. Now might be the time to catch them off guard. They don't seem like the sharpest bunch — might just fall for it.'

'Super-sleuth now, are we?' Mick's sarcasm was back. *Take another puff*, Robbie thought.

Having thought he coordinated the meeting quite well and delegated without ordering, Robbie couldn't believe his ears when the excuses started.

'The Bar in The Waldorf doesn't open till noon…'

'The bank is closed on a Sunday…'

'Finn won't be up yet…'

'The Thirsty Horse won't be open yet either…'

'Rhianna always goes back to bed after feeding the pigeons...'

'ARE YOU LOT FUCKIN' SERIOUS?' roared Robbie. 'After everything I've just said. Two men could be dead — one of them your friend — the corrupt police department's doing fuck all, and you lot want to do is sit around drinking pints and talking about the weather?'

At that moment, with impeccable timing, Princess strolled by.

'What a lovely day, Princess. Another round please — but none for Sir Robbie here — he's working,' Tappie said, winking as she passed. The boys loved Tappie's wit.

'Nice on Tappie...'

'Get in there, Tappie!'

'Oi oi!'

Rudolph nearly knocked the table over again, his spindly legs seemingly at odds with the rest of his frame.

A dejected Robbie resigned himself to the reality of the situation. Excuses they might have been, but they were also the truth.

'Four p.m. then?'

'Aye, we'll see you for happy hour, Boss,' Tappie said, adding insult to injury.

Robbie wasn't sure if it was the lack of sleep, the hash, or the four days of drinking, but he was not in a good place. He was in the horrors. He had *the fear*. Paranoid as fuck, convinced everyone was turning against him.

He had been to some dark places in his life and was in no hurry to revisit them. He was supposed to be here on holiday — relaxing, getting away from the pressures of work — and instead here he was, trying to solve a crime he wasn't even sure had been committed, stuck with a bunch of inebriated reprobates who showed him zero respect and got their kicks taking the piss out of him.

It was not good.

'Text me,' he said, directing his words towards Auld Davie. He could hear the boys sniggering away as he stomped off in something of a huff.

He was close to tears.

Chapter 20

Robbie's childhood

It was too early for the ferry, so Princess called him a taxi. He decided to stop off at the public beach, directly across from his balcony. He had grown up beside the sea and remembered fondly the hours and days that he had spent down at the beach. Not that he had had a happy childhood.

Robbie was the second, and youngest child of a relatively small Catholic family. For years, he thought he was an only child. His brother, Stephen, ten years his senior — or he would have been, were he still alive — had drowned at sea in a horrific accident. Stephen had only been five years old.

His mother had been reduced to a shivering wreck, a recluse, while his father, already a heavy drinker, became an intolerable, abusive drunk who took his grief out on her. She had never wanted more children after that, and Robbie often felt she hadn't wanted him. He wondered if his father had forced himself upon her just to ensure she would give him an heir. On the rare occasions Robbie tried to stand up for his mother, it was he — or sometimes both of them — who ended up on the wrong side of his father's fists.

He had tried to bury these unbearable thoughts and memories, but they clung to him like a heavy cloak. He'd hoped the sea air might clear his head, that the vastness of the ocean might make his own past feel smaller, more distant. But staring out at the restless water, all those memories surged back like the tide.

Throughout his teenage years and early twenties, he battled depression and substance abuse — mostly alcohol, but also weed, amphetamines, acid, and coke. Living so close to the islands that controlled much of the supply, getting drugs had never been difficult. The local authorities couldn't cope, so his father sent him away to St. John of God to treat his addictions — something Robbie neither thanked nor forgave him for. It hadn't worked. If anything, it had only deepened his resentment.

He was more of a binge drinker these days rather than a full-blown alcoholic, but dependency had never left him. And he prayed he hadn't passed those traits on to his only son, Bert Jnr. Unfortunately, there were clear signs that he had. Not that Robbie could blame him for looking for an escape from such a miserable upbringing — he'd done the same.

His wife had tried everything to help him, but his tendency for self-destruction had always outweighed his will to quit. Predictably, she eventually had enough and left him. He didn't blame her now — though he had for a long time. He'd been bitter and, like most addicts, had blamed everything and everyone except himself.

Bert had yet to forgive him, and they rarely saw each other these days — something that gnawed at Robbie.

He knew self-medication wasn't the answer, but he was his father's son, after all — and it was the only way he knew. So, with all the Catholic guilt in the world weighing him down, he poured himself a mood-altering measure of Micil. Then he poured another.

Mick, for all his hostility and crankiness, had readily handed Robbie a nodge of hash when he asked — and quite a generous one at that. Robbie recognised its Pakistani or Afghan origin by its black colour and soft, squidgy texture. It had been years since he'd had proper Paki black. When he was younger, it was everywhere, but Ireland had since become a weed country. Decent hash was now nearly impossible to find.

What was usually on offer these days was a grim concoction of horse tranquiliser and burnt rubber — possibly the worst-quality hash in all of Europe. Then again, Ireland was the last stop in Europe before the Americas.

There was no point in arsing about with single skinners, not the way he was feeling. So, Robbie pinched off a bit and rolled himself a five-skinner. Scrolling through the albums on his phone, he landed on some Black Sabbath, connected it to his trusty JBL Flip 5, sparked up the joint, took a healthy swig of Micil, and wandered out to the balcony to take in the view. Not even the heat was going to rob him of these few minutes of bliss.

Minutes turned into hours, and before he knew it, the bottle was empty, the entire nodge had been smoked, and Ozzy Osbourne's solo material was now blaring through the speaker. He'd missed the start of happy hour, had several missed calls from Auld Davie, and a slew of unread WhatsApp messages from the group.

Fuck. How was he going to explain this one away? He'd been giving out to the boys for days about not taking this matter seriously — about putting their desire to drink before everything else — and now here he was, completely out of his face at four in the afternoon, having achieved absolutely nothing. Needless to say, the fleeting euphoria had given way to a fresh wave of depression and guilt. *Get a fucking grip Robbie*, he could hear his father say.

His only hope was that the rest of the boys would be too rat-arsed to notice the state he was in.

Maybe they had been at it all day too, taking advantage of the radio silence? That would certainly help with his immediate predicament but would do nothing to aid the search for poor Har de Luc. Nor would it help him make his intended return flight in nine days' time. Never in his life had he wanted a vacation to end so badly.

      He found half a percolator full of cold coffee — god knows how long it'd been sitting there. He didn't even remember making it. That would have to do. He smoked the remnants of a roach from the ashtray, gargled some mouthwash, and headed down the pier towards the ferry. It was fuckin' boiling.

Chapter 21

Who's in the bag?

The mood was strangely somber when Robbie finally arrived at the bar—nothing like the raucous rabble he'd expected. You could have cut the tension with a knife. Princess was in tears, and Pablo looked like he'd seen a ghost. Not a single wisecrack was made as Robbie pulled up a chair.

'What is it?' he asked, his voice tight. 'It's like a morgue in here.'

'Have you not heard?' Davie said, stunned.

'Heard what?' Robbie was worried now.

'Rej! Rej is dead.'

A tray of glasses crashed to the floor as Princess let out a wail that could've been heard for miles around.

'Pablo just told us. It was just announced in the *Khaleej Times*.' Eugene said, handing his phone to Robbie.

The headline read:

Police Investigate Death of Pakistani Worker Found in Ras Al Khaimah; Cause Unclear

The article followed with a brief statement:

'Ras Al Khaimah, UAE—A Pakistani national, found dead earlier this week in the industrial area of Ras Al Khaimah, has been named as Rej Khan. Local authorities are refusing to release any further details.'

'What is this?' Robbie asked skeptically, narrowing his eyes at the screen. 'Eugene, have the hospitals confirmed this? Was it *Rej* in the body bag?'

'No,' Eugene replied, shaking his head, 'none of the hospitals reported any DOAs during the early hours of Saturday.'

'Top Shelf,' Robbie turned to him, his tone sharp with urgency, 'did your contact give you anything?'

'Not a thing,' Top Shelf said, exhaling in frustration. 'He won't even answer my calls.'

Robbie ran a hand through his hair and focused on Top Shelf. 'Okay. What's the usual procedure in a situation like this? Would they contact the family? His work? Someone would have to identify the body, surely?'

Top Shelf prepared to launch into one. *Jesus*, thought Robbie, *here we go*.

'First, the police would file an incident report, along with any witness statements. The body would then be taken to a government morgue for examination. If there were no family members available, authorities would request friends or colleagues to identify the body. They'd also assess whether there were any suspicious circumstances — and if so, they'd open a file for investigation.'

He paused briefly, giving the others a moment to process the information — and himself a chance to catch his breath — before continuing.

'The death would then be registered with the Ministry of Health and Prevention, and an official death certificate issued. If he had his I.D. on him, the authorities would likely have tried to contact the family. But in most cases here, it is easier to reach the employer than the next of kin. So Pablo really should have been informed by now.'

'And he hasn't?' Robbie asked.

'No, no one has, and the Pakistani Embassy would've been informed too.'

'Have they?'

'They won't give that information out over the phone — but I doubt it.'

'This fuckin' stinks,' Mick burst out.

'Agree,' said Robbie, then continued, 'OK. Let's say it *was* Rej being loaded into that van. That would normally be an ambulance, right, Top Shelf?'

Top Shelf gave a sort of nod. 'Usually — but not always. Sometimes unmarked vehicles are used to avoid drawing unnecessary attention from the media or bystanders.'

'Did we get anything on the reg, Eugene? Who's it registered to? Can we track it? CCTV? Where did it go after the industrial estate?' Robbie was operating with surprising clarity, given the morning he'd had.

'I've got nothing on the reg—but I think Top Shelf might,' Eugene said, nodding in his direction. 'We've got nothing on CCTV after the van leaves the car park.'

'Fuck!' Robbie screamed in frustration. 'What've you got, Top Shelf?'

'Well, I spoke with Big Finn, like you asked me to. He says their falling out was nothing more than Har being — his words — "a racist bastard." Har was just upset because he'd been thumped eight-nil. He's a sore loser.'

'Okay, so how does that help us?' Maybe the smoke was wearing off, or the hangover was setting in, but Robbie was getting agitated now.

'It doesn't. But when I told Finn what was going on, he offered to help. He's not a bad lad, Finn — and you know he's a tech wizard. Anyway, he hacked into some system and found that registration...'

Everyone was on high alert, waiting on the punchline.

'It's registered to an Abul Ali. And get this — it's a Toyota Yaris. And... Abul Ali is deceased.'

'Jesus, this is getting worse,' Robbie said, voicing what everyone else was thinking. 'So the embassy's no good to us?'

'No, they just told us to collaborate with the police... and we know how that's going.'

'So, how do we even know if there was a body in that bag? And, if there was — was it Rej? If not, who — or what — was it? And why do they want us to think it was Rej?'

'Did anyone else get anything? Dick — Waldorf CCTV. Anything on Har's movements?'

'He arrives at the Waldorf by buggy at nine forty-five. We checked with the golf staff, and Brownie confirmed that he brought him straight from there — so we can rule out anything significant happening during that window.'

'Okay, what about between one a.m. and one forty-five? Can you see who he was with? Was he using his phone? Anything?' Robbie was almost pleading — though he wasn't sure with whom. The gods, maybe?

'We see him drinking with you. You exchange numbers, then he disappears outside, alone.'

'For a smoke?'

'That's what we thought initially,' continued Dick, 'but the CCTV on the terrace shows him talking to two other guys. White, blonde hair, tanned faces — sunburnt, really. Quite well-built. Rugged-looking. Irish, Scottish, Russian maybe? They talk for twenty minutes or so before exchanging what looks like phones. It's hard to tell, though — they're clearly trying to hide whatever it is they're up to.'

'Burners, probably,' asserted Rudolph, shaking his head and rolling his eyes.

Is he winding me up? thought Robbie, before continuing, 'That could explain the missed calls from an unknown number.' He was half thinking out loud, but inwardly searching for affirmation.

'So, what on earth could they have been discussing that prompted Har to call me — someone he'd just met — six times? He must have thought it pretty important. Either he had something to tell me, or he thought I could help him,'

'Did he know you were police?' Mick asked.

It was possible, but Robbie had been so hammered he really had no clue.

'No, no one knew,' he lied.

'Could he have guessed? Maybe something you said, or something he saw in your wallet — or on your phone — when you exchanged numbers? Har was pretty perceptive, and he's had plenty of experience dealing with the Fuzz.'

'It's possible,' conceded Robbie, hoping the lies weren't showing on his face, 'but I'm usually pretty careful.'

'We have to assume he did. Why else would he call you?' continued Mick.

Robbie had to agree.

'Can we find these guys? I presume the CCTV works out the front of the hotel. How did they leave? Taxi? Car? Was Har with them? Robbie asked, turning to Dick and Eugene.

'We'll try.'

'And try to get a copy this time,' Robbie added irritably. 'We don't want to be trekking up to the hotel every time we need to see the CCTV footage.'

It would also prevent the boys from coming up with more excuses to hang around the golf club until the hotel bar opened — not that he was one to be calling the kettle black after his antics.

Robbie noticed he was slipping back into his 'do-be' and 'does-be's.' He tended to do that when he was stressed… or drunk. Reprimanding him over it was one of the few things that his mother and father had agreed on. God, how he'd hated those elocution lessons with Mrs. Murphy, but neither she — nor they — had managed to beat it out of him entirely.

'What about the bird lady? or, or the cat lady… the fuckin' air hostess… what's her face? Ah, Jesus… Diana, Juliana… you know the one, Mick?'

'Fuck, Robbie, breathe,' offered an unusually sympathetic Mick. 'Rhianna's the name you're looking for. And yes, I think so — I'm meeting her shortly, as it happens. She's nearly as paranoid as you and won't speak over the phone.'

'Great. Mind if I tag along? Where are you meeting her?'

'Up in Club Cloud Nine.'

'Where the fuck is that?'

'Just out the road. It's Sunday, so it's Ladies' Night tonight, and Rhianna never misses those.'

'Okay, let's go,' said Robbie, eager to move things along — he'd wasted enough of this day as it was.

'Simmer down, Sherlock.' Mick was trying to get a rise out of him, and it was working. Robbie's blood was beginning to boil.

'It's still happy hour. We'll head when we're ready. She's not be going anywhere.'

'Four pints please, Princess.'

'Same.'

'Aye, me too.'

'Go on then, you've twisted my arm.'

Holy fuck thought Robbie. He felt like he'd lived two days already today — and aged about twenty years.

Chapter 22

The Cat Lady

As usual, Robbie and Davie were the only two without transport. The other five all insisted on driving to wherever 'just out the road' was. Carpooling, conserving the planet, saving on fuel etc., were clearly not top of their priorities — not to mention the severe penalties for drink-driving.

Robbie had been meaning to ask for a while: 'Doesn't anyone care about drink-driving? I thought you got banged up for that over here.'

'Arie, it depends.' replied Dick fairly nonchalantly, twirling his car keys around his right index finger.

'On what?'

'What — or who — you hit basically. If it's a local, you're in trouble. A white expat, maybe. But anyone else? It's not that big a deal, unless you kill them, that is. They might put you away for that.'

Might! Robbie couldn't believe what he was hearing. *Might?*

'Take Top Shelf there, for example,' continued Dick. 'What did you get, Top Shelf?'

'Ten thousand dirham fine, and they impounded my car for sixty days. Fuckers.'

'How long did you lose your licence for?' enquired Robbie.

'Oh, I didn't. They gave me twenty-three black points. You need twenty-four to be put off the road. I had to watch myself for the next twelve months. One more strike, and I was out. It was torture.'

Robbie was dumfounded again. He kept waiting for the boys to burst out laughing, but no one did. Top Shelf seemed genuinely annoyed at the penalty handed to him — felt hard done by. It was incredulous.

The alcohol and hash had surprised him, but now this? *Were there any laws in this land at all*? He found himself thinking out loud again.

'Of course. You get twenty-four points for running a red light,' stated Rudolph.

Off the road for running a light, but a slap on the wrist for being completely smashed. Robbie saw little point in continuing the conversation.

They all paid their separate bills and made their way down the disabled ramp like the bunch of old codgers they were.

Robbie and Davie clambered into big Tappie's people carrier. Robbie wasn't sure if it was the road, or The Sex Pistols' "*Anarchy in the UK*" — that was blaring full blast — but even this *beast* of a vehicle was bouncing around as they thundered through the industrial estate.

'Wait till you hear my karaoke version,' Tappie roared, grinning from ear to ear. Robbie could barely make out his words over the din.

This industrial estate was worlds apart from the one housing the Thirsty Horse. This place had an eerie, forgotten feel, as if time itself had given up on it. Crumbling warehouses with boarded-up windows flanked the dirt track — calling it a road would have been generous.

It felt like the last place on earth that anyone would expect to find a night club. When they finally arrived, the scene was like something out of a dystopian science fiction movie. They were staring at an enormous hanger, looming in the darkness. Robbie half-expected it to house illegal clinical experiments or suspected terrorists. *Guantanamo Bay* sprang to mind.

Inside was little different. It was, indeed, a large, dimly-lit, pretty much empty, hanger. A long straight bar ran along one side, with two pool tables at one end, and a small stage at the other. On the stage, some Filipino band were doing their best to murder "*Dancing Queen"* by ABBA.

According to the posters on the walls, *Super Trouper Stars* played every Sunday night, to be followed by karaoke and salsa dancing. Tappie looked like he was in heaven.

Five women — black women — sat at the bar, dressed in short skirts and tight tops — their cleavage hanging out like overripe melons — scanning the room like predators. They weren't here for the drinks, the music or the atmosphere.

A few locals hovered shiftily nearby, conscious that anyone might recognise them. No one said a word, but it was clear what was happening. 'Don't ask, don't tell,' muttered Mick. Robbie understood — more fuckin' hypocrisy.

Robbie clocked Rhianna straight away — it was hard not to. She was one of only three people on the dancefloor. There couldn't have been more than ten or twelve people in the building, plus the bar staff.

She was wearing a figure-hugging, black glittery jumpsuit, large earrings, and sky-high heels. It was a wonder she didn't topple over the tiny clutch bag that she was dancing around. Her hair was curled into a voluminous perm, and her bold red lipstick, along with the heavy mascara, gave her the look of a seventies' porn star — a look which Robbie liked very much.

She did not look seventy years of age. To Robbie ageing, tired eyes, and in this dimly-lit hovel, she could easily have passed for forty. He made a mental note not to drink too much more. The memory of making that mistake before sent a chill down his spine.

The big sign behind the bar read:

30% off all beers and selected spirits

Another place cheaper than Ireland, thought Robbie as the boys propped up the bar making what small talk the could over the blaring music. Eventually, the dancing queen herself left the floor and joined a younger, flamboyant-looking man at a large round table.

'That must be her son,' said Mick, nodding in the general direction of the table.

They grabbed their drinks and wandered over to join the table. She was obviously expecting them, as there were no grand introductions.

Close up, Robbie realised just how bad his eyesight had become. The glitter on her jumpsuit turned out to be nothing more than cat hair and dandruff, and her lipstick and mascara were smudged all over the place. She looked every inch the seventy-year-old he had seen feeding the pigeons.

The other lad, however — presumably, her son — was quite striking. He was slight in stature, petite, with high cheekbones and a soft jawline that lent him an undeniably feminine appearance.

'This is my son, Elton. Elton, Robbie.'

Elton offered his hand in a soft, gentle handshake, and Robbie noticed the perfectly manicured nails. 'Pleased to meet you,' Elton said, in an airy, silky, high-pitched tone, before kissing Robbie on both cheeks. As Elton's smooth skin brushed against his own, Robbie caught a hint of cologne — or was it perfume?

As he pulled away, a strand of his wispy fringe — part of his modern, chic hairstyle — brushed against Robbie's eye. It almost felt intentional, and as he leaned back in to apologise, he met Robbie's gaze with the most beautiful brown eyes — large and expressive, the kind a man could get lost in — framed by long, dark lashes. He was impeccably groomed, his healthy glow only enhancing his effortless beauty.

Robbie was spellbound.

Cat lady broke the spell. 'You must be the guard,' she began, stating rather than asking.

'That'll be me,' Robbie replied reluctantly, straining to hear. He glowered over at Mick, who just grinned back.

What else have they told her about me?, thought Robbie.

'Could we go somewhere quieter,' Robbie roared in her ear.

'No, they might be listening. It's safer here.'

'Who might?'

'Well, they know that you're snooping about don't they?'

It was a fair point, and Robbie was in no position to accuse anyone of being paranoid.

Right on cue, Rhianna pitched in. 'Just because you're not paranoid, Robbie, doesn't mean they're not out to get you.'

Elton — *could it really be Elton?* — produced another one of those newfangled gadgets. They seemed to change shape and size so often that Robbie found it impossible to keep up. He had struggled with the transition to digital policing a few years back and missed the old paper-based methods, laborious though they undoubtedly were.

Now, he had to contend with e-briefing systems, digital reporting tools, social media investigations — all of which he found overwhelming. With one eye on his pension, he was glad he had spent much of his career using more traditional methods.

Mick had obviously given the Cat Lady some idea of what they were looking for, because Elton had spreadsheets open with flight numbers, aircraft type, crew details, weather conditions, frequent flyers, payment methods, no-fly lists… it was exhausting just looking at them.

Robbie explained that they were looking for two passengers: Har de Luc and Rej Khan.

'Let's start with Rej. Has he flown in the last few days?'

Elton looked like he was on speed. His slender fingers flying across the keys like a madman on a personal vendetta. Words were appearing before Robbie had even finished articulating them.

'He was booked on a flight to Pakistan on Friday but never boarded. You want me to check further back?'

'Yes, can you go back twenty-four months?'

'No probs.'

Super Trouper Stars were taking a break, and Elton's fingers were doing their best to keep up with the high-energy of the pulsating dance music the DJ was blasting.

'Here he is again! He's a fairly frequent flyer,' an exciting Elton proclaimed, tapping his fingers rapidly on the table — almost in time with the bopping up and down of the pint glasses, struggling to keep in sync with the rhythm of the thumping bass.

'Brilliant, Elton. Can you send me all that?'

'No problem, what's your email?

'WhatsApp?'

'Jesus, no, Robbie. They might be listening.'

For fuck's sake, is this a family thing? Robbie thought, as he scribbled his email on a beer mat.

'What about Har de Luc?'

Nothing. They went through the same process of expanding the search window. Still, nothing.

'Try these names,' Top Shelf interrupted, pulling out his phone and scrolling through his gallery. He found the pictures of the four passports Har had stashed in his cheese drawer:

Larry Hutch

Del Church

Charles Dun

Red Chalk

Speedygonzalez was on it in a flash.

'Bingo!'

'I always knew I'd make a great detective; didn't I, Mum?' Elton was now as high as a kite.

Round after round of shots then appeared at the table — Jägerbombs, tequila shots, Liquid Cocaines, Mind Erasers, Cement Mixers… Tappie was giving it large on the karaoke machine — "*I Fought the Law,*" "*My Generation,*" "*Highway to Hell*" and, of course, "*Anarchy in the UK.*"

The salsa dancers had somehow forgotten to leave the floor, creating a surreal clash of styles — a bizarre mix of headbanging, skanking, fist-pumping, air guitar, and salsa rhythms. *You couldn't make it up*, thought Robbie.

Monday 16th June

Chapter 23

The scooters

Robbie woke up in a daze. He could hardly see. He had no idea what time it was or where he was, but the now-familiar roar of pile drivers and bulldozers told him he couldn't be far from his apartment. The machines were relentlessly tearing apart the pier and surrounding buildings, hammering away like a jackhammer inside his skull. They'd even brought in the dredgers to deepen the harbour entrance, preparing for the imminent arrival of the bulk carriers, container ships and HLVs. God love anyone who had recently bought property in the area.

He was in a bed, but it wasn't his own. Naked. Not alone. And definitely not in the mood for poetry.

Fuck.

The last thing he remembered was some guy — Turlip, or Tulip, or something — Irish, if he recalled correctly — singing into the rear end of a pool cue during a game of killer. *That could've been three a.m., or maybe four.* There had been no sign of last orders, of that he was sure — or as sure as he could be, given that he'd clearly blacked out. *What time was it now?* he wondered.

Someone was milling about — clearing away empty bottles, mopping, taking out rubbish bags — none of it helping his pounding head or the growing fear inside him. He was afraid. Terrified. Not just of what he might have done, but more importantly, of whom he might have done it with.

Who the fuck was he in bed with?

God, he was actually praying now, *I hope it's not Rhianna.*

'Good morning, sunshine,' came a sprightly voice from the kitchen.

Through the haze he could just about make out a slim figure in a silky babydoll robe. For a moment, his fear left him, and he suddenly felt quite alive.

'Coffee?'

This was getting better.

'Quite a night eh?' continued the voice. 'We can go through those files when you've woken up a bit.'

Files? What files? The only files Robbie was expecting were from Elton. *Oh, sweet mother of Jesus — that can't be Elton? Can it? What the hell have I gotten myself into this time?*

Robbie rubbed his eyes, only now to see small stars. He felt dizzy, even though he was lying down. Then he heard another voice:

'Morning, sunshine.'

This time it was a gruff, masculine voice coming from under the covers. Someone was still lying beside him in the bed — and if it wasn't Elton, then who the hell was it? He felt sick to his stomach as he gingerly lifted the covers…

Never in his life had he been so happy to see a pair of feet — albeit Mick's smelly feet. They were sleeping head-to-toe… and, indeed, it was Elton prancing around in a babydoll robe. He briefly felt a stirring in his loins, but with Mick still in the bed, he forced himself to closet those thoughts and feeling in the back of his mind. Yet unintentionally — or otherwise — he couldn't, or didn't, push them out completely.

Mick was bursting his hole laughing.

A relieved Robbie squinted around the room, and seeing nothing reached behind his head to find his clothes neatly wrapped into a makeshift pillow. He had clearly been on autopilot.

He pulled them on, and before he could ask, Elton pointed him towards the toilet. He barely made it.

His arse exploded the moment his cheeks hit the plastic rim. He was *literally* pissing out of his hole, and his ring was on fire.

Fuck, what had he eaten? Or was it the Liquid Cocaines? Whatever it was, it was *unpleasant.*

He wiped his arse, and his fingers went clean through the paper.

The second gush of scooters arrived so quickly that the rebound from the bowl splattered all over his cheeks and sack.

The only answer was the bum gun — which, until now, he had avoided — but desperate times called for desperate measures.

By the time he had finished, the bathroom — full of girly touches — was drenched, and Robbie felt pretty guilty leaving such a mess — and stench. He mopped up as best he could, sprayed some lavender air freshener, opened the window, and lit a candle before closing the door behind him, praying no one else needed it anytime soon.

He waddled back to the sitting room, his ring still on fire.

Elton had coffee and croissants on the table, and his laptop open. He was good to go. *Oh, to be young again…*

'So,' he began, 'We have Rej flying out fairly regularly. The last time he flew was January 10th from Dubai to Peshawar. Prior to that, last year — August 9th, March 15th, 2023 — October 13th and May 12th. That's the same day, every five months, and every flight is Dubai — Peshawar.'

'As I said last night, he was also booked on a flight last Friday, but didn't board for some reason.'

'Did he cancel?

'No, just didn't turn up.'

'Last Friday, you say?' Something was ringing in Robbie's head. Why was last Friday significant?

'Yes. Actually, all those dates are Fridays. Initially, I thought that might be because Peshawar flights aren't that frequent, and that's possible, but he always flies on the second Friday of the month. I found that a little bit odd. Don't you?'

'Very.' Robbie agreed. 'Where is this Peshawar?'

'Northwest Pakistan,' continued Elton, 'near the Afghanistan border. It's served by Bacha Khan International Airport. Historically, due to its proximity to the Khyber Pass, it was an important trade route. More recently, it has become a key drug trafficking route.'

Then it clicked. Har de Luc was last seen on Friday, but it was Thursday that had stuck in Robbie's mind.

Rej got paid on the second Thursday of every month — the day he went missing. Har was in The Waldorf, exchanging burner phones last Thursday — the second Thursday of the month. He also withdraws two hundred and ten thousand dirhams, every five months — on the second Thursday of the month.

Had he not just withdrawn money last Thursday? The day Rej went missing — the day before Rej had missed this flight?

There were too many coincidences for this to be anything but deliberate. For some reason, his mind briefly flashed back to "*Friday on My Mind*" by The Easybeats — though he'd first heard it from his childhood guitar hero, Gary Moore. R.I.P.

One of the reasons Robbie had stayed in the Gardaí so long was the kick — the natural high — it gave him. When a case got juicy, the adrenalin replaced his need for artificial stimulation. He was getting that buzz now, but he had been in the game too long to let it show.

'Excellent, Elton. What about Har de Luc? Or Larry Hutch? Del Church? Charles Dun? Red Chalk?' Stupid names, Robbie thought. 'If you were going to invent fake names, why would you choose names like that?'

'I thought that too,' Elton said, 'so I ran the names through some software. They aren't exact, but they're what you'd call partial anagrams or semi-anagrams of Har de Luc. And there are more. We found Claude Rhol, Chad Loure, and Leo H. Duclar, and I've a feeling we are only scratching the surface.'

'Wow! And you found flight details for these passengers?'

'Oh yes, and get this — When do they always fly?

'No fucking way.' Har thought Mick was out smoking on the balcony, but it was clear he had been listening in.

'You guessed it, Mick — the second Friday of the month. Also, to Peshawar. Same exact dates as Rej.'

'So, also every five months? Jesus!' exclaimed Robbie. 'And last Friday?

'Again, a ticket was purchased — business class too — but *Chad* didn't show up either.'

'So, Har withdraws all that money, Rej gets paid, and they both fly out to Peshawar the next day?'

'Exactly!'

'Last Friday was also the day that Har was last seen. So, he withdraws a large sum of money, misses his flight, and ends up in the Thirsty Horse? That makes no sense. What did he do with the money? Where did it go? Was he carrying it when he went in there? Is that why he never came out?'

If Robbie hadn't been convinced a crime had occurred before, those doubts were now well gone. This was about much more than two men falling out over a mince pie.

'Get hold of the boys if you can, Mick. Let's see if they've found anything out.'

'We're meeting later at the golf club, Robbie. Happy hour,' said Mick, trying not to exhale any of his five-skinner.

'Okay,' there was no point in saying anything else. Robbie was too tired to argue.

Elton was now drinking what looked like Bucks Fizz. He had applied some makeup and changed into a knee-length pencil skirt and white blouse. The blonde wig and high heels made him look every inch the sexy secretary. Robbie felt that familiar yearning in his loins again — one he didn't want at this precise moment. Yet it felt good, made him feel alive — but it was instantly followed by a tidal wave of Catholic guilt, or maybe embarrassment — perhaps both.

'Must be off. Some of us have got work to do,' he — or she — chirped. 'Let yourselves out, and don't bother locking the door.' And just like that she was gone. Or he.

Unprovoked, Mick took a long draw of his joint, inhaling deeply for what seemed like forever. *For a small man, he must have extraordinary lungs*, thought Robbie — before Mick finally exhaled nothing but thin air.

'And don't get me fuckin' started on *that*' he said, pointing at the door. Robbie hadn't said a word.

'Them, they, it, enby... fuckin' giraffes. Give me a fuckin' break. Fuckin' weirdos, the lot of them.'

Robbie didn't disagree with the 'they, them, it' sentiment. The PC brigade had been allowed to take things way too far, been given too much rope — a rope he hoped one day *they* might hang themselves with — but he had nothing against trans people. He had spent a lot of time in Thailand and loved the inclusivity of it. He'd had many great nights in the ladyboy bars of Bangkok. He really should have said something, but he didn't — and he felt guilty about that too.

Chapter 24

Call yourself a father?

The sunlight nearly blinded him as he stepped out of Elton's apartment block. He squinted up at the building behind him — MB. At least he didn't have far to walk in the heat, which was too hot even for him to guess. The car park was half-empty, so Robbie figured most people were at work. He still had no idea what time it was.

Elton had just left for work, but airline staff didn't follow regular hours. *Could he possibly be a flight attendant?* Robbie wondered. He knew Thai Airways had made headlines years ago for their pro-trans hiring policies — but Emirates? Homosexuality was still illegal in this country under Sharia law, and the penalties were severe.

Elton was surely far too smart to risk that. Maybe *she* had a date, or just fancied a day out. Either way, Robbie quickly decided it was none of his business.

He might have agreed with some of Mick's opinions, but not with the way he voiced them so openly.

He thought he could hear the faint cry of a call to prayer. It certainly wasn't the morning call; he'd have been lucky to have been out of the club by five thirty this morning. He assumed that it must be the midday adhan, the Dhuhr. That made sense. If he was lucky, he might get a few winks before catching up with the others, but he was losing track of what everyone was supposed to be doing. He was losing track of everything — even the days.

What had started as a few simple questions had spiralled into something far too big for him, a retired PI, and a bunch of god-knows-whats. But without the help of the authorities, they were all he had. And he'd come too far to walk away now.

He'd better check his ticket. It was looking less and less likely that he'd make his return flight. Maybe he could change the dates. *Had he booked a flexible ticket?* Probably not. His thrifty nature usually meant snapping up the cheapest fare available — and how could he have known he'd need to change it?

Eventually he pulled out his phone — it was indeed just after midday. There were several missed calls and WhatsApp messages.

FOR FUCK SAKE ROBBIE

CALL YOURSELF A FATHER

WOULD A SIMPLE PHONE CALL BE TOO MUCH

The lack of punctuation he could understand — although Mrs. Murphy certainly would not. He appreciated that language changes. Communication changes. He wasn't very good at it, but he got it. He also knew that if you wanted to convey any sort of emotion — *angry* emotion — in a text message, bold capital letters were the way to do it.

It was his ex-wife. This was all he needed.

What did she want? She'd have asked him to call back if she needed something. No — this was an attack. A full-blown assault over something he had — or, more likely, had not — done.

A father? *Shite.*

What date was it? He had been so caught up with this Har de Luc nonsense, that he'd completely forgotten Bert Jnr's birthday — his twenty-first.

How could he have forgotten that?

The 14th June — the day the Falklands War had ended.

He remembered it vividly: crawling through the woods, face caked in mud, trusty spud gun at his side, when the news came through of the Argie surrender.

It was the first war he could remember — back when war was still fun and games. Well, it was no fun and games now, and he'd pay for this, no doubt. He'd be back on the cold list for another month or so.

For fuck's sake.

MB to ME couldn't have been more than a hundred yards, but by the time he arrived, sweat was pissing out of him. This outfit wouldn't be passing the *sniff* test. Nor would he. But there was no point showering now.

He grabbed a chilled glass from the freezer, poured himself a cold can of stout, and — after replacing the glass and a couple of cans — sat down to try to extricate himself from the hole he'd dug with his family. Or what was left of it.

sorry Ange. got caught up work.

Ill make it up 2 him ✓✓

Next:

Sorry son. Just got caught up with work

Hope you had a great day. Talk soon ✓✓

Maybe Ange had her blue ticks turned off, but more likely she was ignoring him — and honestly, he deserved that. At least Bert had seen his message, but his lack of a reply spoke volumes. At least there were no messages from the boys to deal with.

He must have drifted off, because when he woke, it was half past two, and the all-too-familiar banging and drilling had started again. *They hadn't mentioned this in the Airbnb listing*, thought a somewhat dejected Robbie. *Could he really have been here only four days? Not even?*

In those four days, he'd ploughed through a carton and a half of Chesterfields. Four hundred smokes would usually last him a two-week vacation, but this was no ordinary vacation.

Then it hit him — the routine medical at work. Jesus, they'd probably sign him off for everything they could think of. Mental breakdown, physical collapse — maybe even commit him.

Maybe that wouldn't be such a bad thing…

With no lift arranged, he made his way down to the jetty, where, sure enough, Top Shelf was waiting for the three forty-five ferry to depart.

'Good afternoon Robert.'

'Terrence.'

'Quizzy tonight.'

What the fuck is he on about now? Robbie was tired and irritable.

'Quiz night,' Top Shelf elaborated, seeing the look on Robbie's face.

Quiz night? Someone might be dead. Quiz fuckin' night? What the fuck am I doing here?

He stared blankly into the murky, stagnant water. He couldn't even see his reflection; it was so black. From nowhere, the thought popped into his head: *what a horrible place to drown*. He wondered if anyone had ever drowned here. *Why was he having these dark thoughts? Where would the body wash up?* The tide seemed to have little effect on the lagoon. *Would it be carried out to sea?* He doubted it somehow.

Not even Top Shelf's incessant wittering, nor the noise of the construction, was loud enough to drown out the voices in Robbie's head. *Sit and suffer, Robbie. Do it or sit and suffer. Do it...*

The gentle bump of the boat hitting the dock fenders was enough to snap Robbie out of his trance.

'You OK, Robbie?' Top Shelf seemed concerned.

'Yeah, yeah. Just tired. Late night, you know.'

'Tell me about it. Where did you end up?

'Don't ask.'

He didn't.

Chapter 25

Saxy the saxophonist

Dick and Eugene had been busy—*productive* might be a better word, for they had still managed to find time to play eighteen holes with Tappie and Davie, who were busy drinking their happy hour spoils, after getting up-and-down on eighteen to secure victory. The mood was jovial.

'Oi, oi. Here's Starsky and Hutch.'

At least they had targeted both of them this time, rather than singling Robbie out for ridicule.

'Afternoon gents,' offered Top Shelf, oblivious to their taunts.

'I hear you had quite the night with Elton?'

Robbie went beetroot, which elicited nudges, winks and sniggers.

'Mick not here?' Robbie asked, trying to deflect the conversation away from whatever they thought might have happened — and possibly almost did.

'No, sunshine,' came the reply, followed by more nudges and giggles, only more animated this time.

What had Mick told them?

'Where's Princess?' asked Robbie, again trying to change the subject.

'Careful now, Rob! Elton might get jealous.'

Jesus, this was becoming intolerable.

'Have you anything worthwhile saying at all?' snapped Robbie.

'Ooooooohhhhhh!' they all responded in chorus, as if they had been rehearsing this one. 'Robbie's tired and cranky.'

'For fuck's sake lads…'

'Alright, alright. Yes, as it happens, we do,' Eugene said, flipping open the lid of his Apple MacBook Pro.

As it took its time powering up, he explained that they had the CCTV footage from the Waldorf — and that Robbie 'would want to see this.'

'Okay.' he continued, 'We see the other two men getting into a taxi, without Har. He appears five minutes later and leaves on foot, heading in the direction of the golf club.'

'Can we see where that taxi goes next?'

'No, but we did get the plate number.'

'And?'

'Dick called the head office and told them he had left his phone in the taxi, couldn't remember where it had dropped him off, and wasn't sure if he had paid the fare.'

And they bought that?'

'Yes. The taxi was pre-paid. It's a company account, and the drop-off was Marjan Island — the new casino.

'Isn't that still under construction?' asked a puzzled Robbie.

'Yes.'

'Did we get the company name?'

'No, they wouldn't give that out, but they gave us the driver's number to ask about the mobile phone, since it hadn't been handed in to lost and found.'

Robbie felt like a greyhound waiting for the traps to go up…

'He said the company account was Vos'hod. They're a development company from Russia. They're planning to build a Nobu Hotel, residences, and restaurant down there, but there are rumours about all sorts going on — money laundering, human trafficking, drugs — you name it.'

'Nobu? Why do I know that name?' Robbie asked.

'It's Robert de Niro's company,' asserted Rudolph, his eyes bulging with pride, eager to showcase his encyclopedic knowledge.

I must make sure to get on his team if I get roped into this stupid quiz night, thought Robbie, before adding, 'Surely he doesn't need to be involved in any of that?'

'No, but he won't have anything to do with the day-to-day running of it. I doubt he even knows where Marjan Island is,' continued Eugene.

Robbie wasn't sure he even knew where it was, despite it progressing so fast that it was now blotting the skyline.

'They can't have been security guards if they were drinking pints at half past one. And if they weren't security guards, what were they doing on-site in the middle of the night? Do employees live on-site?' He knew the answer to that before he had even asked it. 'We need to find out what they're up to. How are we going to get in there?'

'Stick that in your fuckin' Quizzy pipe and smoke it.'

Even the boys liked that one, and roars of laughter and cheering ensued.

'Not a bother, when do you want in?' Mick said, winking at Dick, as if this was something they did every day.

'And how are you going to manage that smart arse? Those lads mightn't have been security, but they'll have security—and quite tight I'd imagine.'

'Leave that to us. We'll go after the Quizzy.'

And that was that. Discussion over. Somehow, these two intoxicated eejits were going to bypass physical security personnel, surveillance systems, access control measures, and whatever else was protecting one of the largest developments in the Arabian Gulf for years. And they were going to orchestrate this while supping pints and answering trivial general knowledge questions.

As if reading Robbie's mind, Mick raised his glass in the air and reiterated 'Not a bother, boy.'

Moving on.

'Okay, anything else? Tappie, Rudolph… you didn't actually make it up to the Thirsty Horse, did you?'

'I did,' replied the pompous Rudolph. 'While the rest of you were busy chatting up the birds, well *some* of them were birds,' he winked at Robbie. 'Or pretending to be Sid Vicious,' he added, looking now at Tappie, 'I was staking it out.'

Robbie was trying to keep a straight face, but it sounded so utterly ridiculous that he couldn't help himself. Everyone was rolling around.

With tears streaming down his cheeks, he managed, 'Seriously...?'

'Aye, I am. I went up there after Cloud Nine. About midnight, I'd say.'

'Fair play, Rudolph. And?

'Well, my understanding was that place was always dead, but there's a lot more going on than you'd imagine. The back door never stopped from the time I arrived until nearly four a.m. My initial thought was drugs — and I wasn't wrong — but it was more than that. Some were collecting, some delivering... it was all cash, and packages of all shapes and sizes — toasters, microwaves, baseball bats. It's like a back-alley Amazon.'

'But get this,' he paused, keeping the lads in suspense to maximise the effect of the punchline, 'there were police everywhere... and they weren't there to stop it. It was almost as if they were regulating it.'

'Great work, Rudolph,' said Robbie, his self-induced gloom lifting slightly. 'That might explain why the police don't want us sniffing around up there.'

'Aye, but if they're orchestrating all this illegal activity from the back alley, you'd have to assume the legal stuff goes through the front. So, it most probably *was* a body we saw being loaded into that van.'

'Indeed. And where did that van go if not to a morgue or hospital?

'There are a number of possibilities,' said Top Shelf, scratching at his two-day stubble. 'It may have been taken to a temporary holding facility — basically a large fridge — or a forensic lab, a law enforcement facility…' he paused.

'But if they just wanted to get rid of a body, it'll either be buried out in the desert or chopped into pieces and scattered across the Hagar mountains for the goats.'

'Fuckin' hell. But, why? And, if it wasn't Rej, whose body was it? And, if it wasn't him, where is he? Why did he not get on that flight? Why did both of them miss that flight?' Every time Robbie thought he was getting somewhere, the answers only led to more questions. He hoped they might have better luck with the quiz.

Saxy, the glamorous quiz hostess, ambled over with the quiz sheets. The boys were like kids in a sweetie shop, clambering over one another to get at their favourite jellies. Robbie couldn't blame them — she was quite stunning. She must have been six foot, with blonde flowing locks that reached her tight, pert arse. Her faded blue denims and worn Converse gave her a shabby-chic look. Robbie was not expecting the harsh Geordie accent, seemingly at odds with her laid-back appearance, which made her all the more memorable.

She had already pre-filled the boys' childish quiz name — "*See You Next Tuesday*" — and they opted to play their joker in the first, general knowledge round. With Big Finn, who had joined the table, proving to be a real font of knowledge, along with the encyclopedic Rudolph and Tappie's under-the-table research, they had little difficulty in securing the bottle of wine for the round prize as early as possible.

They actually had little difficulty securing nearly every round — each team member seemingly having their own area of expertise, from Formula One to "*Fair City"* and everything in between. Seven o'clock came and went, without the usual stampede to squeeze the last drop from the happy hour cow. Robbie briefly thought the boys were taking it easy ahead of their *mission*, only to find out that happy hour extended until eight p.m. weekdays.

In between rounds, both Mick and Dick were busy making phone calls and sending messages. They seemed to have included Big Finn in whatever they were planning. Occasionally, they conferred to tick off boxes on their mental checklists, combining with what seemed like an effortless efficiency — like two peas in a pod. Suddenly Robbie saw these two bumbling reprobates in an entirely new light.

It had been four days since the June Strawberry Moon. The waning moon, still shedding a decent amount of light, cast an eerie, peaceful glow over the lush eighteenth green and fairway. The now empty bar, with the quizzers long gone, felt strangely serene.

Bert Jnr had also replied, leaving Robbie in a far better place than he had been for most of the day.

No worries Dad. Had a gr8 nite. Chat soon

'Right, I hope you're a good swimmer, Robbie?' joked Mick. At least Robbie hoped he was joking as the four men — Finn was accompanying them — made the short stroll to the ferry.

Robbie checked his phone. It was 12.45 a.m.

'Doesn't the ferry stop at midnight?'

'That one does,' said Mick, pointing at the passenger ferry. 'Dick's doesn't,' now pointing at a small rigid inflatable boat, manned by a man in a wetsuit.

'Alright lads,' came the unmistakable shrill of a Sligo accent.

The hull of the small boat groaned as the giant Finn lowered himself in. Robbie hoped he wouldn't sink it.

Chapter 26

The frogmen

'Keith, Robbie. Robbie, Keith.'

While Mick was pulling on his frog suit, Dick explained 'Keith here is the Captain of my scuba-diving sideline. He'll get us as close as he can to the casino development before killing the engine. From there, we'll drift in on the current. Keith and Mick will swim the last stretch, skirting past security. There's a CCTV blackspot at the north end of the development. We installed it,' he said with a wink, before adding, 'They can cut through the wire fence there.'

'They're behind schedule on that development, so they've got shifts working round the clock — you can hear them clanking away all night — and no one will bat an eye when Mick is hoisted into position.'

Position? Hoisted?

'They only install the CCTV as needed — cost cutting. So, the lower floors have security, but the higher ones haven't had them installed yet. Keith is also a crane operator. He'll hoist Mick above the CCTV coverage, and Mick will then lower himself down on a rope and swing in.'

'Won't he need a PIN or something to mobilise the crane?' asked a skeptical Robbie.

'You're right, it's not as easy as it once was to hot wire a crane. Keith's worked this model before — there's a way to bypass the startup lock. Failing that, if it's a keypad, he'll pop the panel and short the relay to trick the system into thinking it's unlocked. If it's remote-controlled, Big Finn can intercept the signal and hijack the commands. Either way, not a bother Robbie.'

And he said all this without the faintest hint of humour, as if it were something that he did every day.

'Mick will have his underwater headset on, so we'll have no communication issues.'

'And do we know what we're looking for if he gets in?' Robbie asked.

'When, Robbie, not if. And more or less. They're probably not storing anything there, so we'll be looking for documents, files — anything that might point to suspicious or illegal activity.'

'How is he going to get past the cyber-security?'

'What do you think we brought him for? His buoyancy?' Dick teased with a grin, pointing at Finn.

Jeez, they've thought this through, or it's not their first time. Robbie decided not to ask.

As the small boat zipped over the water, a fine mist of spray cooled the evening's rising humidity. Keith had estimated that he'd need to kill the engine some 200 - 300 meters out, but with the noise from the development, even at 100 meters, the slapping of the hull on the waves was barely audible.

The two boys dipped their goggles in the pool of water that had gathered in the boat, strapped their dry bags to their chests, and adjusted their gear one last time.

'Don't forget this,' said Dick, attaching the final lead weights to the Pelican case.

Seeing the perplexed look on Robbie's face — he'd only seen these things in the movies — Dick explained, 'Compass, crowbar… a thief's tool kit, you might say. And the weights? Without them, this thing would pop up to the surface like a bloody cork.'

'Don't forget the Rubber Ducky,' added Finn.

Robbie waited for the smirks, the giggles — but none came.

'Rubber ducky?'

'Small device. Plugs into a USB port, injects commands, bypasses security.'

Fuck me...

Mick crouched and strapped the case to his ankle with practiced efficiency. Then with one swift motion, leaned back and rolled off the side of the boat, hitting the water with barely a splash, before disappearing into the darkness.

'Testing, testing. Mick, do you read me?' Dick's voice crackled through the static.

'Loud and clear, Dick.'

'Head left, about thirty meters, then you'll be clear of the camera line.'

'Copy that.'

Robbie's heart was pounding now. Meanwhile, Dick was perched over the side of the boat, dangling his toes in the water and smoking a cigarette. Finn had a massive set of headphones plugged into his phone, and was tapping away to some tune or other — neither of them looking like they had a care in the world.

After what felt like an eternity, the receiver crackled back into life.

'All clear.'

'Mick, head left — there's a narrow path behind the warehouse. Stay low. The crane should be just about thirty meters round the next corner.'

'Copy.'

Things were going far more smoothly than Robbie had imagined, and the communication system was working perfectly. But it only provided audio — no visual communication. Robbie wanted to ask *how the hell Dick was navigating this* but now wasn't the time for questions.

Dick opened a large cooler and passed the boys a bottle of beer, popping the tops off with his trusty Clipper lighter. Then, with the same casual ease, he produced three sets of night vision binoculars. Every maneuver, every prop, every detail seemed to outdo the last. There was no way these boys hadn't done this before. *What the fuck did they really do?* Whatever it was, they were damn good at it.

Robbie was taken aback. In the pitch-black night, every movement, every shadow, was clearer than he'd ever hoped. Through the night vision, he could see Mick clearly, apparently suspended in thin air, the infrared light failing to detect the rope. But he was moving — almost inside now — and then, just like that, he was gone. Invisible again, swallowed by the solid concrete walls.

The receiver crackled again, 'On target. Floor twelve.'

Dick began issuing directions again, in almost military fashion. He seemed to know this place like the back of his hand.

'Right Mick. We didn't install any CCTV up there,' Robbie realised — *that's how he knows.* 'But there might be some in the stair wells. The elevator should be to your right, probably out of service, but there's a service ladder inside. If you can pry the doors open, climb up to the top floor.'

'Finn is working on the Ducky script now. You'll have it by the time you're up. Load it as soon as it comes through.

'Copy.'

Finn, still bopping away with his headphones on, gave Dick two thumbs up, as if to say, *job done.* Nothing Robbie had witnessed so far lent any substance to the tales he'd heard of Finn and his short temper. If anything, he seemed more like a jolly giant. *Maybe he was just good at hiding his mean streak?*

'We're in,' the receiver crackled.

The office had no air conditioning and was damp and mouldy — a glaring oversight. Mick's mind flashed back to the mess he'd made of his own place by leaving the air-conditioning off one summer. When he returned from Thailand, green mould had taken over everything. He had to replace all the furniture and never managed to get rid of the mould entirely, eventually being forced to move out after a series of unpleasant confrontations with his landlord.

'Problem: The devices all require two-factor authentication. The Rubber Ducky's no good. What now, Finn?'

'You've got a small Stingray device in your Pelican — looks like a tablet or small laptop. That'll intercept the OTP before it reaches the real device. Just plug it in and proceed as you would with any two-factor authentication.'

'Copy that.'

Almost immediately followed by: 'We're in.'

'Next?' asked Dick.

'The sun will be up in a few hours, so we don't have time to clone the entire system, but I've loaded a portable RAT onto the USB stick. Plug that in, and it'll install the backdoor on the Operating System. We'll have all the access we need after that.'

'Job done.'

'Great. Get the fuck out of there,' said Dick, some relief and emotion finally showing on his face.

This lad is as cool as a cucumber, thought Robbie. *They all are.*

Mick had obviously secured the rope when he entered, because a few minutes later he was swinging through the air like something out of Tarzan. When he and Keith re-emerged from the water, it was 1.35 a.m. The entire operation had taken less than one hour. Dick popped the tops off another four bottles, Mick sparked up a joint, Keith put the small vessel into overdrive, and off they sped, as quickly as they had arrived.

'Club Cloud Nine, anyone?' asked Finn.

Robbie was surprised by Mick's retort.

'It's alright for you, ya lazy bastard, poking around on your laptop. Some of us have been doing real work. You try swimming over there with all that shite tied around your ankles. You're all welcome to come over to mine for a drink, but I'm not heading up to that kip again.'

Keith dropped them off at the marina before scuttling away to wherever the boat was moored. Before Robbie headed to his apartment, they agreed to meet at 10.00 a.m. in the office — as the boys were now calling it — leaving Dick, Mick, and Big Finn to party on. Robbie had to admit; they deserved it.

Robbie trudged wearily back to his apartment, fished half a joint from the ashtray, and lit it slowly, careful not to singe his now-heavy growth. He stuck some Tom Petty on the speaker, poured a large whisky, and let his mind wander through the day's events — alone, drained, and reluctant to face anything else.

He stumbled into the bedroom and flopped onto the bed, fully clothed. His body sank into the mattress, and sleep claimed him before he could finish the thought: maybe, just maybe, tomorrow would be a better day.

Tuesday 17th June

Chapter 27

The slow, painful solution

Fuck, I'm glad that day's over, was Robbie's first thought at five thirty, roused by the now familiar sound of the screecher. The first blast — the call to prayer — woke him with a shudder, but by the second wave, he was caught in that hazy space between sleep and consciousness. A dreamlike state where he could control the plot and characters. His immediate thought? To introduce Princess, or Elton. Or both.

He reached for his phone.

Elton:

Can we meet? Tonight, 8pm?

I'll send you on the location xx

Robbie's pulse jumped. *Was he being daft? Why had Elton sent two kisses? A simple mistake? A Freudian slip? Intentional?* It all felt strangely covert. Mysterious. He stared at the message again, as if the meaning might change if he looked hard enough. He felt like a teenager on his first date — unsure whether to be excited or cautious. But the truth was, it mattered, and he wasn't sure why.

Complete dehydration had set in after five days on the sauce. He dragged himself out of bed. Everything hurt — his back, his knees, his shoulders, even places he didn't know existed — and it wasn't from the boat. These were the familiar pains of a drunken tumble. He wondered where he had tumbled. Lately, he was starting to pay for all those falls over the years. God knows what state he'd be in if he ever made it to real old age.

His mouth tasted like an ashtray — it was revolting. He was absolutely polluted. If he wasn't careful, he'd be the next one in a body bag — and no medical facility in the world would touch him. Organ donation was out too. Alcoholics Anonymous might put his liver in a glass case as a warning to any youngster fooled into thinking drinking was glamorous.

He tried everything — brushing his teeth, mouthwash, Diet Coke — but nothing could rid him of the disgusting taste in his mouth. He was sure he reeked of booze too.

Robbie had been considered quite tough back in Ireland. He could drink for days while others had cried enough. His ex-wife could never understand why he didn't suffer from hangovers. *Was he bulletproof?* she'd ask.

But out here, in this *dry* land, these men had put that to the test — and he had failed miserably.

This was a humdinger of a hangover, a hangover from hell, the kind you only get after days on the lash… and no food.

Yep, he'd really done it to himself this time.

He could barely see, but when did manage to look in the mirror, he didn't like the person looking back at him. Bloodshot eyes, flaky, dry red skin, acne, big black rings under his eyes — he looked about a hundred years old.

The shakes had progressed, from his hands to his entire body. He was afraid he'd slit his own throat if he tried to shave off six days' worth of stubble. Afraid he'd topple over if he tried to get under the shower. Afraid of the water.

In fact, he was afraid of everything. His own shadow. Every noise made him jump.

He was in the horrors.

He'd also entered the *out-of-body* phase of the hangover. He didn't mind this feeling when it was induced by the mind-altering substances he'd experimented with in college — but this was involuntary. And it was terrifying.

The only thing in his favour was that he'd been here before. There was very little he didn't know about drinking or being hungover. He knew what he needed to do.

There were only two ways to get out of this, and if he had any hope at all of meeting Elton that evening, he couldn't take the obvious, short-term solution. If he started drinking now, he'd never make it to eight o'clock. And if he did, he'd be absolutely plastered — no way was he letting that radiant beauty see him in that state.

So, it had to be solution number two.

The slow, painful solution.

But it was tried, tested, and it worked.

Step one — the jakey rehydration sachets, intended for babies with diarrhea.

Step two — yoghurt.

Step three — banana.

Step four — pot noodle.

All of the above would require the two-handed approach just to get anywhere near his mouth. Then, assuming it all stayed down…

Step five — go back to step one.

Fuck, he forgot he was supposed to meet Dick, Mick and Finn at the club. *What time was that again?*

'Alexa, do I have any reminders?' he asked.

'Good morning Robbie. Yes, you are meeting Dick, Mick and Big Finn in the golf club at ten a.m.'

'Thank fuck for Alexa...' he muttered.

'I'm sorry, I don't know that one.'

'Shut it.'

'I'm...'

He ripped the plug from the socket.

While fumbling around on his laptop, bouncing between cleaning up his inbox and paying bills, Robbie remembered that Royal Ascot — one of his favourite race meetings — started today. A bit of form studying would do nicely to take his mind off his hangover.

He knew gambling was illegal out here, but between the drink, drugs and prostitution, there had to be a way of getting a bet on. *Didn't they host the World Cup at Meydan Racecourse?* The boys would surely put him right when he met them later.

Robbie had worked in a betting shop during his students days — weekends and holidays — and loved it. But things had changed. There was no Sunday racing back then, and evening racing was just starting to take off — two nights a week. No fruit machines, no online gambling, and none of that *fuckin' cartoon* racing. The industry was a relentless machine now, and despite all their talk of responsible gambling, the bookmakers were squeezing the punters for every last drop.

It had been a good job in his day, though — one of his favourites, better even than stacking shelves in Tesco. He actually felt for anyone who worked in the industry now, but it hadn't killed his love of the sport.

Not that he was mad about the *Royal* aspect of the five-day meeting. In fact, he wasn't mad about anything royal. Robbie was a republican with no time for those *welfare royals — outdated parasites, scroungers of the state.* Don't get him started on that *big-eared, useless cunt* — and he wouldn't listen to anyone who tried to tell him otherwise.

He'd never forgiven them — and never would — for tearing his beloved Ireland apart.

But it was a feast of racing, showcasing the finest equine talent from all over the world. He didn't mind looking at the fashion either — particularly the women's — and figured it might be a good icebreaker with the lovely Elton later.

Come to think of it, *what was he going to wear? Did he have anything suitable? Suitable for what, though?* He didn't even know where he was going. Was it a date? *Why the hell was he even thinking that?* They were supposed to be investigating a possible murder, and all he could think about was what to wear — to impress... who? Him? Her?

He really hoped *she* showed up rather than *he.* Was that shallow of him?

Jesus, *did he even have anything clean?* He'd been here five days now and was getting through two or three outfits a day. Nothing was passing the *sniff* test in this heat.

He decided he'd better head to the mall and pick up some new clothes. Despite being out every night since he arrived, he hadn't spent as much as he'd expected, so he could afford to splash out a little.

The mall was much smaller than Robbie had imagined. Aside from handbags, sandals, makeup, and the food court, there wasn't much on offer. A few designer shops — well out of Robbie's reach — sold abayas and kanduras, but nothing he'd ordinarily buy. Eventually, he stumbled across an H&M, the closest thing to Penneys in the mall. He picked out a plain white cotton shirt, a colorful Hawaiian shirt, and a pair of beige slacks. He wasn't going to win any fashion contests, but at least they were clean.

He knew he was on the mend when he couldn't resist a New York Cheesecake donut from Krispy Kreme stall. Looking down at his ever-expanding waistline, he sighed — seeing his toes was getting harder by the day. But he wasn't about to let that ruin the moment.

'Fuck it,' he muttered as the filling oozed onto his T-shirt. At least it wasn't his new threads.

Chapter 28

Drive for show, putt for dough

Robbie spotted the three boys through the window as he entered the club — sitting, as always, at their round table. It was still too early for him if he wanted to make date night — but he couldn't face the inquisition if he appeared at the table with a coffee or, worse, a mineral.

Fuck, he also had his H&M shopping bags. They'd tear him a new hole if they knew he'd been out shopping... and they'd want to know why.

He stuck the bags behind the bar just as he spotted the Guinness 0.0%.

He wasn't a fan of non-alcoholic beers, but zero-zeros had been taking Ireland by storm that summer. Might as well give it a go.

Wilson —*no sign of the lovely Princess?* — poured it from one of those newfangled surger cans. It looked the part, Robbie thought, watching it settle. More importantly, the boys fell for it.

'Good morning, Chief,' said Dick.

Robbie ignored him, his mind elsewhere.

'Morning Robbie,' Dick tried again, more animated this time. 'Anyone in there?'

'Jesus, sorry, Dick. I was a million miles away.'

What the hell was he doing?

Sweet Princess, who made pulling pints look like an art form, would jump at the chance of a date with him. Yet here he was, fretting over a date with Elton — a bloke he barely knew, who liked to dress as a woman. If the boys were going to ridicule him for drinking non-alcoholic beer, what the hell would they say if they found out about this?

He shook the thought away as the pint settled in front of him. One thing at a time. He took a hefty slug, and had to admit — it didn't taste half bad.

'Sorry, what were you saying?'

By the time Robbie focused, the other three were already huddled around Big Finn's laptop, their eyes glued to the screen.

'We're in,' Dick said, emotionless. 'Backdoor's set up, just like we planned last night.'

Robbie wasn't surprised. After last night's shenanigans, nothing these three did would shock him anymore.

'Great work, lads.'

'This isn't work, we do this for fun,' Finn said, grinning. 'But it's more than that now. We've got something.'

As Big Finn dug deeper into the system, he walked the boys through the usual files — plans, blueprints, financial reports — nothing unexpected. The kind of stuff you'd expect from a casino development project.

'But look at this,' he said, opening folder within folder — almost as if it were buried, 'Duel Arch.'

'Duel Arch?' Robbie's interest was piqued, but it meant nothing to him.

'For fuck's sake Robbie, I thought you were supposed to be the detective,' said Mick with not a hint of sarcasm.

Then it hit him. He could see it plain as day now. In fact, he couldn't not see it.

His mind flashed back to *Countdown*, and Carol Vorderman with her conundrums. *She was a cracker,* he thought. Ever since they'd finally gotten more than three channels, men all over the country had fantasized about Carol — she'd been the thinking man's tottie for twenty-six years.

Rachel had been an impressive replacement, but he still found it hard to watch these days.

'Robbie?'

He'd drifted off again.

'What the fuck's wrong with you today?' an even more irritable Mick demanded.

'Sorry. Yes, of course, *Duel Arch*'

It was those conundrums again, or anagrams, or whatever the fuck they were called. *Har de Luc — Duel Arch*. God bless Carol.

They opened the *Duel Arch* folder, and immediately, the complexity of what they were looking at hit Robbie.

Financial transfers — numerous ones — flowed in and out, each one directed to an account belonging to *Har de Luc*. The amounts were consistent with Har's salary.

'Take a look at this,' Finn said, his voice tightening.

They all leaned in, scanning the details.

'Matches up with his bank account,' Dick muttered, pointing at the screen. 'Same amounts. Same dates.'

The pieces of the puzzle were beginning to fall into place.

'But look at this,' Finn continued, now opening another folder labeled *Jan Kher*. He paused, waiting for their reaction.

They all looked at each other, perplexed.

'Jesus lads, Har de Luc — Duel Arch. *Jan Kher*???'

'Fuuuuuck — Rej! Rej fuckin' Khan!' blurted out Mick.

'Exactly,' Finn said, pointing at the leger entries. 'And they've been paying for his flights too.'

As they continued to scroll through the folders, Robbie's eyes narrowed on a new set of data — cargo deliveries.

'Open that Finn.'

Finn's fingers paused on the keyboard, scrolling slowly. 'Hold on,' he murmured.

He pulled up the shipping manifests, and there it was — several entries for shipments arriving at *Al Hamra Docks*.

'Look at the dates,' Robbie said. 'Every shipment is logged after *Har* and *Rej* fly out to Pakistan.

'And look at this,' Finn said, his voice tinged with disbelief. He pulled up a list of ships due to dock. 'These are scheduled to arrive tomorrow.'

Robbie leaned in closer, his mind racing. 'That's no coincidence. All these ships coming into Al Hamra... What the fuck is in those containers?'

Dick tapped his fingers on the table. 'Are we all thinking the same here?'

They were, and all nodded in unison.

'So, Har and Rej go out with bundles of cash, and arrange some sort of delivery, and it's shipped back to Al Hamra?' Robbie asked.

'Looks that way.'

'What time are those ships arriving tomorrow, Finn?'

'Midnight.'

'And the cargo is still scheduled? Isn't that a bit odd? If Har and Rej didn't make it to Pakistan, then how was the order placed? By whom? And with what? Har had all the cash.'

'Good point,' agreed Dick.

'We need to be there,' Robbie said, his voice firm.

Dick rubbed his chin, thinking. 'Yes, we'll need a way in. Docks like Al Hamra — security's not tight, but it's not a walk in the park either.'

'Exactly,' Robbie replied. 'We need to keep it quiet. No attention.' He turned to Mick. 'Any ideas?'

Mick nodded, a sly grin spreading across his face. 'Not a bother, boys. Wee Al will get us in.'

Who the fuck was Wee Al?

'We could give him a shout now if you like,' suggested Dick. 'Fancy a few holes Robbie?'

'Jesus, I'm shaking like a leaf, Dick.'

'Have a few more of them,' Dick said, nodding towards the Guinness. Little did he know it was non-alcoholic.

Robbie had come here hoping to play some golf. It had been pishing down all summer back in Ireland, and he hadn't managed to get a game in for weeks.

'Isn't it boiling?' he asked, wiping his forehead.

'Arie, it's not too bad,' Dick replied. 'You're in the buggy most of the time, so you're not out in the sun much. And they give you a cool box for your beer. There's a wee cart that sells cans and bottles too, if you run out, and a couple of huts around to grab a drink or take a pish.'

Robbie had plenty of time before meeting Elton, and maybe the fresh air would do him good. He had to admit, Dick was doing quite a good job of selling it. It would also give him something else to talk about in case he got tongue-tied over dinner. But he'd need a few *real* beers before teeing off, or he'd never get the ball off the ground.

Mick shouted a round of beers from Wilson. Robbie pretended to go to the toilet, and sneakily asked Wilson to pour him a real Guinness, though he'd genuinely enjoyed his 0.0%. He made a mental note to try it again. It might prevent some of his blackouts if he could alternate between that and the real stuff. Of course, that was easy to say at eleven in the morning. Would he entertain a non-alcoholic beverage at midnight? Not a fuckin' chance — though he probably wouldn't be able to tell the difference by then anyway.

After a full Irish breakfast and several pints of Guinness, the memories of this morning's horror show were firmly put to bed. He was actually feeling quite good now, and growing in confidence by the time Wee Al arrived and was introduced. Al worked down the docks apparently.

Of course, he fuckin' did, thought Robbie.

Al was the harbour master, ex-military, from somewhere in the North of England — Loughborough, or somewhere equally obscure. *At least he wasn't one of those southern fucks*, Robbie thought.

Robbie had spent the summer after graduating working on the buildings in London. He'd enjoyed it, and the genuine Londoners — the Cockneys — were alright, but anyone south of the capital had that arrogant, Germanic manner, and he fuckin' hated them. *Weren't the royal family fuckin' German? What was it with that country?* England, not Germany. It — and they — annoyed the shite out of him.

But Al seemed okay. A smallish man with a goatee beard, in his late fifties maybe, liked cricket — liked most sports, it seemed — divorced, and now remarried to a Filipino, or Thai, woman named Concorde, or something like that. All the boys seemed to be married to Asian women — and punching above their weight. Robbie couldn't blame them — he'd nearly gone down that road himself with Pang and still harboured feelings of guilt and regret over it.

Al explained that, whilst it was a working port, security was moderate at best, and if they could fabricate some sort of work-related visit, he could arrange access. They'd meet in his place at eleven. Once again, Robbie marvelled at how effortlessly these two men — whom he'd once written off as drunken wasters — had solved a problem of this magnitude with such ease.

They somehow decided that Dick and Mick would take on Al and Robbie. Scramble format. The losers to buy the first round.

Robbie smelled a rat instantly, but that feeling faded as Wee Al boomed his tee shot 300 yards down the middle of the first fairway, leaving it just short of the green. Dick and Mick followed suit, both effortlessly popping their own drives down the middle, leaving Robbie shitting it on the tee. His nerves were at him.

He could hear his father's voice. It had annoyed him endlessly when he was younger, and it was annoying him now — though he knew it was good advice.

Keep your head still and your eye on the ball — see the club hit the ball.

'Fuuuuuk,' he screamed as his ball trundled a measly 30 yards to the ladies' tee. He could feel the embarrassment rising.

'Take another, for fuck's sake,' said Mick. 'We'll call that your mulligan.'

He did, and this time, he got it away — a bit low and not very far, but at least it was straight. He breathed a sigh of relief as he heard the familiar crack of a can opening. This time, it was he that followed suit.

The game ebbed and flowed, and Robbie was impressed — it was obvious the boys played regularly. His own game was the usual blend of the sublime and ridiculous.

Al outdrove him on almost every hole, but Robbie's short game had always been his strength, and he held his own — made his contribution felt.

It was three o'clock when they finally reached the last green — all square. By now, Robbie's head, neck, forearms, and calves were red raw. He'd applied the sunscreen way too late. The boys kept telling him, but Robbie *'knew his own body'* and *'could always take the sun.'*

Twenty-five degrees in Ireland? Maybe. Fifty degrees under the midday sun in the middle of the Gulf? *I don't fuckin' think so.*

For fuck's sake, he thought, *now I'm going to look like a fuckin' beetroot over dinner*. He hoped Elton would choose somewhere suitably dimly-lit.

Dick and Mick both missed their birdie putts. Al was up next, leaving his three feet short. Robbie, having studied Al's line — and with a shot at glory —

thundered his ball at the hole. There was no way he was leaving this short.

He could see their opponents giggling away.

'Whoa, calm the fuck down, Hercules.'

'Jesus, that's gonna go further than your drive on the first, Sherlock.'

On it thundered, but it was bang on line. 'Take the stick out, Al,' roared Robbie, 'Quiiiick!' The flagpole could send this thing off in any direction.

Al ripped it out just in time for the ball to strike the back of the hole with such ferocity that it leapt a foot in the air before dropping into the base of the cup.

Robbie was jumping up and down, delirious, and screaming, 'Ya fuckin' daisy! Get in there!'

The boys were stunned.

Robbie winked at them as they shook hands. 'Drive for show, boys, putt for dough.'

He knew he should go home, but he was going to enjoy the pint he'd won. He took a cold Punk IPA, knowing full well it was the most expensive pint on tap.

'Sneaky cunt,' was all Mick said as they clinked glasses.

Chapter 29

The haircut

'Right lads, I'm off,' Robbie said. He'd had two — one more than he intended — but pretty tempered all the same.

'What?' cried Mick in disbelief, as if it were the most ludicrous thing he'd ever heard. 'Happy hour starts in five minutes. Are you feckin' mad?'

He made some excuse about having to check in with the station back home, and with the three-hour time difference, it was difficult to coordinate the calls. They seemed to buy it.

'Alright, fuck off then. You'll not be as lucky the next time.'

His bill paid, he grabbed his shopping from behind the bar, phoned the captain of the ferry and slipped out the back entrance, heading down the delivery ramp toward the jetty. Thoughts of last night's very successful, covert operation immediately sprung to mind. He wondered if tonight's evening with Elton would be just as successful?

God, there were the butterflies again. And there was his father's voice — *Get a grip, Robbie, for fuck's sake, get a grip. Don't be a pussy all your life.*

Was it any wonder he still had issues?

A pang of guilt suddenly washed over him. Yes, his father was a cunt, and a cunt of the highest order — but was still his father — and in some way, no matter how small, he had surely loved him at one time or another. Robbie memories of him were of a big man, strong and imposing. But the last time he saw him — drinking cans with the homeless *jakes* in Eyre Square — he was stick thin, barely recognizable. Robbie hadn't even said hello. Maybe that had been *his* opportunity to be the big man, but he was no longer sure he had that empathy in him.

He stepped onto the boat, thinking, *That cunt left us. His choice. Fuck him.* The guilt was long gone by the time the ferry reached the marina.

Now, as he stared at his sunburnt face in the mirror, he realised that if he ripped off his six days' growth, he'd look like a fucking idiot — a reverse raccoon. He was going to have to manicure this thing, and he hadn't a clue how to start. Hope Elton liked the *distinguished* look — something he'd never pulled off before.

God, I hate beards, he thought, staring down the barrel of his Bic one-blade disposable razor. This was going to be torture. The fucking thing would be blunt by the time he got to the other side of his face.

He remembered seeing shaves and haircuts being advertised somewhere — but where? And why couldn't he remember?

There was no real history of dementia in his family, except maybe his grandmother on his mother's side, but it worried him when he couldn't recall things — word search, that sort of thing. He knew his lifestyle didn't help.

People had always said he took after his mother, in looks if not personality, and that concerned him too. She had been a bit neurotic, a bit OCD — *wasn't everyone?* — but had died too early to tell whether she would have gone the same way as her own mother. One of the reasons he'd stuck with the job so long was that it kept his mind sharp, the cogs well-oiled, and prevented him from being put out to pasture before his time.

Fuck, he'd have to ask Alexa. Hopefully, she'd be in a talkative mood today. Even that concerned him. *She's not real Robbie... it's a fuckin' machine...*

The obliging Alexa directed him to Al Jazirat — that's where he'd seen it — loads of them — when he and Auld Davie drove up to the police station that day.

He ordered a Careem and, almost immediately, was notified that Mohammed, his captain, had arrived. *Wonderful little app*, he mused. He knew Uber operated in Galway, but taxis were so prohibitively expensive that he almost never used them. Plus, traffic was so bad in Galway, it was often quicker to walk or cycle. But there'd be no walking or cycling in that fifty-degree heat.

From the outside, the taxi looked immaculate — fresh from the car wash, he supposed. But the minute he opened the door, it hit him.

The stench was overpowering: a foul mix of BO, curry, and stale cigarettes. Mohammed was filthy. He looked like he hadn't washed — or been home — in days. *Had he been sleeping in this?*

He pulled down the window, but the hot, humid air only seemed to amplify the rank smell.

Ghhrrrk! Ughhh! He was dry retching now — he'd never been good with smells. His mouth started to water. He swallowed, but the water kept coming.

Oh fuck. He pressed his hand over his mouth and nose, but it was no use. When it came, it came. The vomit erupted from him, and his fingers only helped give it the blunderbuss effect.

It splattered everywhere — on the seats, the windshield, Mohammed... the only thing it didn't hit was Robbie.

Thankfully, Mohammed had a roll of toilet paper in the car. Robbie almost gagged again at the thought of wiping his mouth with it, dreading where it might have been — but it was all he had.

He doubted it would mop up the mess in the car... or off Mohammed. But *fuck it*, he thought, *he fuckin' deserved it, the smelly bastard.*

He got out and slammed the door, Mohammed shouting profanities after him.

I thought they didn't like the 'bad' word.

He allowed himself a small, bitter giggle. *Schadenfreude*. How he loved that word!

From the road, he'd thought Al Jazirat pretty run-down. Now, immersed in this mess of a metropolis, he'd have to drop the *pretty* from that conclusion. It was a fuckin' dump. A kip of a place. Falling to pieces, rubbish everywhere. It was a bigger version of Mohammed's taxi — only, after Robbie's visit and left to rot in the baking sun.

From the dozens of barbershops, he chose the cleanest-looking one. It wasn't an easy decision, and he was already beginning to regret coming up here. That fuckin' Alexa had a lot to answer for.

Inside, he was greeted by Mohammed. *Another fuckin' Mohammed. Jesus.*

The place had a faint whiff of BO, poorly masked by incense. It was stuffy — no air conditioning. Just a small fan circulating warm air, made warmer by the completely unnecessary use of hair dryers.

An older local man was having the grey patches on his beard painted over. Another was receiving a shoulder and neck massage. They were busy.

An ancient-looking, white-haired man sat on a bench, waiting for the next available chair. He didn't have much hair left — nor much time on this planet — so Robbie wondered what the point of his visit was.

There were no appointments. No system, it seemed.

'Welcome to Tony & Guy,' the stranger said.

'Gav.'

Robbie caught the accent. Irish. Belfast maybe? Antrim? Possibly even Cavan, but it had that certain lilt, musicality that northern accents carried.

'You must be Robbie?'

How the fuck...???? This village was beginning to do his head in. He thought Ireland was bad for nosey bastards, but this place took the cake. Everyone knew everything about everyone. He'd a good mind to tell this — Gav — to go fuck himself, but that would only get back to the boys, and *he'd* end being the bad guy.

'Yep,' he said, hoping to put Gav off.

It didn't work.

'Sure, 'tis a grand day for it...'

Oh, sweet mother of Jesus...

''Tis, so, 'tis.'

'Sure, what else would you be at?'

Well, I wouldn't be fuckin' here if I knew this was what was in store.

'Arie, you know yourself.'

'True. True. Some craic though.'

'Yep,' said Robbie, inhaling as he did so.

'You in for the ould slap?'

I'll fuckin' slap you if you don't wind it in....

'Next.' Mohammed voice cut the tension — tension that only Robbie seemed to be feeling.

'You speak English?' Robbie asked as Mohammed fastened the dirty cape around his neck.

'Of course, sir.'

Robbie explained his predicament.

'Of course, sir.'

'How much?'

'Of course, sir.'

Mohammed had a lot to live up to. Robbie was used to the delectable Clodagh's soft hands running through his hair in "*Clodagh's Clippers*." Mohammed, however, attacked him with a spray gun, clippers and a slit-throat razor. Robbie said a silent prayer.

Oh, sweet Mary, mother in heaven....

Twenty dirhams later, Robbie had to admit that Mohammed had done a reasonable job. His colleague — Ahmed — was busy slapping Gav about the face, which at least silenced the wittering imbecile for a bit. However, just as Robbie was about to up and leave, Gav couldn't resist getting the last word in.

'I never made a mistake in my life. I thought I did once, but I was wrong.'

With the memory of his taxi experience still fresh in his mind, Robbie decided against ordering a Careem. Too risky. Outside, lay a line of waiting taxis stretched along the potholed road. He opened the doors of three before finding one that didn't reek. Mohammed took him home for ten dirhams. Shave, haircut and taxi home for seven euro fifty. Maybe the village wasn't that bad after all.

Chapter 30

The date

He was hungry now. It had been some time since his Pot Noodle, and he hoped Elton would text soon. He went for a quick shite, hoping to get rid of any potential scooters later on.

Memories of stuffing his soiled underpants into the cistern of Abrakebabra — right in the middle of Galway city — came flooding back. And then there was the time he'd had to fling them out a fourth-floor window, only to watch them land square on some poor bastard's skylight.

Funny pub stories years later, maybe — but there was nothing more humiliating than getting short-taken on a date.

How should he play this tonight? It wasn't even confirmed as a date. All he had were the two xx's Elton had tagged onto the end of his text message. Robbie had often made that mistake, embarrassingly so, to work colleagues and mates. But there was something about the way Elton looked at him that night — something in the way he had lingered — told him this was a date.

Should he act otherwise? Surprised? Or should he prepare to impress? A small gift maybe? Flowers? Would that be too much?

He was pacing the room now, checking his phone every two minutes. *Come on Elton.* He turned on the TV and was delighted to find a racing channel showing Royal Ascot. Mick had explained the virtues of the VPN in this country — '*Good for racing and other things,*' he'd said with a wink — so he'd topped his Paddy Power account.

He wasn't sure if he was more excited about the upcoming Queen Anne Stakes or meeting Queen Elton. Both could be winners.

Ping.

Elton:

The Huddle

Citymax

xx

Alexa informed him that the Citymax Hotel was up in the city somewhere. He'd been so caught up in the goldfish bowl of village life that he'd almost forgotten Ras Al Khaimah was home to nearly half a million people — mostly expats.

More kisses. Okay. You don't make that mistake twice. Fuck Queen Anne…

After a quick shower he slipped into his new threads. Beige slacks with a plain white cotton shirt. The fabric was cool against his skin, a far cry from the stifling humidity outside. He left the top two buttons open. Fuck it, three. It was a baggy loose fit, so his belly was partly hidden. He pulled on his pink converse to add a bit of personality and give it a more casual look. It was also a reminder to himself that he didn't need to play by anyone's rules. He didn't dance to anyone's tune. Still, part of him hoped they would signal something to Elton — not that he thought Elton needed his approval. Or sought it.

It was still a bit early, but he didn't want to be late either. He hated *late* people. Late people, loud people, royal people, bores, whingers, arrogant people, rude people, *me me me* people… If he got there early, at least he could have a couple to settle his nerves, which were starting to creep back up again.

Now wouldn't be the time to strap on the blood pressure monitor his doctor had tried to force him to buy. He'd had that discomfort once before, when they made him wear one for twenty-four hours. It nearly strangled him every half hour as it buzzed to life and squeezed the bejaysus out of his arm —

sending his BP rocketing. He'd had an irrational fear of that thing ever since — white lab coat syndrome.

Buy one? I don't fuckin' think so — what you don't know can't hurt you.

He selected the *Comfort* option on Careem, hoping to avoid another stinking Mohammed, and was pleasantly surprised when he opened the door of Ansar's hybrid Toyota. Ansar looked a bit like Freddie Mercury — but the Arabic music? Too much.

He was better than he'd been most of the day, but that *fuckin' plink-plink* shite — the endless jingly noises and tinkling cymbals — was pounding on his fragile temples. It wasn't that he couldn't appreciate the craftsmanship, but right now, all it did was gnaw at the edges of his nerves.

He popped in his iPods and struck up "*The Silver-Tongued Devil*." Hard to beat a bit of Kris.

The Citymax was an unassuming building, tucked a little off the beaten track. He wondered why Elton had chosen this location. Was it purely business? Had it anything to do with Har de Luc or Rej? If it were business, couldn't they have met in his apartment? During the day, even? 8.00 p.m. in some nondescript hotel bar?

Inside, he was shocked. It almost felt like an old Irish bar — before they'd been given the Celtic

Tiger facelift. Dark, dingy, and cramped. The air was thick with smoke, and it was hard to make out the dart board, which hung dangerously close to the pool table, taking up half the pub. Locals, expats, and hookers mingled effortlessly, the whole place buzzing. Happy hour, which had kicked off at noon, seemed to be doing its job. There was no sign of Elton, so he ordered a pint and a double Jack Daniels.

He nearly choked on his pint when Elton strutted through the door. Long blonde hair, tiny leather miniskirt, fishnet stockings, slutty knee-high boots with six-inch killer heels, dark mascara, and ruby red lips. She didn't look out of place amongst the other hookers in the place, and no one — except Robbie — blinked an eye. She, and it most definitely was *she,* looked *amazing.*

She approached him with an air of grace and elegance, casually parading her feminine assets like she owned the room. Robbie was dumbstruck. As he stood to greet her, she pushed him back into his seat with feline authority and leaned in to whisper in his ear. She smelled wonderful.

'Hi Rob. Call me Elle.'

Elle knew the place, and the place knew Elle. Francis, the Filipino waiter — more than a little camp himself — arrived with two pints of Guinness and two tequila shots before she'd even settled. She casually swung one leg over the other, revealing just a glimpse of flesh.

Robbie couldn't believe his luck, though it was hard to hide his nerves. He was petrified. This really was a date — and he hadn't been on one in so long, he wasn't even sure what to do. What to say.

He could feel his face reddening, though she probably wouldn't notice under the sunburn.

'Getting a bit of sun are we Rob?'

It broke the ice and they both fell about the place laughing... and the laughter never stopped.

Robbie's nerves eased with every pint, and before long, they were flirting. The body language was red-hot. She stroked and teased him, playing with him, and he was putty in her hands.

They talked about everything — music, dancing, poetry, art, food, books, film, football, England, Ireland, the weather. Everything but work.

It was like chatting to your best mate — only a stunning best mate.

They'd only just met, and he felt like he'd known her forever. His mind raced. He wondered if they had rooms here. Of course they did. Was that why she'd wanted to meet here? Was he getting ahead of himself? He didn't think so. Robbie was a pretty good reader of people, and he was reading *this* one loud and clear.

Robbie was in a bit of a pickle. He knew he had to be at Al's place by eleven, which was thirty minutes away, and it was already half nine. Time was running out, but he desperately wanted to be with Elle — really be with her — and he might not get the chance again.

But this couldn't lead to anything serious, could it? He was in Ireland; she was in the UAE. It was nothing more than a holiday fling, a one-night thing. Sure, wasn't it even illegal? She had no intention of moving to the West of Ireland, and, much as he was warming to the place, he had no intention of sticking around here.

So, it was now or never. And with every pint, it was getting harder and harder to exercise any form of restraint.

As if reading his mind — or more likely, his body language — their hands were all over each other now. She grabbed him by the hand. Saying nothing, she led him to the lift and pressed number nine.

As the door closed behind them, she leaned in and gave him a long, lingering kiss. The restaurant was on the fifth floor...

Elle had been more than understanding when Robbie explained why he had to go. She wanted to do it again… and so did he. He wanted to do it again right now. *Fuck Har de Luc.* Though, without him, he'd never have met Elle — but *fuck him anyway*.

Sitting in the taxi now, the old Catholic guilt was creeping in again. What had he just done? It wasn't the illegality of it — it was the moral dilemma. Elle was Elton. She was *he*. Robbie was straight, or at least he'd always thought he was. Did this mean he wasn't? He wasn't attracted to men. He'd nearly had a heart attack when he woke up next to Mick. He shuddered at the thought.

But Elle? She was different. It was different. Somehow. He didn't understand it, but it felt right. Somehow.

Chapter 31

The Docks

The taxi pulled up outside Al's villa, just behind a beat-up old Ford Transit van. "Butler" could just about be made out from the fading signage. Robbie could hear shouting and singing. Someone was playing a guitar, a harmonica and what sounded like some kind of a drum. It was a full-blown session.

In that moment, he was transported back to his musician days. God, he missed those days. Sunday afternoons in Galway. Away from the madness of the big weekend nights, Sundays were all about chilled drinking. Music was everywhere. It started in the Crane Bar at two p.m. (Irish time) and didn't stop until the Róisín Dubh — if you were still standing, and still allowed in, around three in the morning.

He'd rarely made his Monday lectures, opting instead to join the lads in the Monday club. He'd rarely made his Tuesday lectures, either. Come to think of it, after his first year, he'd hardly made any lectures at all. He really should have done better than a 2:2, but fuck it — it got him to where he was now, didn't it?

'Looking very swanky Robbie. You been on a hot date or something?' joked Tappie, putting his guitar down. Big Finn was banging away on the bodhrán, Dick had the harmonica, and Al was puffing away on a tin whistle. Mick was puffing away on an enormous joint.

Robbie started to blush. There was no way they could have known what he'd just been up to. Was there? In this fuckin' village, you never knew.

This time, he was delighted to have a sunburnt face.

'We thought you'd need some muscle,' said Mick, pointing at himself, Finn and Tappie.

'And them?' Robbie said looking at Rudolph, Top Shelf, and Auld Davie.

Al cut in before Robbie could say another word. 'We need to cover a lot of ground. The docks are huge. We need three teams — one on the surveillance cameras, one on the ground, and a one ready to follow if necessary.'

'Follow?' Robbie didn't.

'Unless customs inspect the containers, those guys won't be hanging around. They'll have them loaded straight onto a flatbed, then shift them to a warehouse — out of sight. We need to be ready to tail them.'

Robbie rolled his eyes but bit his tongue. The boys were good at playing dumb, but he knew better. They had their talents. Al had mapped everything out.

'Keep these on at all times,' he said, handing out what looked like World War II-era walky-talkies. 'But keep them silent.'

He had a 'work order' for Butler's to carry out some routine maintenance on the dock's surveillance system. It looked legit — professional, well-prepared. Butler's had been handling maintenance on the system for years, so the guards wouldn't think twice about their van rolling up. It was the perfect cover.

With a bit of luck, they'd breeze through, get inside, tap into the cameras, and watch everything coming off the boats in real-time.

Al, Dick, and Robbie would monitor the CCTV from the control centre. Mick, Tappie and Finn would be out in the yard, while Rudolph, Top Shelf and Auld Davie would be ready to follow any cargo that left the docks.

It was almost too easy. And that made Robbie uneasy. But the more he thought about it, the more it held up. Al had done his homework, and after yesterday, Robbie had to admit — the other deadbeats weren't as useless as he'd thought.

Top Shelf and Auld Davie clambered into one van with Rudolph. Robbie, Mick, Tappie, and Finn squeezed into the back of Dick's van, with Al riding shotgun. Each one had their own nervous energy, and the tension was palpable. Robbie could feel it pressing on his chest.

'Just stay quiet,' Mick muttered. 'We get in, we get out. Simple as that.'

Robbie, always the pessimist, shot him a look. 'And if the guard decides to check the van?'

'Not gonna happen,' Mick replied with a slight edge in his voice. 'If anyone's going to question us, it'll be after we're in. But by then, we'll be monitoring the whole damn place.'

Al, sitting in the front, gave them a brief nod before starting the engine. 'This is my job lads," he said, his tone serious. 'Don't fuck it up.'

Robbie felt the weight of those words. The docks weren't just a target — they could be the key to the whole thing. What would they do when they discovered what was coming in on those shipments? What could they do? They couldn't go to the police.

The Guard in Robbie wanted to solve this riddle, but the man just wanted it over and done with, so he could enjoy the rest of his holiday with Elle.

Maybe slope off somewhere for a few nights — somewhere like Thailand, where she could be herself.

'Focus,' he muttered under his breath.

Mick, sensing the tension, leaned forward from the back of the van. 'You okay, Al?' he asked, his voice low.

Al forced a smile, nodding quickly. 'Yeah, just thinking.'

'Just don't think too much,' Mick replied, his voice carrying a slight chuckle. 'Just act normal.'

Nobody spoke again. The silence stretched as the van snaked its way through the village's dimly lit streets, past children caught up in the latest craze — electric scooters. No helmets, no lights, barely out of primary school. Mothers, clad in black, pushed prams against the flow of traffic.

Robbie had seen enough carnage in his time, and this was an accident waiting to happen. God love the families when it did. And it would.

Dick made a sharp turn, and Robbie saw the docks up ahead. They were almost there.

Stevie, the security guard, was a big, burly lad. Polish or Russian, maybe — Robbie couldn't quite place the accent, but it was definitely Eastern European.

'Ev-en-ing, sir.'

Al leaned over Dick. 'Evening, Stevie.'

'Ah, Meester Al. All is fine, da. Everything alright, sir?'

'Yeah, we've some maintenance to do on the surveillance system. Routine stuff. You know Dick don't you?'

'Yes, sir. Hi mister Dick.'

Dick just nodded.

The van was already on a list of pre-approved vehicles, so all Stevie needed was a quick scan of the paperwork before raising the boom barrier. They were in.

If Robbie had been expecting a tin-pot dock, he couldn't have been more wrong. Al Jazeera was a fully functioning, working port. The smell hit him first — that old, familiar mix of salt air and diesel, thick and clinging. Beneath it, the faint, sour tang of fish guts lingered, a ghost of the past that remained long after the fishing boats were gone.

It took him back to his old Dublin days again. Shipbuilding and traditional cargo-handling had all but disappeared by then too, replaced by containerisation, but the North Wall and Alexandra Basin were still bustling with freight.

Here, though, Al Jazeera was alive. Shipbuilding, maintenance, dry-docking, wet-berths, warehouses, workshops, jetties, barge-ramps… It was impressive. *A place where a man could easily get lost — or hide,* he thought.

He was glad Al was with them. He knew the place like the back of his hand.

'So, what now Al?' Robbie asked.

'That's ours.' Al nodded toward the water. 'The wee tugs are bringing her in now. There's a bit of paperwork before the gantries move in and lift it on to the straddle carrier. Usually, it would then go off to the stacking yard, or straight to customs for inspection.'

'How that fuck are they gonna get past customs if they're bringing in what we think they are?

Al scratched his jaw, eyes scanning the port. 'If they're bringing stuff in regularly, they'll have it figured out. Either it's well concealed in the container, or they've got someone in here —' he paused, 'which makes me decidedly uneasy — making sure that the inspectors turn a blind eye.'

'Jesus, Al. And you honestly know nothing about this?

'Do I fuck.' Al spat on the ground. 'And It's not really the kind of carry-on that I want in my docks, to be honest.'

The party atmosphere of "*The fields of Athenry*" was long gone now. Al was serious. He'd be the one left carrying the can if it all went tits up.

Auld Davie confirmed that they were in position outside. Al relieved the guard on surveillance, explaining that he'd take over whilst Dick and his team carried out the maintenance.

Al explained that the cameras operated on a rotation. The system automatically cycled through different feeds every ten seconds. They could manually override it to focus on specific areas if needed, but with fifty cameras and only sixteen monitors, that meant thirty-four cameras were effectively blind at any given time.

There were also blind spots, bad angles, temporary obstructions, and a myriad of possible technical issues that could hinder their surveillance.

He unfolded a map of the docks, and they all huddled around it. The *ground* team, now in their Butler's overalls, would be maintaining the cameras beside the container. They were to make themselves visible, but act like they were busy minding their own business.

All they had to do now was sit and wait. And it wasn't long before an imposing white Mercedes-Benz G-Wagon rolled into view.

'Come in Davie.'

'Copy.'

'Story with that G-Wagon.'

'Breezed through — same as you.'

'Copy.'

First out were the two bruisers they'd seen Har swapping burner phones with. Then, an older man stepped into view, wearing a dark green blazer and a beret — a blazer that Robbie recognised from the police station.

'That's…' he began.

Dick completed the thought. 'Mohammed fuckin' Alshahari.'

'Fuck.'

Next, two businesswoman stepped into view.

The first wore a flashy, expensive suit, high heels clicking against the silent night, and hair pulled tightly back so tightly it must've hurt. Hard to place her age. Forty? Fifty? She reminded Robbie of the waitresses he'd seen during his brief career as a TEFL teacher back in Poland — almost rude, sultry, moody, sexy. Then, just as quickly as she appeared, she was gone.

'What the fuck Al? Is that coming back in ten seconds?' Robbie asked.

'No, the feed's still live. It's as if she knows exactly where the blind spot is.'

'That's the fuckin' Viper,' added Dick, 'Petra Ivanova. Norwegian. Real estate. Auld Davie bought a villa off her years back. She's a big player in the casino development.'

Then came the second woman — smaller, but just as flashy. Her suit was tailored, sharp, her spiked hair making her look younger. Thirties, maybe? But like the first, she slipped out of view almost instantly.

Dick scrambled for his walkie-talkie. 'Who the fuck was that Mick?'

'It's her, Dick. The Red fuckin' Widow.'

'Who?' Robbie asked, a confused.

'The Red Widow — Valentina Orlova,' replied a stunned Dick, 'A mean, cold, calculating bitch. Russian cartel. What the fuck have you gotten us into Robbie? This is serious fuckin' shite.' Robbie was beginning to realise that — fast.

'How the fuck did they just breeze through, Al?' he asked.

'Who authorized the Merc, Stevie?'

'Pre-authorised, Mr. Al,' Stevie replied, 'it's always in and out.'

'Wouldn't you usually still submit a list of passengers?' Robbie asked.

'Usually, yes,' Al admitted. 'But you've got the Russian mafia, a police Major, and one of the wealthiest real estate agents in the Gulf down there — and they're being escorted by Tyson Fury and his twin. There's nothing usual about this.'

The LED flashed on the walkie-talkie. 'Top Shelf, Davie, get ready. This is going straight onto a flatbed. Alshahari's chatting with Sinbad, the security guard. Looks like he's slipping him something — brown envelope. This thing isn't going anywhere near customs.

'Copy that.'

'Davie, Al here. Get yourselves round to the service exit. Aside from Sinbad, there are no patrols on that route — and they've already taken care of him by the looks of it. There's a little dirt patch just off the road. Wait there, and we'll let you know when it's moving.'

'Right, Mick. Wait till it's moving then get back here ASAP. Davie, keep your location on. We'll be right behind you.'

'Copy that. Over and out.'

Wednesday 18th June

Chapter 32

The impound yard

Rudolph was on it the minute the flatbed truck emerged from the services exit. The roads were quiet, making it easy to maintain their distance while staying locked onto their target. The truck moved steadily, leaving the village behind, and heading towards the old truck road.

'Looks like it's heading for the impound yard,' said Top Shelf, remembering to click his walkie-talkie as he spoke. 'Dirty fucks cost me two months' car hire and a thousand dirhams to get it out.' The bitterness still lingered from his drink-driving conviction.

'Fuck me, those bastards are up to their necks in this,' added Rudolph. No one had to ask who he meant. 'Slimy, dirty shower of useless cunts. Fuckin' law mongrels. Scumbags. Filth.'

Al and Dick had caught up with Rudolph's Mitsubishi Pajero but the time the truck entered the yard.

'Welcome to the jungle,' grinned Mick.

The impound yard was a graveyard, a paupers' cemetery for the forgotten and discarded. A place where cars, once symbols of freedom and purpose, were left to decay — stripped of their dignity, their rusting chassis a sad testament to their former glory. No one wanted to end up here — abandoned, alone, and imprisoned in this mechanical purgatory. A place where time stood still, and the elements slowly reclaimed what was once sleek and proud.

Their fellow inmates had been impounded for similarly minor violations — unpaid fines, expired registrations, reckless driving. Others, guilty of greater transgressions — DUI crashes, hit-and-run crimes — perhaps deserved their fate, their exile a form of justice. But many were simply victims of circumstance, condemned not by law but by poverty.

Early release was an option. Even a full pardon. But at a hundred dirhams a day, who would come to their rescue? A poor construction worker earning less than that in wages could hardly afford to retrieve his car. Hell, it was more than the wreck was worth. And so here they remained — vehicles not yet dead but already mourned. Forgotten by their owners, disowned by society, yet left on display as a silent warning to others. A deterrent. A shameful exhibit of what happened to those who fell afoul of the law.

It was as sad a sight as Robbie had seen in a long while.

From their vantage point they could see the big white Mercedes parked near the entrance, Valentina waiting beside it with her Meatheads flanking her sides.

Mohammed Alshahari snapped his phone shut and strode towards the container, a large set up keys swinging in his hand. He hesitated for a moment, eyes flicking around the yard for any lurking dangers — but the boys were well-hidden behind the old, abandoned reception building.

There was a deranged excitement in his expression, like a man about to unwrap a long-awaited gift but unsure if it was gold or a live grenade.

The boys held their breath. What the fuck was inside? Drugs? Weapons? Contraband? People — God forbid.

A heavy silence settled over the yard, broken only by the groaning, tortured squeal of metal scraping against itself, hinges protesting with each slow, reluctant movement as Alshahari pried open the container door.

His expression twisted — excitement turning into shock, then something darker. He turned, slow and deliberate, toward Valentina and Petra. For a moment, it seemed as though he might choke on his own fury.

Then it erupted.

A raw, unholy roar ripped from his throat, bouncing off the surrounding hills and ripping into the barren desert beyond. It was a sound of betrayal, rage — pure animal fury.

'It's fucking emptyyyyyyyyyyyy……………………'

He swung wildly, caring not where his fist landed. It connected squarely with Valentina's face, a stomach-churning crunch cutting through the night. She dropped, her head cracking against the hard, unforgiving concrete.

The sound ricocheted through the yard like a pinball, bouncing off rusted wrecks and forgotten machinery. Blood smeared across the ground in an instant.

Alshahari froze. Half-stunned. Waiting. He'd wanted to make his point — scare someone — vent his fury. But not this. Not dead.

The Meatheads moved fast. Before Alshahari could reach for his weapon, two guns were already jammed against his skull.

'Drop it. Don't fuckin' move.'

Valentina was back on her feet, blood dripping down her face, her head throbbing with rage. You do not do that to The Red Widow.

Major or not, he would not get away with this.

'You filthy fucking camel jockey. Treacherous little rat. Desert rat. Fucking sandcrawler.'

Alshahari was on his knees now, hands raised, pleading to the all-merciful Allah for his life.

'Your Allah won't help you now, you sunburnt dog.'

Her voice was a venomous snarl as she whipped her gun across his nose. A sickening crack echoed through the yard, sharp enough that even the boys — two hundred yards away — felt it.

Then she turned on Petra.

'You fucking bitch — was this you? You set us up?'

She didn't flinch. Her face, hard as stone and twice as cold, betrayed nothing.

'If I had, you'd already be dead.'

Alshahari wiped the blood from his face, breathing hard.

'Don't you fucking move. I'm not finished with you.'

The Meatheads twitched, fingers hovering over triggers, waiting for the order.

It wasn't Valentina who gave it. It was Petra.

'Calm the fuck down.'

Cold. Measured. Like she'd been through this a thousand times before. She wasn't shocked. If anything, it was as if she'd expected this.

'I knew I shouldn't have trusted you cunts.'

That only made it worse.

As the dust from the confrontation settled, the weight of the situation began to sink in. The yard, once full of adrenaline and violence, now felt eerily quiet. The scent of blood mingled with the rust and oil in the air, the looming question of the empty container hanging over them like a storm cloud.

Valentina's eyes were still locked on Alshahari, her fury not yet fully extinguished, but now a darker thought began to form in her mind. She took a step back, scanning the faces around her.

'Why is it empty?' Her voice was low, measured, the fury replaced by cold calculation.

Alshahari, still kneeling, wiped the blood from his nose, his gaze flickering nervously from Petra to Valentina. He was still processing the pain. His jaw clenched as he struggled to speak.

'I… I didn't…'

'Cut the shite,' Valentina snapped, her eyes flashing. 'This was business as usual. So why the fuck is it empty?'

Petra stepped forward, her demeanor as calm and calculating as ever, but the tension in her eyes was unmistakable. 'Har de Luc and Rej should've sorted this. They were the ones on the ground in Pakistan. The flights were paid for. The whole operation was supposed to be airtight. So why is it fucking empty?'

'Maybe because Rej is fucking dead, you stupid bitch.'

'What?' she screamed as she delivered another vicious crack across the face.

'He's dead. He was carried out of the Thirsty Horse in a body bag on Friday night.'

'So, who arranged the delivery and why is it fuckin' empty?'

The question cut through the group like a blade. No one dared move or speak, the reality of the failure settling like a weight in the pit of their stomachs.

'You think I know?' Alshahari spat, his voice full of frustration and fear. 'Do you think I'm responsible for your screw-up? I only handle the delivery here; I'm not the one making deals in Pakistan.'

Valentina's eyes narrowed as she stepped closer to him. 'So, who the fuck is responsible? Tell me, Alshahari, because if I find out you're lying to me, I will cut your fucking balls off and feed them to your camel-loving children.'

Alshahari flinched under her glare, but his defiance returned, albeit weak. 'I don't know. Ask your people in Pakistan. Maybe they fucked up.'

Petra was already shaking her head, her mind working, piecing things together. 'No. This wasn't someone else. If Rej is dead, this has to be Har de Luc's doing. And Rej or no Rej, they were paid to make sure this was done. They fucking know what happens to people if they fuck up. So why hasn't that bastard de Luc packed the container right?'

Valentina turned to Petra, her lips curling in a sneer. 'You trust him?'

Petra's eyes met hers, cold and unwavering. 'I don't trust anybody.'

The silence stretched out as the realization hit. Someone was playing them, either from within or outside their circle.

The tension in the yard thickened again, the failure gnawing at them.

'We go after Har de Luc,' Petra finally said, breaking the silence, her voice decisive. 'If he's fucked this up, or screwed us over, he's dead.'

'Fine,' Valentina muttered, the fire still burning in her eyes.

The boys looked at each other. Jesus. As the tension simmered and plans were forming in the yard, it was clear: if they wanted to find Har — alive — they'd better find him before these goons. As for Rej? Was he dead or alive? They still couldn't be sure.

Chapter 33

Super-sub

The boys waited for the yard to empty before making their way back to the village.

'Cloud Nine?' suggested Tappie. 'It's the only place we'll get one now.'

'What about the Horse? Isn't that open till after two?' asked Mick.

'Good call,' said Top Shelf. 'We've unfinished business up there. Something happened that night, and we still don't know what it was. Maybe we'll get some answers now that the dust has settled.'

The boys agreed. It was only a short drive back down the truck road.

As they trundled through the dark, putrid, rat-infested streets, again passing the bicycles with no lights, and the men still sat under trees, Robbie wondered out loud 'Don't those guys have work in the morning?'

'They do, but they don't give a fuck,' Mick said. 'Would you for a dollar a day?'

Robbie had to admit he wouldn't. It was bad enough getting up in the morning without having the total piss ripped out of you by some privileged, penny-pinching, slave driving, tightwad cunt. This was another of those contradictions that he had been so blindly unaware of prior to coming here. This land had been, and still was, built on slave labour.

Under British influence, the Arabian Peninsula had abolished slavery in 1962. He'd therefore assumed that everyone out here would be well paid, from the street sweepers to the city slickers. How wrong he had been. They could tart it up however they liked, but this was twenty-first century slavery, and it didn't sit right with Robbie — not that he was going to lose any sleep over it.

The Thirsty Horse was dead. It looked like an old-school canteen — barren. Plastic tables and chairs. Plastic cutlery. A foosball table and some weird-looking board game at the end, beneath the TV, which was playing some random cricket match. No one was watching, but all five TVs were showing cricket. The rotten, stale smell of curry — the same one that had turned Robbie's stomach in the taxi — clung to the walls, where a small opening, masquerading as a bar, had been carved. Budvar was the only beer pump on display, standing lonely and untouched.

Behind the bar stood a small, wiry man — not far off a midget — who looked like he was used to squeezing through tight spaces. His skin was deep brown, almost black, from long days under the sun. A scrawny, caterpillar-like moustache perched on his upper lip, and his hair — it was hard to tell if it was the result of too much oil or days of not being washed — was greasy and slicked back. Whatever it was, it nearly turned Robbie's stomach.

But it was the tattoo that stood out.

Curled around the side of his neck, just below his ear, was an inked cobra, mouth open in a silent hiss.

He didn't even see them come in, didn't so much as acknowledge them. But when Auld Davie dragged him away from his Snapchat, TikTok, or whatever the fuck *Tok* had him glued to his phone, he had the nerve to look annoyed.

Davie cleared his throat, 'Ah-hem. As-salamu alaykum. Tis'aa kuous min fadlik.'

The barman looked as lost as the rest of the boys.

Sensing their bewilderment, Davie added 'It means nine pints, please.'

'I know what it means, that but that cunt doesnae,' replied Tappie.

'*La 'Arabi,*' the baffled Mohammed added.

'*Ingleezi?*' offered Davie.

'*No Ingleezi.*'

'Nine fuckin' pints,' shouted a now irate Mick, his nine fingers nearly in Mohammed's face.

'*Ah.*'

'Aye, fuckin' *ah!*'

'No ten, sir? One — nine dirham, two — ten dirham.'

'Fuck it, give us ten then.'

'Right, Inspector Cluso, where are we gonna get these answers from?' smirked Mick. 'That wee bobbly-headed fuck wouldn't know his arse from his elbow.'

'We need a translator,' offered Davie, 'I'm not sure Mohammed fully understood me.'

That did it. The boys were bursting their holes laughing at the poor ould sod, taunting him with:

'*Moo lo da ba zi koo*'

'*Yo fa ha ra ka no*'

'Vee sha koo bi go'

'Very funny lads. Why don't you try if you're so clever,' a visibly offended Davie, replied.

'He's right, though. We do,' came Top Shelf, the voice of reason.

'Aye, but even if we get a translator, who are we going to ask?,' added Mick, looking around at the empty room.

Rudolph was wobbling his head — mimicking Mohammed — and licking his lips now. He was limbering up, pacing the sidelines, waiting for his call. *His call*. His fifteen minutes of fame. The super-sub, ready to take his shot at glory.

'I know how to get these lads to talk.'

The boys were all ears.

'Alright, John Hewitt,' mocked Tappie, old enough to remember the club legend's winning goal in the 1983 European Cup Winners' Cup final against Real Madrid, securing a 2-1 victory in extra time.

'Booze!' was all he said.

The wait was agonizing.

'We go down to the all-night offie, buy two crates of Red Horse — the strong one, the sixteen percenter — and join the boys under the trees. They'll be singing like canaries after two of them. And, if they're not, we'll refuse to give them anymore until they squeal.'

The lads had to admit; this was one of Rudolph's better ideas. He might just have put the ball in the back of the net, deep into injury time.

'So, who's going?' said Tappie.

One by one, the excuses began.

'Well, it was my idea.'

'I ordered the pints.'

'Eh! I ordered the fuckin' pints.'

'Jesus… all right. I'll go,' said Robbie. 'Where is it?'

'Just back at the roundabout. Two minutes. Premium Cellars. Cannae miss it. If you do, dinnae come back.'

They were off again — clinking glasses, rolling around, slapping each other on the backs.

For fuck's sake, thought Robbie, as he accepted the offer of Rudolph's keys.

'Don't forget the fags,' shouted Tappie as Robbie disappeared from sight. 'Let's hope he gets lost eh!,' he winked as he held up ten fingers to

Mohammed. The message well and truly understood this time.

Chapter 34

Snake-neck

The lads made their way to the car park — an open patch of dirt — and slowly approached a group of Indian lads. They were always there, sitting under the trees in the shade, cans of cheap beer in hand, eyes dull from long hours of hard work, or hard drinking — it was difficult to tell.

Top Shelf knew they wouldn't talk to them freely. These men lived in the shadows; their voices too small to be heard.

'Don't make it obvious, don't startle them,' he whispered.

The Indians motioned for the boys to join them. All their hopes were now pinned on these forty-eight cans of Red Horse doing their thing. By the second can, the magic potion had begun to take effect. As the alcohol worked its way into their blood, tongues began to wag.

Yes, there had been rumours. They hadn't been there personally, but it was a close-knit community, and people talked. And let's face it, they had very little to talk about so this was a juicy bit of gossip. Top Shelf only hoped they hadn't embellished it for their own entertainment.

There had been a fight, and it wasn't just a drunken brawl. Someone had gone missing. No one knew who, and when the police arrived, they found a body, bagged it up, and took it away.

But that was the problem — no one knew who it was in the bag.

Some of the lads had heard whispers. Some said it was Rej; others said it was someone else. Nobody knew for sure. But Sanjid — who had been working the alley that night — might have seen something, and he would meet them tomorrow at the Thirsty Horse at ten a.m.

Just in case anyone was watching, Mohammed would let them in through the back door.

The next morning, the lads regrouped at their usual spot. Mick and Dick, leaving no stone unturned in their pursuit of cold beer, had submerged their pints in buckets of ice. They raised their eyes in a morning salute as they sucked on their plastic straws. Fuckin' paper straws — no wonder Trump banned them. At least he was good for something…

'So, who is this guy?' Robbie asked, squinting his eyes to avoid the morning sun. 'Why is he willing to talk all of a sudden? Can we trust him?'

No one answered straight away, but the answer was in his gut — this kind of man only spoke when he had no other choice. Had he seen too much? Was he now so scared that he had to talk to someone? What was in it for him? Money? Or did he think the boys could protect him?

'He'll talk,' Top Shelf said finally, his voice low. 'But you know how it is. Some people say it like it is, and some say it like it isn't — like they're told to say it.'

The lads all exchanged looks. It might be a waste of time, but they had no other leads, no other choice. They had to talk to him. Still, something gnawed at Robbie — something didn't sit right. He had a bad feeling in his gut, and it wasn't just guilt or self-loathing. It was something darker, a sense of dread that he couldn't shake.

They reached the Thirsty Horse at ten on the dot. No sign of Sanjid.

Robbie's gut twisted. Something was wrong. He could feel it.

'C'mon, round the back's this way,' muttered Tappie.

'Wait,' said Mick, scanning the area, making sure they hadn't been followed.

Tappie knew something wasn't right, too. This place should be quiet at this time of day, but it wasn't. There was a buzz — an unnatural one. Almost feral.

As he turned the corner into the back alley, he saw it.

The crows descended like a curse, blackening the sky in a rolling, shrieking swarm. Their caws were not calls but cries — hoarse, guttural things that scraped against the soul. Wings beat like burial shrouds in the wind. They clawed at one another with blind fury, driven by the scent of something dying. It wasn't clear if they'd come for the dead, or to kill.

Robbie's stomach dropped. He was already moving before he fully processed why.

The man lay slumped, face down, a dark stain spreading beneath him. The birds tore at his flesh with sharp, merciless beaks, their beady eyes flicking up only to challenge each other.

Mick stepped up behind him. His voice was quiet.

'He's dead.'

Their only source — who'd been willing to talk just hours before — was gone. And with him, any chance of finding out what really happened to Har and Rej that night.

Robbie stood motionless, staring down at the body. They knew who was behind this, and that was a scary thought. They were tying up loose ends and wouldn't stop at this.

He swallowed hard. *We could be next. I could be next.*

'We need to get out of here,' he muttered, pulling his gaze away from the gruesome scene unfolding before him. 'We're not safe.'

No one argued. Grim-faced, they turned and made for the cars.

As Dick twisted the key in the ignition, something caught his eye — a small piece of paper wedged under the wiper of the Transit van. Robbie hopped out. It was a note, scrawled messily on a receipt from the Thirsty Horse.

The note read:

Go home Mr. Policeman

The receipt read:

Date: 17/06/2025
Time: 01:37
Server: Mohammed

Items:

Budvar (Pint) x20 @ 9 AED each

Subtotal:

20 pints x 9 AED = 180 AED

   Discount for 2 - for - 10 AED Offer (10 sets): - 80 AED

Final Total: 100 AED

'Fuck…' he shouted. Robbie slammed the door of the van shut and took off like a man possessed. He tore around the corner into the back alley, startling the gorging crows. As the dust began to settle, he could just make out, on what was left of the dead man's neck, through the mud and blood, the flared hood of an inked cobra.

'Fuck…' He was out of breath when he returned to the van. 'Go.'

'Spit it out.'

'That wasn't Sanjid, it was Mohammed.'

'What? Snake-neck Mohammed? What did he ever do to anyone?'

'Exactly. And where the fuck is Sanjid?'

How were they going to track this Sanjid down now? They had to go back to the industrial estate. Back to the boys under the trees. But if people had been reluctant to speak to them before, what reaction were they going to get now, with the news of Mohammed's murder starting to spread? Nobody would want to get involved. And The Red Widow and The Viper could be lurking, or worse, their Meatheads.

There were no cameras where he had been bludgeoned to death, *they* had made sure of that. Sanjid was more likely than most to have seen something. He should have been there — he must have witnessed something, more than he should have. The boys knew who was responsible for this, but Sanjid didn't. Now, he would be hiding, terrified for his life, knowing that it could be him next.

Robbie's gut twisted at the thought, but they had no choice. Sanjid was the key, and unless they found him, they'd never get to the bottom of what had really happened that night between Har and Rej.

The boys peered into their pints. Glasses half-empty. There were no jokes, no high spirits. They were tired and hungover, but more than that, they were deflated now, the thrill of the adventure gone. For once, no one was rushing to finish their drinks. Even Princess seemed to know something was wrong. The auto-order had been cancelled. Auld Davie's system broken. No one was in a hurry to talk.

Robbie felt the onus was on him to start. He owed these lads. He'd dragged them into this. He stated the obvious. 'We need to get into that industrial estate.'

'Oh, fuckin' great, Plod. How the fuck are we supposed to do that with those two bitches watching our every move?' Mick was in no mood for Robbie's pish.

Tappie broke the mood. 'Fuck this lads. This is fuckin' miserable. We need some fuckin' Red Bull. That'll sort us oot.'

'Princess...' he roared, somehow mustering the strength to smile.

Like the pot of gold at the end of the rainbow, Princess floated through the door like an angel, her smile breaking through the clouds, her long legs lifting them from the gloom, her voice like a heavenly choir — soft and soothing.

Balanced delicately on her tray, like cruise missiles poised in their silos, ready to launch, to strike, to put fire back in their bellies — nine Jägerbombs. The lads stared at the tray, then at Tappie.

'You're a fuckin' genius, boy,' said Mick.

Taking the compliment in his stride, Tappie winked at Robbie. 'You know what else we need?'

Robbie didn't get it.

'Donuts.' He turned to Mick. 'Get Talabat up.'

Mick thumped his fist off the table, nearly sending the Jägerbombs flying. 'Jesus, Tappie, that's it —'

The boys just stared at each other — bewildered, lost, dazed, and confused. It was too early for this cryptic shite.

'Talabat,' Mick continued, 'that's how we get into the industrial estate.'

The boys stared at each other again, their puzzled expressions shifting to awe.

'Jesus, Mick,' Tappie conceded. 'It's *you* that's the genius.'

Chapter 35

Duncan Donut

After several rounds of Jägerbombs, the boys had the bit back between their teeth. Ideas were flying around like a pinball in a machine, toing and froing, bouncing off the walls, until the ball finally dropped.

'Right, lads,' began Dick. 'Here's the plan. We'll order some donuts. When the driver arrives, we'll give him some cash to borrow his scooter and uniform. They earn nothing, so he won't say no. Then one of us heads up to the Indians — maybe even take a pizza for authenticity.'

'And who's going to squeeze into that stupid little orange uniform?' asked Tappie, visibly relieved it wouldn't be him. 'I'll no' fit, for sure.'

'That rules me out,' said the giant Finn.

'My head's too big for the helmet,' added Robbie.

One by one, the excuses piled on until they were all left staring at Mick.

'Ah Jesus, no fuckin' way. Pick on the little guy is it? You shower of scumbag fucks. No fuckin' shame at all, have ye? Call yourselves friends? Friends, me arse. Fuckin' rotten bastards. Cunts.'

They were still staring at him.

'Nice one Mick,' as if his rant had been some kind of acceptance speech.

Robbie's predicament now was how to keep these vagabonds from going on the lash all day. There was no way Mick going to abstain and watch the rest of them get annihilated.

He considered suggesting a round of golf, but the last time he'd played with these boys, they'd had at least eight cans, several joints, and a wee break on the tenth tee to down a bottle of Buckfast. *Fuckin' Buckie*, Robbie had thought — *do grown men really drink that shite?*

Their bodies may have been creaking under the strain of middle-to-old age, but no one had thought to tell their minds. These guys were like kids — willing to do anything to avoid a day of honest work, still laughing at infantile jokes and playground humour.

No, golf would not do.

He was about to suggest they go home for a nap when Mick announced that Duncan had arrived with the donuts. Duncan Donut took very little persuading to part with his scooter and was down to his underpants in a matter of minutes.

'Well, you'd better give him yours, Mick. Poor Duncan will get fried alive standing there in his Y-fronts,' said Tappie.

'You fucks owe me big time,' grumbled Mick, peeling off his designer gear. 'And he better not soil them.' He shuddered at the thought, before adding, 'Look at the state of his own fuckin' skegs.'

It was a fair point — they were filthy. Robbie wondered how many days he had actually had them on. They looked stuck to him.

'Just get on with it and stop your whinging, Mick.' Tappie was enjoying this.

Mick pulled on the T-shirt.

'Lovely, Mick.' Rudolph was getting in on it now.

'Shut it, ya red-nosed fuck.'

'Now, now, Michael.' Even Dick was getting into the spirit.

Next, he tried to pull on the black trousers.

'Need a hand there, fatso?' howled Tappie.

The boys were pissing themselves now as Mick writhed around on the ground, trying for all he was worth to get them on. But despite their stretchy material, he just could not get the zipper up.

Auld Davie was splitting his sides, his shoulders were nearly hitting his ears, he was laughing so hard. 'Want me to have a go? I'm good with crotches.'

'I bet you are, you dirty old bastard. You're getting nowhere near my fuckin' dick.'

When he eventually got them on, they were so tight that he could hardly walk.

'Jesus Christ, Mick, you look like a burst sausage,' cackled Tappie.

Mick took a stiff-legged step forward and winced. 'My balls are nearly in my fuckin' throat,' he groaned, adjusting himself in a way that made everyone laugh even harder.

'Better not sit down, lad, or you'll do yourself an injury,' said Dick, wiping a tear from his eye.

Auld Davie, still gasping for breath, gave him a once-over. 'I'd say they suit ya, but I don't think they're meant to be spray-on.'

Mick gritted his teeth. 'Are we done takin' the fuckin' piss?'

'Ah, give us a twirl there, Mick,' said Rudolph, spinning his finger.

Mick shot him a look. 'You cunts better remember this, 'cos I'll not fuckin' forget it in a hurry.'

But as he took another step, the seams of the trousers let out an ominous rip. The group went silent for a split second before erupting into hysterics.

'Oh fuck, he's gonna blow!' howled Tappie, clutching his sides. 'You should've shaved your arse if you were planning on givin' us a show.'

Mick stood there, fists clenched, his face contorted in rage. 'Right, that's it. Duncan, take your fuckin' kecks back. I'd rather ride bollock-naked than suffer this humiliation.'

Poor Duncan was inconsolable — his only pair of work pants, destroyed. Dick clapped him on the back. 'Don't worry, lad. We'll sort you out. Mick'll pay.'

Mick, still fuming, yanked his own trousers back on and let out a relieved breath. He shot one last glare at the lot of them. 'Right, dickheads, if I'm not back in an hour, either The Viper, The Widow, or Duncan's fumes have got me.'

'Wait...' said Dick.

'What now?

'Well, your face.'

Mick was getting right pissed off now. 'What wrong with my fuckin' face?'

'It's too white. You'll stand out like a nun in a knocking shop.'

Mick rolled his eyes. 'Oh, for fuck's sake. What do you want me to do, get a tan in the next five minutes?'

Tappie snapped his fingers. 'Hang on, I've got an idea.'

Before Mick could protest, Tappie grabbed a handful of grime from the wheel arch of Duncan's scooter and smeared it across Mick's cheeks.

'Oi! You dirty bastard!' Mick recoiled, swiping at his face, but Tappie was already going in for another round, smudging it in like war paint.

Auld Davie nodded approvingly. 'Aye, that's better.'

Mick glared at them all, seething. 'You cunts better pray I don't make it back.'

He jammed his helmet on, revved the scooter, and tore off down the road — or as fast as a Talabat scooter could manage — leaving the others still pissing themselves behind him.

Tappie cupped his hands around his mouth. 'Mind the speed cams, Mick!'

Chapter 36

The broken nose – part II

True to his word, Mick was back within the hour. As he was climbing the steps to the golf club, his phone rang. He didn't recognise the number but, for some reason, answered.

'Allo,' said the voice in a weird Pakistani, or Indian, accent. 'Fifty-seven donuts please.'

'What? Who the fuck is this?'

Inside, the boys were rolling around on the ground, howling.

'Sir, I need very urgent delivery. Many, many donuts. Please bring fast, Talabat man.'

Realisation hit Mick, and he slowly stepped onto the patio, locking eyes with the lot of them, doubled over in laughter.

'You cunts,' he growled.

His trip had not been wasted however, and as Princess delivered tray after tray, Mick filled them in.

He'd found the boys under the tree — hammered. They could barely string a sentence together but managed to point him towards a villa of sorts — more of a run-down shack.

A rickety metal gate, barely hanging on its hinges, had led him to a filthy yard, thick with the stench of decay. Broken-down scooters lay scattered across the ground, half-buried in piles of garbage. Beady-eyed rats scurried between old, crushed fast food wrappers, rotting fruit, and half-eaten sandwiches, their noses twitching in the air.

There, in the middle of it all, stood Sanjid — a small, bony Pakistani — stringing up his oversized uniforms and threadbare T-shirts on a makeshift clothesline stretched between two battered trees. His Thirsty Horse security shirt had seen better days.

He'd nearly run off when Mick suggested that he might have heard or seen what went down at the pub that night — but his reaction was all Mick needed.

'What did you get, Mick?' asked Top Shelf.

'Sanjid had been working the back door as security,' Mick explained, 'while the police managed their usual back-alley market — weed, coke, pills, and such. Inside, Har and Rej had been arguing — something about the next delivery. It sounded serious, but Sanjid didn't know exactly what it was about. Har had been furious — fuming, apparently.'

'There was a lot of shouting. People were staring, but no one wanted to get involved. Then Rej grabbed Har's bag — tried to yank it from him — and Har snapped. He punched Rej square in the face. Rej went down, cracking his head off the ground.'

'What was in the bag?' Dick asked.

'Sanjid didn't know,' Mick said. 'He just said Har stormed off, and Rej lay there for a while — stunned. Then… then things got worse.'

'Worse?'

'Out back, there was trouble. The police were there, doing their thing, but something was wrong that night. Something about a deal gone bad. Sanjid didn't know for sure, but people started arguing, fighting, and the next thing — there was a body on the ground. The police covered him up quick, shoved him into a body bag like he was nothing. Then they were gone. Clean. Fast. Like it never happened.'

'And Har?'

'Sanjid didn't see him after that. He was gone.'

'And Rej?'

'Same. Left out the back door, and Sanjid never saw him again.'

'So, Rej's alive?'

'Yes. If you can believe that head-wobbler.'

'And the body on the ground? Was he shot? Stabbed? Just saying there was a body on the ground is a bit vague, isn't it?'

'I agree. I pushed him on that, and he got a bit jittery. Couldn't really answer it, but it sounded like it just… appeared. No gunshots, no knives — just a body.'

The boys let that settle, the pieces rearranging themselves in their minds.

Robbie was too long in the tooth to buy this shite.

'So, Har and Rej fight over a bag. Har storms off. Something happens out the back. A corpse shows up — then gets hauled off like rubbish. Then Rej just wanders off.' He paused. 'And through all of this, Alshahari wants us all to think that Rej is dead. He nearly got beaten to a pulp protecting that story. Why would he do that? There are holes all over that fuckin' story.'

Could this Sanjid — a security guard earning less than the price of a pint per day — be trusted? If the local police already had the entire docks in their pocket, were peddling all sorts of contraband out of the Thirsty Horse, was it safe to assume security — Sanjid — was also on the paylist? He'd sing like a bird for a packet of peanuts.

But, if he was telling the truth, who was in that body bag? It wasn't like they could strap this scarecrow up to polygraph. He probably barely had a pulse anyway.

More to the point, did they really care? If it wasn't Har or Rej, why should they? Robbie hadn't come here to solve crimes — nor was he getting paid to — and the others didn't really give a fuck.

Yet the question just wouldn't leave him. He hadn't risen to Detective Sergeant by walking away or sticking his head in the sand. Where the fuck were Har and Rej?

Could he put Princess's mind at ease? That would certainly earn him some brownie points. He drifted off, wondering how she might thank him… in kind.

Earth to Robbie

Jesus — Princess, Nong, Elle, fuckin' Cat Woman, Saxy the saxophonist, Magnolia… *did he think he was Casanova or what?*

Robbie and the boys sat in silence, pondering their next move. Har and Rej were alive. They hadn't boarded that flight to Pakistan, hadn't arranged the delivery, and somehow they'd made sure to cover their tracks.

FUCK!' Mick screamed. 'I've just about had it with these cunts. We've been chasing our tails for a week now.'

'Time and patience, Mick,' said Robbie. 'It took a snail to America.'

'Look, Plod!' Mick snarled, now irate. 'Why don't you just fuck off back to Ireland and let us get back to our golf and pints?'

Robbie snapped. His patience had worn thin. 'You think I fuckin' want this? Need this?' he shot back. 'I'm supposed to be here on holiday, not arsing around with you shower of drunken fucks.'

Mick's eyes flashed, his temper flaring. Robbie didn't have time to react before Mick shot up from his chair and, in one swift motion, smashed his head — brutally — into the middle of Robbie's face. The crack of Robbie's nose breaking was sharp and sickening. Blood poured from his nostrils, dripping down his chin and mixing with the adrenaline pumping through his body.

'Fuckin' hell!' Robbie staggered back, his hands instinctively going to his face, but Mick wasn't done. This time, he punched Robbie in the face, knocking him over the table.

'Don't talk to me like that, Plod.' Mick bent down and spat in his face. 'You got us into this shite, ya culchie fuck.'

Robbie wiped his bloody nose with the back of his hand. His head was spinning. 'Get out of my face, ya Limerick scumbag.'

He pulled himself to his feet, and for a moment, the two men stood there, face to face, seething — neither one willing to back down.

Dick stepped in. 'Pull your shit together, both of you,' he snarled. 'Take five minutes, then we're back on this. We finish what we started, and if they're alive, we're gonna find them.'

Robbie wiped the blood off his lip, glaring at Mick. 'Fine,' he said.

'Mick?'

'Fine.'

Princess arrived with her mop, brush, pan, and paper towels in hand, and did her best to restore some order to the place. Auld Davie led Robbie away to the toilets to wash away the filthy mix of blood and spit from his face.

Mick lit a smoke and shrugged his shoulders. 'What?' he shouted at the boys. 'He's had that comin'.'

Robbie reappeared from the toilets, but Mick went at him again, lunging across the room. Big Tappie caught him and threw him back into his chair. Robbie was escorted to another.

'Calm the fuck down, both of you.'

'Right, Top Shelf, you take this. He's in no fit state,' instructed Tappie, nodding towards the sulking Robbie.

Top Shelf needed no further encouragement to take the reins.

'Okay. Could they have left the country another way? he asked, his mind racing through possibilities. 'Money talks, and they'd have the means. Maybe a boat, a private plane?'

Robbie coughed; he wasn't about to let this geriatric, retired private dick run the show. 'What if they never left? What if they're still here, hiding in plain sight?'

The lads mulled it over. If they hadn't left, then where were they? Some small villa, a quiet getaway?

The thought nagged at Robbie.

'What if they're playing us?' Robbie suggested. 'Pulling the strings the whole time? They've got the money — maybe they've been planning this all along. You said Har was clever?'

'Too clever,' said Dick, 'for his own good.'

'Maybe that's why he called me? He knew the Guard in me would come looking for him — for them. He knew we'd track them down eventually. And when we do, it won't be some dank corner of the world — they'll be living it up, somewhere nice, somewhere we'd never guess.'

'Hmm,' Mick said, not really buying it. 'Why disappear if you want to be found?'

'Well,' Robbie replied, 'he wants *us* to find them. He doesn't want that other crowd finding them.'

A few moments passed in silence before Mick, considering the possibility that Robbie's theory might actually carry some weight, spoke again. 'Okay, so where the fuck are they, then, Colombo?'

Robbie shook his head. 'Fuck knows, but if it's the last thing I do, I'll find these cunts. I'm not getting outsmarted by a Paki waiter and a fuckin' baguette-waving, garlic-breathed, cheese-eating frog.'

'Here, here,' shouted Mick, as if they were the best of buddies.

Chapter 37

Hop-a-Long

Just as the boys were discussing their next move, a strange-looking individual hobbled into view. Dressed in combat shorts and a sleeveless T-shirt, one sandal on his left foot, and a Doc Martin attached to the other, on what appeared to be a prosthetic limb.

He had a sunken, hollow appearance, not helped by his bald head, his big, pockmarked, drinker's beacon, or the chunks missing from the lobes of his ears. He looked like a boxer, or a war veteran, someone for whom everything that could've gone wrong, had. He was easily one of the queerest looking individuals Robbie had seen in a long time.

Thoughts of Har and Rej faded as they watched him limp across the floor — his uneven gait echoing with each second step, a dull thud vibrating through the wooden boards. He carried no cane.

Yet, despite his obvious physical disabilities, he exuded a strange confidence — an air of authority. Calm and poised, he shuffled up to them and slid something across the table.

A crumpled McDonald's napkin, used and stained with a suspicious blob of ketchup.

The boys looked at each other. Mick picked it up, skeptical of its hygiene, then unfolded it cautiously, wary not to drop any ketchup on himself.

Inside, scrawled in red ink, a brief but chilling message:

```
We know you're looking for him
Keep going
We'll be watching.
```

'That's fuckin' disgusting,' said Mick, revolted. 'Fuckin' ketchup.'

Dick paled. His voice was tight. 'Fuck. That's not ketchup—that's The Red Widow's symbol.'

A heavy silence fell over the table.

'And if she's watching us… Jesus, she's probably watching us now. Watching us all day. Watching Mick get into that stupid fuckin' Talabat suit…' He trailed off. He didn't need to finish. They all knew.

'And us, skulking around like fuckwits, thinking we could hide from her.'

'Well, if she thinks I'm doing her dirty work for her, she can go fuck herself,' Mick muttered.

Robbie exhaled. 'Look, she'll find them —' he paused, '— hold on— she'll find him. She thinks Rej is dead too.'

He paused again. 'Anyway, with or without us, they'll find whoever they're looking for. On the plus side, they'll want them alive — at least until they get their money back.'

'Yeah, but if we find Har first, we'll only lead those two bitches straight to him — and maybe Rej too. How long do you think they'll last after that?'

'Not long, granted. Which is why we need to be smart — smarter than them.'

'Lads,' Auld Davie said, nodding at the strange-looking errand boy, 'walls have ears. Old rubber-lugs there, Peg Leg Jake… is still here. Say nothing, and keep saying it, until we get out of here… until we lose this guy.'

'That shouldn't be too difficult,' joked Tappie. 'Just chuck his leg in the water, and he'll be swimming round in circles trying to find it.'

That did it. The poor bastard went red in the face and started foaming at the mouth, 'ya… ya… better… fuc…'

'Spit it oot hop-a-long. You gonna hit me with your leg?' Tappie was goading him now.

Auld Davie, weary, continued, 'I don't know how they're doing it, but these snakes are watching us, maybe even listening—they seem to know our every move. So how the hell are we getting out of here without being seen?

'Dick? Mick?' They'd had all the answers before. Robbie was hoping they'd pull another rabbit out of the hat.

'Well, there's always...'

'Yep.'

'You think?'

'Don't see why not.'

'Fuckin' spit it out,' roared Tappie, his humour gone. He was getting exasperated with this telepathic game of ping pong.

Suddenly, Rudolph shouted, 'Where's Clubfoot?'

'And where's Donut?'

Poor Duncan had rather been forgotten in all this chaos.

They all looked around. Neither of them were anywhere to be seen. But the commotion coming from down the steps was unmistakable.

While everyone had been distracted, Peg Leg had scurried off down the steps and was attempting to steal Duncan's scooter. The old Honda Hobbit had a kickstart mechanism, and Peg Leg was struggling to get any rhythm out of his prosthetic limb. Meanwhile, Duncan, now fully aware of the theft in progress, was bopping Peg Leg's shiny, bald head with his helmet, trying to knock him off the bloody thing.

This chaos was the perfect distraction. With all eyes on Peg Leg, it was time to rally the troops and make their escape.

'Let's go,' Mick ordered, his voice sharp. The crew fell in line, slipping through the clubhouse and down the service ramp. As they weaved through the bushes toward the water, Dick grabbed a small backpack.

What the fuck? thought Robbie.

At the shoreline, Dick unzipped the bag and rolled out a deflated rubber boat onto the sand. He shot Robbie a look, as if to say — *why are you so surprised?*

Kneeling, he yanked open the inflation valve and rammed in the pump. Big Finn held the nozzle steady while Dick worked the foot pump like a madman, stamping furiously, his face already beginning to change colour. With each frantic press, the boat started to take shape.

By the time it was fully inflated, Dick was dripping with sweat, panting hard, and his head had turned a beetroot-purple. He looked like he was about to explode — or have a heart attack!

'Spliff?' offered Mick.

Un-'fuckin'-believable Robbie thought, but after already being battered today, he decided to keep that opinion to himself.

The boat was ready. It looked sturdy enough, but with nine men piling in — one of them *ten-tonne Tessie* — Robbie had his doubts.

They shoved it into the water. Big Finn climbed in first, and the tiny boat dipped alarmingly under his weight. The others hesitated, but time was running out — The Viper and The Widow would soon realise they were gone. One by one, they followed him in.

By the time Mick clambered aboard, the boat was packed tight — sweaty armpits and crotches in faces. The water was just inches below the rim.

'Jesus Christ,' Robbie muttered. 'This thing is going to sink.'

'Not if you sit still, ya retard,' Mick warned, voice low. 'Now shut the fuck up and paddle, unless you want me to lighten the load.'

Robbie wanted to hit him, but there wasn't enough room to swing. And after earlier, he had no doubt that, given any excuse, Mick would toss him overboard.

He grabbed a paddle. Time to go.

Robbie had assumed they'd be making the short trip across the water to the marina — the route the ferry took. But as the neared the jetty, Dick instructed the crew to veer left. *What the fuck?* Robbie knew little about boats, but surely this thing wasn't designed for this kind of trip. *Where the fuck were they headed anyway?*

Dick said nothing. Mick was sucking on his reefer, staring out into the distance. Big Finn — the one they surely needed to paddle — had given up entirely. Either they knew something Robbie didn't, or something was off about this.

He tried to shake the feeling off as the boat drifted out to sea, but somewhere in the distance, he caught the glint of something on the water ahead.

'What's that?' he muttered, barely able to make it out with his deteriorating eyesight — which seemed to be getting worse with every passing day in this lot's company.

Dick didn't react.

'Is that another boat?' Robbie pressed, squinting into the sun, his pulse quickening.

Mick shot Robbie a disdainful look. 'What the fuck are you on about now?'

Whatever it was, it was getting closer, and it was moving fast — too fast.

'Fuck,' Dick muttered, suddenly spotting it too.

'What's going on?' Robbie asked, trying to keep his voice steady.

Dick didn't answer. He motioned for everyone to be quiet. As an eerie silence — only disturbed by the faint hum of the casino development—settled over the uncontrolled vessel, the men sat there, staring into the inevitable abyss that awaited them. Slowly, the shape of the other boat slowly came into full view. It was massive — far larger than theirs — and it was heading straight for them.

Robbie's clenched his cheeks. Never mind the embarrassment, or the shame — this was no time to be taken short. Was this some kind of ambush? Had The Widow already figured out their plan? Or had they been tracked?

The boat was almost on them now, its engine humming, slicing through the water as the small dinghy bounced up and down in its wake. There was no way they could outrun it.

With chilling simplicity, Dick said, 'We could be fucked here, lads.'

Chapter 38

Panda boy

The massive boat slowed as it approached, its bow casting a shadow over the dinghy. The engine noise softened to a low growl, but the threat remained.

A makeshift rope ladder dropped over the side, landing with a slap against the hull. It dangled just above the water, just out of reach, as if some kind of test. The boys stared at it, frozen.

Then, a voice. An annoyingly familiar voice. Squeaky. Arabian. The kind that makes you want to punch someone in the face. Half-Indian, half-Pakistani — yet smooth, clipped, and full of authority.

'Climb aboard, gentlemen. Let's have a chat.'

Robbie looked at Dick, his expression unreadable. Mick flicked his reefer into the water, with his usual cockiness.

'Who the fuck is that?' Finn muttered, barely above a whisper.

Dick swallowed. 'Alshahari.'

A quiet chorus of 'fuck' rippled through the group. Major Alshahari was everywhere in this. He'd been at the Thirsty Horse. Had he arranged the body bag? The unmarked van? Fuck, had he even arranged the dead body? He'd been at the police station when Robbie first visited, and he had known Robbie was coming. He'd been at the docks, the impound yard... They'd even heard him admit — to The Viper and The Widow — to arranging the delivery of whatever it was they were bringing in. He was as bent as a three-bob bit. And now, he was here. And that meant someone had given them up.

Mick looked around at the faces of his so-called allies. 'Right, who's the rat? The snitch? Which wee piggy went squealing off to the market? I'll rip your fuckin' throat out. There'll be no more squealing once I'm finished with you. C'mon. Which of you rotten cunts gave us up?'

The ladder jerked again. 'I won't ask twice,' Alshahari called down. 'Don't keep me waiting.'

Robbie glanced at Dick, looking for some shred of hope, some way out — but they didn't have a choice.

'Up we go,' Dick murmured. 'Just keep your mouths shut — if that's possible. Let him do the talking.'

One by one, they climbed. As soon as they reached the deck, Alshahari's men had them on the ground — hands and feet tied like terrorists, blindfolded and gagged. The tension was thick enough to cut with a knife.

Alshahari stepped forward and ripped the blindfold from Robbie's face. Robbie had remembered him as an unimposing man, but now, kneeling before him like some vengeful God, his presence was overwhelming. His eyes seemed to stare straight through him — assessing, calculating, wondering how best to gut his catch.

'Now, why,' he said, clasping his hands behind his back, voice cold and deliberate, 'did you not walk away when I asked you? Why do you English always crawl back like rats?'

That lit a fire in Robbie. 'I'm not fuckin' English —'

Alshahari cut him off with a sneer. 'I don't give a fuck where you're from, you worthless infidel. We should have wiped your kind off the face of the earth fifty years ago — but here you are, still stinking up my country like a rotting corpse.'

He paused, letting the words settle. Robbie had done nothing to this guy — hell, he didn't even know him — yet here he was, standing over him, ready to unleash all of Allah's wrath.

Sweet mother of Jesus... Robbie tipped his head back and stared at the heavens, as if God Himself might reach down and pluck him from this nightmare. But there was nothing — only the sharp, ragged cawing of hungry gulls circling overhead.

He looked around, throat dry as sandpaper, at his crew — lined up against the bulwark, bound and gagged — but there wasn't a thing he could do.

All except Eugene.

The bastard stood off to the side, untied, untouched — like he was one of them. Arms crossed; lips curled in a smirk he didn't even bother to hide.

Robbie's gut twisted. So Eugene had sung — handed them over to Alshahari like pigs to the slaughter.

He stared at him, speechless. Shattered. Empty.

Finally, the words stumbled out, brittle and broken.

'You? Eugene?'

From along the line, he heard muffled gasps from the others.

'Why?'

Alshahari smiled faintly, as if he already knew the answer. 'No matter. Let's talk, shall we?'

Robbie, frightened though he was, found something from within — maybe anger, maybe pride — he didn't know.

'There'll be no talking, you lowdown scumbag, not until my men are untied. Who do you think you are, you fuckin' sand snake?'

Crack.

Alshahari snapped the back of his hand across Robbie's face, sharp and fast, bursting fresh blood from his already shattered nose. It wobbled on his face, broken and useless.

'Shut it, panda boy,' Alshahari sneered, his own eyes still black from the back of The Widow's gun. 'You're not in control anymore. You might boss around your little leprechaun brigade back in Ireland, or this shower of useless dogs who defy the true faith. Out here you're at the mercy of Allah.'

The anger drained from Robbie, leaving only raw fear. Was this the end? It wasn't supposed to happen like this. His thoughts flashed, scattered — Bert Jnr, his father, Elle… Would he see his mother again if he met his maker today?

He looked up at his aggressor, hopeless, pitiful, a broken man. He'd take whatever mercy Allah had to offer.

'What do you want? I have nothing.'

Alshahari hissed, 'I had this sorted. Do you think I let that bitch Valentina beat me for nothing? Everything was running like clockwork until you showed up. Why are you looking for my men?'

My men? Why the hell is he saying, "my" men? Robbie thought, but kept his mouth shut.

'I don't know,' Robbie replied honestly. 'Har is their friend. They just want to know he's okay. That he's alive.'

Alshahari crouched down, face level with Robbie's. His breath stank of stale coffee and cigarettes. 'Oh, he's alive alright... no thanks to you. Now I've got The Widow and The Viper breathing down my neck. What do you think they'll do to your friend when they get wind of our little plan?'

Plan? What plan?

'You're poking around in places you don't understand, O'Malley. Asking questions that'll get you killed.'

Robbie could feel the blood trickling from his nose, warm and slow. He wanted to spit it at the man, but what good would that do now?

Alshahari grinned — he knew he had the upper hand.

'You think this is about drugs? Guns? Some street-level racket?' Alshahari's voice dropped to a whisper, but the menace in it was deafening. 'You have no idea what was in that container, do you?'

Robbie frowned. 'It was empty.'

Alshahari's eyes glinted, as if he were speaking to a child who just didn't get it.

'Empty?' He chuckled darkly. 'Of course it was empty, my friend.'

He stood up suddenly, turning his back on Robbie, pacing the deck with his hands clasped behind him.

'Let me give you a lesson, O'Malley. Women like The Viper and The Widow don't care about money. They care about reputation. About fear. And if word gets out that their shipment was taken — by me, by Har, by Rej, by anyone — what do you think happens next?'

Robbie had nothing. No plan. He swallowed the blood in his throat and whimpered. He didn't know why he said it, or what he hoped to get from it. 'But Rej is dead.'

Alshahari turned sharply, leaning down again. His voice was calm now, almost friendly — which made it all the worse.

'Don't play dumb O'Malley. You and I both know that's not true. I made sure of that — why do you think *I* let them run?'

Alshahari was beginning to enjoy this. Seeing this poor, worthless kāfir suffer. 'Those bitches will burn us all. Every last one of us. You. Your friends.' He gestured casually at the others tied up on the deck, as if their lives were no more than cards in his hand. 'Me. Har. Rej, this boat…'

He sniggered.

'There's no mercy from women like that, O'Malley. They'll drag us to hell for this.'

Robbie swallowed again, trying to find his voice. 'So what, you're… what? Running? Hiding?'

Alshahari's eyes gleamed, but there was no humour in them.

'No. I'm buying time — moving pieces. And until I figure out my next move, you're going to stop meddling and do exactly as I say. No more Bear Grylls bullshit.'

He rested his hand on Robbie's shoulder — not heavy, but deliberate — like a man mollifying an anxious child. The grip tightened just enough to remind Robbie who was in charge.

'And if you *don't* —' he smiled without warmth —'well, let's just say you'll wish those bitches had burned you.'

Robbie stared up at him, heart pounding, mind whirring. Everything he thought he knew — about Har, about Rej, about this whole mess — was crumbling.

Alshahari gestured to his men —'untie them.'

The boys were cut loose, wrists raw and faces pale. Mick was the first to speak, his voice rough and broken. 'What about that cunt?' he muttered, nodding toward Eugene, who stood frozen, white as a sheet.

Alshahari didn't even look. He gave a small flick of his fingers to one of the guards — a gesture as casual as swatting a fly.

The guard nodded once, drew his pistol, and levelled it at Eugene's head.

'Let the sharks have him,' Alshahari said flatly. 'He's no use to me now.'

Eugene opened his mouth to beg, but the shot cracked before a word could leave his throat. The bullet punched clean through his forehead, and his body toppled over the rail, vanishing into the water with a hollow splash.

Alshahari straightened his jacket, then looked back at Robbie, voice like ice.

'Now get off my boat, and out of my water.'

Shaken, the men lowered themselves, one by one, back into the small dinghy. Finally, as Robbie stepped over the bulwark and gripped the rope ladder, Alshahari leaned in close — so near that only Robbie could hear.

'And if you think Eugene was the only rat you've got, think again.'

Robbie felt his heart sink.

Chapter 39

Limerick, my dear

Robbie's entire head was beating like a drum. He could barely see through his swollen panda-like eyes, barely breathe through his shattered nose. His hands were torn raw — bloody and blistered from rowing this godforsaken rubber dinghy, and he'd pissed himself under the oppressive muzzle of Alshahari's pistol. He was stinking, hungover, hungry, exhausted — mentally and physically — and all he wanted now was to go home.

This was it. The last straw. If he didn't get out of here, he was going to die. Whether at the hands of some bent cop, the Russian mafia, or a Norwegian property tycoon. What terrified him even more were his own dark thoughts. Maybe he wouldn't have the strength to fight them. Maybe he'd give in. Let the weight of it all pull him under. His demons had been circling for far too long — and now they were closing in.

Mick snapped him out of his self-indulgent cesspit.

'Oi! Fuck-face. What the fuck was he whispering in your shell-like? You better not be in cahoots with that smelly Arab fuck.'

And as if things weren't bad enough, he was now absolutely petrified of one of his own men — and he knew Mick could smell it. He had finally broken him, reduced him to a shell of the man he used to be — shaking and unsure of himself. *But why? What had he ever done to this man? What was Mick getting out of this sick little game?*

Robbie was still trying to make sense of it all. The container had been empty, but Alshahari had known that from the start. He'd planned this with Har and Rej before orchestrating their disappearances. Whether they now had the contents, or the money meant to buy them, one thing was clear — The Viper and The Widow wanted it back.

Their colleague, Eugene — who had turned out to be an informant — had been shot dead before their eyes, but what if he wasn't the only rat? Who else was feeding information to Alshahari? To someone even worse? The Widow? The Viper? Every glance now, every hushed conversation suddenly reeked of betrayal.

Mick and Dick had an almost telepathic connection, their unspoken exchanges setting Robbie further on edge. Paranoia slithered into his fraying mind like a disease, twisting his thoughts, making him second-guess everything.

Who could he trust?

And, still, they didn't know why Har had called him that night. Was he seeking Robbie's help? Did he want to escape Alshahari's grip and control?

Robbie stood, shaky but firm, and wiped the blood from his face. He really didn't want to start another fight with Mick, but he'd seen his father bully his mother — and he'd sworn never to become a victim himself.

'Right now, Limerick, my dear' — directing his insult straight at Mick — 'I don't trust a single one of you. But we can't stay here, and we sure as hell can't go back. So you can carry on with your bigotry and insults, get yourself shot like you're little rat pal Eugene, or you can shut the fuck up and think of a way to get us out of this mess.'

Mick was startled — taken aback by the strength of character Robbie was showing. He wasn't used to being challenged. His reputation carried weight in the village. This was why he didn't like fresh blood, new faces. This was his manor, but maybe he should've given this guy a little more respect.

He looked at Dick. Dick nodded.

'Come on. We've got work to do.'

As they pulled away from the looming shadow of Alshahari's boat, Robbie couldn't shake the feeling that this could only get worse — far worse than anything he'd imagined.

They rowed as instructed by their captain, Dick, moving as if on autopilot. Robbie had nearly reached a state of acceptance — his fate was no longer in his hands. What would be, would be. This emotional rollercoaster would end, one way or another. All he could do now was hang on and hope.

Que sera, sera was quickly replaced by a sense of *déjà vu* as the small boat slipped into the docks, weaving among the fishing vessels. The steady hum of engines and the occasional shout from a fisherman provided the perfect cover for their arrival.

Dick spoke into his walkie-talkie. 'Al. Come in, Al.'

It was almost a relief when Al responded. He seemed to be one of the more normal people in this whole escapade. What were they up to now? Robbie had no idea — but he'd be glad to set foot on dry land again.

Al met them as they slipped off the boat unnoticed and led them to an old, abandoned warehouse to wait.

The door was unlocked, and they hurried inside. The air stank of salt, aged wood, and diesel. Crates and pallets were stacked high — some draped with tarps, others left open, revealing tangled nets and coils of rope.

Robbie leaned against a crate, exhaling sharply. 'Alright, someone tell me — why the fuck are we here?'

Mick wiped sweat from his forehead. 'Because if we want to find those two losers — Har and Rej — we need to follow their trail. And if they didn't fly… well, they hardly walked, did they?'

Robbie frowned. 'What are you getting at?'

Mick rolled his eyes, his patience thinning. 'They didn't fly out, fuckwit. Are you fuckin' thick or what? No records, no tickets. If they left, it had to be by boat.'

Robbie let the words sink in. 'So we're just assuming they took a boat to Pakistan?'

Top Shelf, who had been quiet up until then, spoke up. The day's events — watching Eugene get shot in cold blood — had shaken him, but he hadn't lost his sharpness. 'Makes sense,' he said, his voice steady. 'Fake their deaths, let the records show they never left the country, then disappear. And that container wouldn't have left Pakistan if they hadn't been there to arrange it.'

Dick nodded. 'Al's sorting us a boat. Tomorrow.'

Robbie glanced around at the darkened warehouse. A rat scurried over the concrete floor, disappearing behind a stack of wooden pallets. He sighed. 'Fuckin' great. Just what I wanted. A fucking sleepover in this miserable, stinkin' shitehole.'

Mick grinned and patted him on the shoulder. 'Could be worse. You could be coming up threes with Eugene out there.'

Robbie collapsed onto the crate, exhausted — on the verge of tears again. Okay, Eugene had been a rat, but for Mick to carry on as if nothing had happened? Did that heartless fuck feel nothing but rage? Robbie curled into a ball, praying to wake up and find it had all been just a bad dream.

'Before you even think about nodding off, get your fuckin' phone in there,' Mick said, shoving a rusted old bucket into view. 'You don't trust us? Well, we don't trust you either, Sergeant Bacon. In fact — everyone, phones in the bucket. Walkie-talkies, keys… I don't give a fuck. You can keep your fags and your cash, but anything that can track us or get a message out — bucket. No exceptions.'

Reluctant as he was, Robbie knew it was the right thing to do. There could easily be another rat — maybe more — among them. He tossed his phone into the bucket, almost relieved to be rid of it. It had brought him nothing but bad luck since he got here… well, except for Elle.

As he drifted in and out of reality, hallucinogens began to swirl around his brain. The world shimmered and breathed, almost like it was alive. The walls pulsed with colors that seemed to ebb and flow in waves, while patterns twisted and warped in ways that defied logic. The air felt heavy, charged with an electric hum that vibrated through his body. Sounds became distorted, growing louder and more intricate, like the rustle of leaves turning into a full orchestra.

Time warped. Minutes stretched into hours, and seconds seemed to last an eternity. He felt as though he were floating outside himself, observing his own actions like they belonged to someone else. His thoughts became fragmented, jumping from one idea to another with lightning speed. Some thoughts seemed profound, others nonsensical, yet it all felt deeply connected.

The room reeked of diesel and urine. Somewhere in the distance, he could hear the faint sobbing of an older man. The sound wove itself into his fevered hallucinations, and he couldn't tell whether it was real or just another trick of his decaying mind. He rolled onto his back, staring up at a ceiling that shifted and undulated like water, trying to latch onto something real.

As his sense of self began to dissolve, isolation hit — an overwhelming sense of being alone, lost in his own mind. The lines between fantasy and reality blurred as his surroundings morphed and shifted in a dance between wonder and chaos — where joy and fear existed side by side, and the boundaries of what was real seemed to evaporate into the void.

Thursday 19th June

Chapter 40

The rat

Robbie jolted awake with a sharp inhale, his body slick with sweat. His heart pounded against his ribs as he forced himself upright on the crate. The warehouse was still dark and humid, but no shifting walls, no glowing lights, just the grim reality of their situation. He exhaled slowly, pressing his palms to his face.

Jesus. How long had he been out?

A muffled sob cut through the silence. Robbie blinked, trying to shake the remnants of sleep from his mind. He turned his head and saw Auld Davie, tied to a pallet, his aging frame sagging against the rough wood. A pool of piss had gathered at his feet, and an oily rag had been stuffed into his mouth, damp with saliva and god knows what else. His eyes were red and swollen, tears streaming down his weathered face.

Mick loomed over him; his face twisted in fury. 'You fucking rat, Davie. Admit it!' His voice was low and venomous, each word spat like a curse.

Davie whimpered, shaking his head, his entire body trembling.

'Lying bastard,' Mick snarled. He ripped the rag from Davie's mouth, and the old man gasped for air, coughing violently.

'Mick, please, I wasn't —'

The slap echoed through the warehouse before Davie could finish his sentence. His head snapped to the side, a fresh welt blooming across his cheek. Mick grabbed him by the collar, yanking him forward. 'I caught this fuck trying to get his phone out of the bucket? What were you planning, eh? Gonna fuckin' squeal on us again? Sell us out?'

Davie sobbed like a child, shaking his head. 'No, Mick, I swear —'

Another punch. Harder this time. Davie buckled, wheezing.

Mick wiped his knuckles on his jeans, then stuffed the rag back into Davie's mouth, shoving it deep enough to make the old man gag. 'Don't you fuckin' lie to me.'

Robbie watched, his stomach twisting. The dream had been terrifying, but this — this was worse. This was real. He wouldn't have minded if Mick was tied to the pallet — he deserved it — or Tappie or Finn — they were big enough to take this. But Davie? He was almost eighty. This could kill him. *Surely, Davie wasn't a rat?*

'Jesus, Mick, that's enough!' Robbie roared. 'He's an old man! Why the fuck would he rat us out?'

'Shut it, Bacon Boy.' Mick didn't even look up. 'Get his phone.' His voice was low, measured — dangerous. He turned back to Davie, eyes cold. 'I swear to God, if I find so much as a single number on that thing, you'll be wishing Alshahari had put a bullet in your skull.' He leaned in. 'I'll skin you alive — then I'll fucking cook you.'

With that, Mick upended a billy can of diesel over Davie's head — and lit a cigarette.

Auld Davie let out another gush, his crotch darkening with piss. The stench of fear, fuel, and urine thickened the air.

'Open that thing, ya old cunt.'

Davie's hands trembled so badly he couldn't press his finger to the sensor.

'If you don't get that open, I'll rip that finger clean out of its socket and do it myself.' Mick was fuming now, his patience gone. He jerked Davie's chin in the direction of Robbie. 'Stick his finger on that stupid fuckin' sensor yoke, Plod. Try to be useful for once.'

Robbie swallowed hard. He knew Mick was dangerous — violent, volatile — but was he really going to torch an old man?

Who knew?

'It'll be okay, Davie,' Robbie said, his voice soft, reassuring.

Gently, he took Davie's trembling finger and pressed it to the sensor.

God, he hoped it would be okay. *Please, God, let there be nothing on this phone.*

Davie was white as a sheet.

The phone jolted to life, its sudden buzz splitting the heavy silence like a blade.

No, Davie, no... not you too.

He said a silent prayer...
*Holy Mary, sweet Mother of Jesus,
keep Davie safe in this dark hour.
Please, God—
spare him.*

But there it was, plain for all to see. There would be no denying this. No way out.

Robbie's heart sank.

Davie's head dropped as if he'd been shot.

Alshahari. Valentina. Petra.

Mick spat in Auld Davie's face. 'I fuckin' knew it. Let's torch the old cunt.'

He gripped his cigarette between thumb and middle-finger, and was ready to flick it and watch the old traitor burn.

'Stop. Stop.' Robbie was pleading now, begging. 'Give him a chance to explain.'

He gently removed the rag from Davie's mouth.

The old man gasped for air, sobbing uncontrollably. His breathing was ragged and uneven. Terrified. Ashamed. Traumatised. Broken.

The others gathered round as he began to speak, hoping that he could somehow explain this away.

All but Mick.

Mick just stared, cigarette smouldering between his fingers, waiting.

There had to be an explanation. A mistake. A reason.

What could have made him betray his friends — his family — like this?

Auld Davie begged, and lied, then lied and begged some more. He was going round and round in circles, each lie building on the last, growing more unbelievable by the second. He'd needed money, sure. The boys understood that. But why hadn't he come to them? No, this was more than that. This was greed. The greedy old bastard thought he could have it all — have his cake, and eat it too.

The only thing left… what to do with him now? If Mick had his way? *Jesus*…

Dick was leaned against a crate, arms crossed, staring into the darkness. 'Can't believe it. First Eugene, now you Davie.'

Mick scoffed. 'Fuck them. Fuckin' rats.'

Silence settled between them. Yes, they were rats, but they were still their own. They all knew this was no longer a game, but watching Alshahari have Eugene executed — so casually — had taken it to a whole new level.

If Mick didn't set the old man on fire, Alshahari surely would. Either way, it didn't look good for Auld Davie.

They could set him free, let him run and take his chances, but Alshahari had eyes everywhere. How far would he get? Take him with them? Forgive his indiscretions? Mick wouldn't have that. Torch him?

Robbie had seen plenty of charred bodies in his time, and it wasn't a sight easily forgotten. He couldn't live with himself if he was party to creating that memory. Drown him? Talk about a rock and a hard place...

Top Shelf sat nearby, gnawing at his fingernails, his face drawn and haggard. Robbie wiped a hand down his face and shook his head, just as another rat darted past his feet.

Then, as if the Good Lord himself had heard Robbie's desperate pleas, footsteps echoed from the far end of the warehouse, and a figure emerged from the shadows — scruffy, a cigarette hanging from his lips. He stared at them, long and hard, before muttering in a foreign tongue, 'Let's go.'

Robbie stretched his stiff limbs and exhaled. *Phew. Had the old fool been saved by the bell?*

'So we're really doing this? Pakistan? Once we're on that boat, there's no turning back.'

'We don't have a choice,' Dick muttered. 'Har and Rej are there, and we need to get to them before anyone else does.'

Robbie exhaled and nodded. Time to move. Time to get the hell out of here and into a whole new nightmare.

As he untied Auld Davie from the pallet, the old man slumped to the floor, wailing... begging... pleading for mercy... one last chance... but his cries fell on deaf ears.

'Leave the auld cunt to rot,' were Mick's final words as he stomped out of the warehouse.

Robbie wasn't sure what toll the whole terrifying ordeal had taken. Auld Davie looked as if he'd aged a hundred years — like a corpse, if truth be told — but his eyes were that of a vulnerable child, sobbing, struggling to catch his breath.

He hugged the old man. He had no words, none that could offer him even the slightest solace.

He was absolutely stinking — piss, shite, blood, diesel, fear. It was heartbreaking. Robbie didn't care what he had done—no one deserved to end up like this. But if he got on that boat with Mick, he wouldn't survive the journey.

Oh, sweet Mother Mary...

Friday 20th June

Chapter 41

The voyage

The Al Saqr was a rusting cargo ship, the kind that should have been scrapped years ago but somehow managed to survive, passed from one desperate owner to the next. Its hull was pockmarked with corrosion, its deck cluttered with tangled ropes, dented barrels, and the broken remnants of old crates. The scent of oil, salt, and decay filled the air.

But it wasn't comfort they were after — it was distance. And the Al Saqr would get them to Pakistan, one way or another, or so their captain — Bilal — told them.

The crew of four were a rough lot, hardened by years of smuggling across the Gulf and the Arabian Sea. They spoke little English — barely spoke at all, in fact — but moved with the quiet efficiency of men who had ferried all kinds of cargo: smugglers, runaways, corpses — without asking questions. They didn't care if you lived or died.

Bilal, a wiry, sun-darkened man with yellowing teeth and a cigarette still dangling from his lips, ushered them aboard.

'Get on. Stay out of the way. No trouble.'

That was the deal.

The Al Saqr pulled away under the cover of darkness, its engines rumbling low and steady. The coastline, barely visible through the murky morning mist, shrank into a dark smudge before vanishing entirely. Soon, there was nothing but open sea, stretching in every direction like an endless void. The ship moved at a sluggish 8 knots — not built for speed, but steady enough to carry them forward.

Inside, the lower deck was filthy — a sweltering cave of rusted walls and leaking pipes. They were crammed into a corner near the engine room, where the air was thick with heat and the constant, bone-rattling hum of machinery.

'This is fucked up,' Robbie muttered.

'Aye, well, it's the only way,' Mick said, stretching out his legs with a groan. 'Unless you fancy swimming to Karachi.'

The reality of it settled over them like a weight. Four days. Four days of hunger eating at their guts, of sweat pooling in the small of their backs, of exhaustion sinking into their bones. Four days trapped in this coffin, rocking endlessly with the sea, their muscles slowly stiffening, their tempers fraying.

Tappie was already miserable, his arms crossed tight over his chest, his usual sharpness dulled by exhaustion. 'This is gonna be a cunt of a journey. Four days on this floating shitepile.'

By the second day, the boat lurched through heavy swells, the wind shrieking through the vessel, waves smashing against the hull with enough force to send them sprawling. The sky had darkened, thick with bruised clouds, the promise of a storm lurking just beyond the horizon. Rain lashed against the deck, soaking them to the skin, the wind ripping through their thin clothes.

They clung to anything they could — ropes, crates, each other. The sea was a living thing, a monstrous entity with a thousand hands, dragging, pulling, twisting. Sleep was nearly impossible. Between the stench of sweat, diesel, and the relentless rocking of the ship, no one could truly rest.

Hunger gnawed at them constantly, and stale flatbread, dry dates, and cups of lukewarm water did little to ease their suffering. Patience was wearing thin. Mick and Dick nearly came to blows over a cigarette, while Top Shelf glared at anything that moved. Robbie sat with his back to the wall, trying to shut out everything, thoughts, emotions — anything at all.

The physical withdrawal from alcohol was starting to kick in too. Forty-eight hours had passed since Robbie's last drink, and it was brutal. His body trembled with the desperate, endless craving for a drink to numb the pain. His skin was clammy, his head throbbing with a dull, pulsing pain that seemed to come from deep inside his skull. He grew more irritable with each passing moment. His energy drained. Even the simplest tasks felt monumental. Simply existing was hard.

He was dizzy and disoriented, his thoughts sluggish and tangled, like he couldn't remember how to string words together. His eyes burned from lack of sleep and food, and everything around him felt distant, muffled. Every moment dragged, but there was no escaping it. Withdrawal gripped him tight, relentless and unyielding.

By the time they reached the Pakistani coast of Balochistan, they were running low on fuel. The Al Saqr veered toward Gwadar, a smuggler's paradise — a dusty, lawless port where anything could be bought for the right price. Guns, drugs, fuel, people — everything moved through Gwadar.

They anchored just beyond the main port, where a small fuel barge chugged toward them, guided by men who looked like they'd slit a throat for a fiver. No questions were asked. Stacks of dirty banknotes changed hands, and within an hour, the barge had siphoned enough diesel into the Al Saqr's rusted belly to get them to Karachi.

The engines stuttered back to life again, and the Al Saqr churned back into the open sea, ready to complete the last brutal twenty-four hours to Karachi.

Hunger, exhaustion, the weight of what lay ahead — everything was closing in, and they had no idea what awaited them.

Then came the storm.

The Al Saqr bucked wildly, thrown about like a toy in the hands of the waves. Every groan of the hull sounded like a death rattle. Robbie clenched his jaw as the boat tilted, sending him skidding across the deck, his ribs slamming into a wooden crate. He heard someone shout — Mick, maybe, or Dick — before another wave crashed over them, drowning the words in a deafening roar.

They were going to die here. Out in the open water, nameless, forgotten. Another set of bodies swallowed by the sea.

Monday 23rd June

By the fourth day, the storm passed.

As night fell over a grey, heaving sea, the water churned but had calmed, no longer violent. The Al Saqr crept forward, battered but still afloat, hugging the coastline, careful to avoid prying eyes as they made their way toward Karachi.

They had survived the sea. Now, they had to survive what came next. The reality of what awaited them in Pakistan loomed heavier with each mile. There was no turning back now.

The aging cargo ship groaned as it limped into Karachi's chaotic port — a vast industrial monster of rusted cranes, battered cargo containers, and the thick scent of diesel and salt. Even at this late hour, the place buzzed with life — dockworkers shouting, trucks grinding along the battered roads, men in loose shalwar kameez haggling over goods.

Bilal said nothing as he nudged the vessel into a forgotten corner of the docks, where rusting trawlers sat half-submerged, waiting for time to finish them off. No formalities, no questions — just a place to crawl off and disappear.

They staggered onto solid ground, legs weak from days at sea, the heat of the Karachi evening pressing in. Mick wiped sweat from his brow. 'Fuckin' hell, never thought I'd be glad to set foot in this stinking country again.'

Fucked as he was, this was the first time since leaving Ireland that Robbie wasn't nursing a hangover. After four days without a drink, a strange clarity settled over him. The cravings had almost vanished, leaving behind an unfamiliar quiet in his mind. His body still ached, but the pain felt distant now, fading by the hour. For the first time in days, he could think clearly — like the world had snapped into focus.

But the others weren't there yet. Their voices were louder now, more insistent. Mick was already getting fidgety. Dick, too, was growing restless, biting his nails. Even Top Shelf, usually the most controlled, had that twitch in his hand, the one that betrayed the need for something to steady him.

'We need a drink,' Mick muttered, eyes flicking toward Robbie. 'No?'

Robbie didn't answer, his mind still clear, but the temptation nagged at him. He could feel the pull of it in his gut, just not as powerful as before.

'No,' Robbie finally said, his voice steady. 'We don't.'

'You mightn't,' Mick shot back, his tone growing more aggressive, 'but after four days on that stinking hell-hole, I've got a thirst that'll fucking destroy me if I don't drown it.'

Robbie didn't meet his eyes. The urge to reach for the bottle was there, lingering like a shadow, an unwanted friend. He didn't want go back to that place. Not again. But his thirst was growing stronger, and he knew his will was weak.

'No,' Robbie repeated, but the word lacked authority, and he could feel the others sensing it. His father's voice echoed in his mind again. He had been no use to him when he was around, yet in his absence, his words still found ways to hurt. *Go on, you pussy. Take a fucking drink. Call yourself a man? You fucking poof...*

As if Mick could hear those thoughts, he sneered. 'Go on. Have a fucking drink. Just one. For the thirst, like. We're gonna be waiting for some guy to take us to Peshawar anyway, and God knows when he'll turn up. You know what these fuckin' curry-munching, shoe-shiners are like.'

Robbie didn't.

He'd naively assumed that alcohol would be easy to find here. *Where did the fishermen drink? Where was the early house? Where was Podraic's?* God, he missed that smoky little shit-hole of a pub down at Galway Docks. Jammers at five-thirty a.m. with everyone — doctors, lawyers, dole-heads, fishermen, teachers — everyone. Smoking, drinking, fighting, shagging, playing pool… Then that fucking eejit went and forgot to renew the licence. Arsehole!

He had assumed wrongly. Not a bar in sight.

Mick pulled a roll of dirty notes from his pocket and motioned that he wanted a drink. Bilal's eyes lit up.

He led them to a crumbling shack, tucked away in a forgotten corner of the Karachi docks. The entrance was hidden by rusted shipping crates and the constant hum of the nearby port machinery provided the perfect cover for the place's secretive existence.

Inside, the air was thick with the pungent mix of stale alcohol, diesel fumes, and sweat. The dim, yellow light was barely enough to reveal the grimy bar counter, where cockroaches scurried about between chipped glasses and scratched bottles of cheap homebrew beer.

Big Finn had to crouch to avoid banging his head off the low, sagging ceiling, while a decrepit fan struggled to move the heavy, humid air. Old plastic tables were shoved together, covered in greasy stains and cigarette burns, each hosting a ragtag group of men who had seen the darker side of life. Paranoid eyes darted across the room, making no effort to disguise their interest in the strangers. Workers from the docks leaned over their drinks, their hands calloused, faces drawn, avoiding the light, yet eager for their next sip of forbidden liquor.

The bartender, a wiry man, scowled at them as he wiped down the counter with a filthy rag that hadn't been washed in years. His movements were slow, deliberate — he didn't need to hurry. Bottles of Pakistani "*beer*" were stacked behind him, alongside rum and whiskey smuggled in from who knew where. There was no menu, no orders — just the exchange of cash for drink, a silent understanding that this was a place of refuge for those who didn't care for the law, or for anything else.

In one corner, a hookah bubbled quietly. This was the sort of place that didn't need a name — just a whispered address passed between those who needed to know.

Chapter 42

The Shaheen Hotel

Mick peeled off a few grubby banknotes, and laid them on the bunker. Holding up nine fingers he motioned to the barman. No questions were asked.

He peeled off a few more and handed them to Bilal. 'English' was all he said.

Bilal took the money without hesitation, stuffing it into the pocket of his sweat-stained shalwar kameez. He gave a single nod before slipping out the door, disappearing into the thick, humid night.

Robbie sat with his back to the wall, arms folded, watching. He could still feel the old thirst stirring in his gut, and the beer was screaming at him. But after four days dry, his mind was sharper than it had been in a long time. He knew he couldn't have the *one*. It didn't work like that. It was all or nothing with him. Sink or swim. Feast or famine. And Mick wasn't helping one bit.

'Just take one,' Mick muttered, pushing a lifeless pint in front of him. 'Just to take the fuckin' edge off.'

Robbie ignored him.

The others lunged for their glasses, like men who hadn't seen a drop in years. Three glasses sat on the bunker... and it hit them. They were no longer nine. Seven. Eugene shot in cold blood. Auld Davie, abandoned in a stinking warehouse. Was he still alive? Would they ever see him again?

The camaraderie was gone. The laughter, the fun, the games — over. What had started with rambunctious revelry had left them angry, bitter, suspicious. Robbie wanted to rip Mick's eyes out, and if he got a chance, he just might.

Bilal returned five minutes later, leading a short, thickset man with a pockmarked face and tired eyes. He wore a dusty brown suit that had seen better days and carried himself like a worn-out car salesman who still knew how to close a deal.

'He Rafiq,' Bilal said, nodding toward the man. 'He know England. He know road Peshawar.'

Rafiq stared at them for a moment before sitting down, hands folded on the table. 'You wan go Peshawar,' he said in slow, deliberate English. His accent was thick but understandable. 'No easy. No for men like you.'

Mick exhaled through his nose. 'Can we not just get a fuckin' bus?'

Rafiq smiled, a sly, cold grin. 'Bus go take you, but road long, and too much eye, too much question. You no look like local. Somebody go see, somebody go talk.'

Mick scoffed, leaning back in his chair. 'So what? Who's looking for us here? It's just a fuckin' bus ride.'

Rafiq held his gaze. 'Maybe yes, e-e-be no. Karachi have many eye.'

Silence settled over the table.

'What are you saying?' Robbie asked finally.

Rafiq drummed his fingers against the table. 'You want safe, you pay more.'

Mick sat forward, muttering a curse as he rested his elbows on the table. 'We've got money. But can we trust that sneaky wee, rupee-counting, curry-sniffing cunt?'

Rafiq sat there, that glaikit look on his face, and nodded. 'I know, man. He have bus. Not new. Not fast. But take you.'

Mick exhaled sharply. 'How much?'

'More you like pay. Less you life cost.'

Robbie exchanged a look with Mick. They both knew they didn't have a choice.

'Okay,' Robbie said. 'Do it.'

Rafiq nodded once. 'You ready. We go before sun come up.'

With that, he stood, smoothed down his crumpled suit, and shuffled off into the murky depths of wherever he came from.

Mick snorted. 'Great. Another fuckin' magic carpet ride. I hope Ali fuckin' Baba knows what he's at.'

Robbie leaned back, letting the distant hum of the docks settle around him. His eyes, though, kept drifting back to the beer that sat in front of him, taunting him with its cold promise. The road to Peshawar was going to be a bastard.

They had nowhere to go. Stay in this shithole all night or find some grimy little motel — those were the options. Mick peeled off a few more notes and signaled to Bilal that they needed a place to sleep. Bilal nearly took his hand off before scurrying back into the sticky night.

This time, he returned with a scrawny little man whose slicked-back hair was greasy enough to fry an egg. His filthy shirt was stained with god knows what.

He looked up at them slowly, eyes vacant. When he spoke, his thin lips barely parted, revealing too many yellowed teeth. 'You want room?' His breath reeked of stale curry, and his accent was so thick the words were barely decipherable — the way only a man who spoke little English could manage. 'Good room, cheap room. You pay, I give key.'

The place was tucked in a back alley, tucked away like it was trying to hide its shame. The flickering neon sign read *Shaheen Hotel* — it might as well have read *Shite Hole*.

The lobby — if you could call it that — smelled like damp, old towels and something faintly rancid, like rot. The floor tiles were cracked. Mick shoved a few notes into Ahmed's grubby little hand, before they were led down a narrow hallway that reeked of mould and stale cigarette smoke.

As they reached the door, he fumbled with a key, jiggling it in the rusted lock. 'Ah, yes, yes... You very lucky. No one take room this time, no more customers tonight, yes-yes.' He leaned into Mick, speaking in a hushed voice as if sharing a secret, 'You want more? Good time? I know man. You give me good tip, I tell you who. You know?' He winked.

'On that?' Mick looked absolutely disgusted.

The room was stinking — *that* kind of smell, the one that made you want to gag. A thin mattress sagged in the middle of the bed, stained with what could only be described as a "history" of human neglect. The air was thick and humid, the windows sealed shut with grime that hadn't seen a rag in years. The walls were so thin they could hear the muffled sounds of shouting, crying, and something —someone — hitting the floor next door.

'Yes-yes. Room clean. Yes-yes. You no sleep long time, maybe wake in morning.'

'Aye, and maybe no wake at all, you grubby little goat-herding fuck.' Mick was in fully racist mode now, and Ahmed seemed totally oblivious to the venom in his words.

A single, flickering bulb in the corner cast long shadows, making everything look even worse. The bathroom had no door, just a tattered curtain that did little to block the sight of the cracked, filthy sink. The toilet didn't flush, and the showerhead had a steady drip of brown, stinking water.

Mick grunted. 'Jesus, what a fuckin' dump. There's no way I'm sleeping on that disease-ridden flea pit. You wouldn't know what the fuck you'd catch.'

Robbie just stood there, eyeing the bed, the walls, the floor. 'What choice have we got?' he muttered, voice flat, defeated.

'Plenty fuckin' choice. I'd rather sleep in the bar, or not at all, than sleep on that.'

Robbie tenderly perched himself on the edge of the bed, then shot back up like he'd been burned.

'Fuckin' hell. Something moved.'

'Right. Fuck this. I'm going back to the pub. You coming?'

Jesus. It was the last place Robbie wanted to go, but he couldn't stay here. It was like something out of a horror movie.

'Bus leaves in a few hours, so you'll get fuck all sleep anyway.'

No one had much to say after that. They traipsed back to the makeshift bar, dejected. Somewhere, a cat screeched, followed by the sharp bang of something being thrown. H*oly fuck, they might be lucky to see sunrise*... and there was only one way to settle the nerves.

Mick ordered seven beers and seven shots of local moonshine. The fire burned in Robbie's belly, the first shot transporting him straight back to that old familiar place — relief, guilt, failure.

He took another shot... and then another...

Top Shelf let out a long sigh. 'You think Alshahari's got eyes over here?'

'If he does, we're fucked,' Mick snorted.

Top Shelf inhaled. 'Very comforting, Michael.' He wiped sweat from his forehead. 'Right. So, if we make it up there, what then?'

'Find Har and Rej.' Robbie said simply.

'Aye, cheers for that, Sherlock. I mean, how? We've got fuck all to go on.' Angry Mick was back.

Robbie exhaled, rubbing his temples. 'It was your fuckin' idea.'

Composing himself, he took a breath. 'They flew to Peshawar regularly. That means someone knows them up there. Someone's seen them. Then they had to arrange transport from there to here, and from here to the Al Hamra. Someone loaded their shipments. They must've drank here, so someone's seen them here too.'

Mick cracked his knuckles, before adding, helpfully, 'That stinking, curry-munching fuck better not be selling us out.'

They sat in silence for a while. The noises of the docks outside, never-ending. Trucks, ships, horns, screams… The night passed slowly by. No one slept.

Tuesday 24th June

Chapter 43

Stinky-pants

When the first hint of dawn touched the sky, through the solitary, filthy window, they could see Rafiq waiting by a battered minibus, talking to someone. Mick drew the short straw and was sent out to greet him. He turned, like an old Indian tracker, when he heard him coming. His pockmarked face split into a grin — the last thing Mick wanted, or needed, to see.

'You late,' he said, before waving his hand. 'No worry. We go now.'

Mick gave him that look — *the shut the fuck up or I'll batter you* look. 'How long?'

The driver, an undernourished man with deep-set eyes, stared at him. 'Road to Peshawar long,' he said as they clambered in. 'Maybe one day, maybe two. Maybe yes. Maybe no. But we reach. Inshallah.'

Mick motioned for the boys to come out, then climbed in and slumped into the seat furthest from the driver. 'Brilliant. Smelly bastard.'

One by one, they clambered aboard the bone-shaker, the heat inside even worse than outside. The seats were torn, springs jutting through the stuffing. The air was thick with the scent of unwashed bodies and stale cigarettes. It'd be a miracle if this thing got them there, but there was no way back now.

Rafiq had told them to sit near the back, away from prying eyes, and keep their heads down — though surely no one could see them through the grime-stained windows, Robbie thought.

The engine coughed to life, and the bus jerked forward, rattling onto the road.

They were on their way. The road to Peshawar had begun.

Mick squirmed uncomfortably in his seat, scanning the faces of every stranger they passed on the road with suspicion. He only said what everyone was thinking. 'We're sitting ducks here — and if Alshahari doesn't get us, we'll either be baked alive, or get a rusty spring up our holes, in this fuckin' thing. I hope you've had your tetanus, Plod.'

Robbie shrugged. He didn't have the mental strength the rise to Mick's taunts. They had no choice.

Top Shelf wiped his forehead with the filthy sleeve of his shirt — the same one he'd been wearing for days. He grimaced. 'I'm fuckin' parched… and stinkin.' You think Alshahari's watching us now?'

Rafiq's warning rang in Robbie's ears. *Too many eyes, too many questions.*

'Where can he get us?' asked a miffed Finn. 'We're in Pakistan already. There'll be no border checks. Nobody looking for passports, surely?'

'Exactly,' Robbie sighed. 'We keep our heads down, act normal.'

Mick snorted. 'How the fuck did you ever make detective? You're about as much use a cock-flavoured lollipop. There'll be checkpoints everywhere. This is fuckin' Paki-land. They're a bunch of smelly tinkers. There's no way we're getting through the Khyber Pass without running into some roadblock. That's if the Cream-crackers don't cut our throats before we get there.'

And this was coming from a guy from Moyross, Robbie was thinking, one of the biggest Tinker communities in Limerick, if not all of Ireland. He had a lot of nerve... so he did.

The bus rattled over potholes — worse than anything Connemara had to offer — as it crawled north from Karachi, bound for Peshawar. Sweat streamed from every pore in Robbie's body, and it wasn't just from the unrelenting heat blasting through the windows. His stomach twisted, a seething, molten mess of regret. That curry — *why the fuck had he eaten in that stinking watering hole?* Tasty though it was, it had turned against him, waging a merciless war deep in his gut.

He swallowed hard, clenching his ring as another violent cramp rolled through him. Not here. Not on this sweltering bus with nowhere to run. He took a slow, steady breath and tried to compose himself — tried to think of anything other than the impending catastrophe brewing in his bowels.

The boys were scattered around him. Mick had his hat pulled low, feigning sleep. Finn flicked through something that looked suspiciously like a Pakistani porn mag. Top Shelf sat with his arms crossed, staring out the window. The others were lost in their own thoughts, their own anxieties. None of them knew the battle Robbie was fighting.

The bus jolted, slamming over another pothole, and Robbie gripped the seat in front of him. A fresh wave of agony ripped through his stomach. *Jesus Christ.* His insides were a cement mixer of molten regret, the curry making its final, merciless descent. He clenched every muscle he could still control. Another pothole. Another lurch. Another brutal warning shot. If they didn't stop soon, something biblical was going to happen. The second coming... *Focus Robbie, focus...*

'Driver, stop,' he screamed.

'No stop, sir. Danger. Too much.'

'Fucking stop.'

He was about to erupt. This journey was hellish enough without the stench of green bile seeping through the rips and into what little cushioning of the seats remained, swirling around the feet of these men — men who had seen it all, but would remember him for this. Maybe only this. Marked for life. The man who shat himself on the road to Peshawar.

He lunged for the door, nearly sending the bus onto two wheels as the driver slammed the brakes, tyres screeching on the makeshift road. His trousers were already down to his knees as he leapt, mid-motion, from the steps. The first wave hit before he even reached the ground — a molten, unstoppable burst of fierce cannon-fodder, splattering the steps behind him.

He could hear them.

'Ya smelly cunt.'

'Uugh.'

'For fuck's sake, O'Malley.'

But he didn't care. He staggered forward, gasping for air, hands on his knees, trying to regain control of himself, of his own treacherous body.

Then came the second wave.

Just as violent. Just as vile. His stomach twisted, muscles spasming as the cursed remnants of last night's curry claimed their final revenge. He was at the roadside now, knees shaking, as cars and buses whizzed past, drivers craning their necks to see the foreigner losing his battle with dignity.

Jesus. He could only pray Alshahari wasn't nearby to witness this.

He looked around in vain. No hope of a docken leaf out here. Just dust and rocks out here in this unbroken stretch of barren waste. An old, disease-ridden plastic bag tumbled by in the wind, but that would only smear the disaster further.

No, it was either the sock or the jocks. And he needed the jocks — his last line of defence in case a third wave struck.

With a deep, shuddering breath, he yanked off his stinking, sweat-soaked sock, the fabric both damp, and stiff, from days of wear. *Christ.* The humiliation was almost worse than the affliction itself. He crouched, bracing against the heat, and dabbed at the ungodly mess between his legs, wincing with every wipe. Hard to tell if he'd properly cleaned up — his sock was already black with filth long before today.

Gingerly, he pulled his trousers back up, every movement a fresh nightmare. And then, with the weight of disgrace clinging to him like the stink of that curry, he made the long, agonising walk of shame back to the bus.

'Oooh… here he comes. Old Stinky Pants O'Malley. Are you okay, Robert?' Mick was grinning ear to ear, milking every ounce of Robbie's suffering.

'Jesus, shut it,' Robbie muttered, climbing the steps, still half-traumatised, half-clenching.

'He reeks,' Finn gagged, pulling his shirt over his nose. 'You wipe with your bare hand, did ya dirty bastard?'

'No, no, no,' Mick shook his head, waving a finger. 'That, lads, is the smell of a man who has just shat out his soul.'

'For fuck's sake, O'Malley,' Rudolph groaned. 'Could you not have at least gone downwind?'

Top Shelf just leaned against the window, arms crossed, smirking. 'You burned the socks, right? Please tell me you burned the socks.'

'Used his jocks, I'd say,' Dick added. 'Or the sleeves of his shirt — go on, lift your arms, show us the damage.'

'Fuck off, the lot of ye,' Robbie growled, sinking into his seat.

The bus jolted forward, the air thick with heat, dust, and now, the undeniable stench of shite... and regret.

Robbie buried his face in his hands. This was never going to be forgotten.

Chapter 44

The Khyber Pass

The laughter had died down long before they reached the Khyber Pass.

The landscape grew harsher, more treacherous, the road winding through sheer rock faces and jagged cliffs. The bus crawled uphill, engine groaning, the driver tense behind the wheel. Everyone felt it now — the shift in the air, the sense that they were heading into something dangerous.

Robbie shifted uncomfortably, but it wasn't his stomach this time. He glanced at Mick, who was watching the road ahead, jaw set. Finn had put his magazine away. Tappie, who usually had something smart to say, was silent, fingers tapping restlessly against his knee.

Up ahead, a checkpoint came into view.

Makeshift barricades of sandbags and rusted barrels. A handful of men standing in the road, AKs slung over their shoulders, dressed in a mix of military surplus and local garb. They weren't Pakistani soldiers. This was Alshahari's crew.

'Fuck,' Mick muttered under his breath.

The driver tensed. He didn't stop immediately, rolling forward slower and slower until one of the gunmen banged a fist on the bonnet, demanding a halt. The driver threw a quick glance at Robbie and the boys, then killed the engine.

A man stepped forward from the group, tall, gaunt, sharp-eyed. He wasn't carrying a rifle, but he didn't need one. The others watched him, waiting for his cue.

'Papers,' he demanded in Pashto, voice flat.

The bus fell dead silent.

This was it. If Alshahari had their names, their faces, or even a whisper of suspicion about who they were — this would be the end of the road.

The air in the bus thickened, a slow, suffocating dread settling over them. Outside, the guards watched, expressionless, unreadable, the kind of men who had seen blood spilled before breakfast and would spill more before lunch.

The gaunt man held out a hand. 'Papers.'

Robbie forced himself to move, reaching into his bag. For a moment he considered running, but to where? Fighting? Fists against firearms? No. There was no winning a firefight here. No escape. Just a choice — to bluff or to die.

One by one, they passed their passports forward. The gaunt man flipped through them, barely looking — until he reached Mick's. He frowned, turning it over in his hands.

'You are… Michael Quinn?'

Mick nodded, slow, cautious.

'Irish.'

Another nod.

The man glanced at Dick's passport. 'Richard Butler?' He looked up, something unreadable flickering in his face.

Then, instead of pressing further, he kept flipping. Checking each one, searching.

That's when Robbie saw it — the tension in the other men. They weren't just checking random travellers. They were looking for someone.

The gaunt man's fingers twitched slightly, impatient. 'Where are the others?' he asked the driver.

The driver hesitated. 'Sir?'

'Har de Luc. Rej Khan. Valentina Orlova. Petra Ivanova.' His voice was sharper now. Demanding. 'The Red Widow. The Viper. Where are they?'

The guards shifted. One of them adjusted the rifle on his shoulder. Another glanced up at the bus, scanning the faces again, as if piecing something together.

Robbie cleared his throat, forcing his voice steady.

'Who?'

The gaunt man's eyes snapped to him, sharp as a knife.

Robbie shrugged, shifting in his seat. 'Never heard of them.'

A long, horrible pause.

Then the man exhaled sharply, flicking his wrist.

'Go.'

The driver didn't wait. The engine groaned to life, gears grinding, the bus lurching forward. Slowly at first, then faster. Past the barricade, past the rifles, past the men who had been a second away from deciding they were all dead men.

Robbie didn't unclench until the checkpoint disappeared behind them, swallowed by dust.

Finn let out a low breath. 'Well. That was fucking close.'

Mick shot Robbie a look. 'Who?' he mimicked, shaking his head. 'I'll give you that one, lad.'

Robbie wiped the sweat from his forehead.

Too fucking close.

It was one of the few occasions that Mick had acknowledged anything positive in Robbie, and the fleeting moment felt oddly satisfying. Robbie had recently decided that Mick was one of the worst humans he had ever met. Possibly the worst.

There was something about Mick's brand of cruelty — it wasn't loud or over-the-top, just a quiet, insidious malice that seeped into every conversation, every gesture. But here, in the middle of the road to Peshawar, Mick had given him a rare nod of respect.

It wasn't much, but it was something.

The tension still hung in the air, thick and unnerving. They'd barely escaped. The Khyber Pass behind them now felt like a near-death experience, something they'd survived by the thinnest of margins.

And yet, it didn't feel like survival.

The gaunt man's words echoed in Robbie's head: *Har de Luc. Rej. The Viper. The Red Widow.*

These names weren't just whispers of trouble; they were a lit fuse. They were trouble, trouble they'd need to outrun — yet here they were, heading straight towards it.

Peshawar loomed ahead, thirty miles or so. Would they find answers there? Were Har and Rej there? Were they waiting for them, or had they already vanished? Had they even left the UAE?

If they were there, and if The Viper and The Red Widow knew, then Alshahari knew. And given what they had witnessed at the impound yard, that was a lethal concoction — one that wouldn't end well — for anyone.

But for now, all Robbie could do was stare ahead, his heart still pounding in his chest as the bus trundled forward. It might have been only thirty miles, but it was thirty miles of winding mountain roads and, given that Alshahari's men had been at the last checkpoint, there was a chance they had lookouts further along the road.

Still, after nearly two days on this boneshaker, his soiled briefs stuck to his arse and his whole-body stinking, the thought of a shower, and a cold beer was very welcoming. *Fuck sobriety*. Depending on road conditions and stops, it would take two more hours to reach their destination.

Thursday 26th June

Chapter 45

Peshawar

As the bus rolled into Peshawar, it felt like a place full of shadows, like it knew more than it was letting on. Har and Rej — two names that seemed to grow more elusive by the minute. If they were here, they could be hiding in plain sight, working with Alshahari or against him, or maybe both.

Har had contacted Robbie at the start of the whole mess. Why? The only thing that made any sense was that he needed Robbie's help. Whether that was part of some twisted scheme to use him, or about getting this crew — his friends — back together, he still didn't know. But whatever Robbie had told him that night, Har had obviously seen something in him. Was that a compliment or an insult? Was Robbie just a sacrificial pawn, taking the heat off while Har swanned off with the spoils? That remained to be seen.

And as for Rej, what the fuck was his deal? His story had more holes in it than a piece of Swiss cheese. He was a fuckin' local, he knew this country, and maybe had the contacts to source things. It made sense for him to be pulling the strings out here. But

Har? An ageing fifty-year-old with a bad back and dodgy knees — he wasn't muscle, so what was his role?

Then there was the rivalry. These two were supposed to hate each other, yet they'd worked together for years. What was that all about? Har had smashed Rej's head off the ground in the Thirsty Horse. That seemed a bit much if the hatred was just a front. And then there was the stolen mince pie incident — if they didn't hate each other, they sure as hell wanted people to think they did. Maybe they were after the same thing: power, money, and a way out. Har was skint. Rej made shite money. No one could blame them for wanting to ditch the sandpit.

Had they fooled everyone? Even Alshahari? Had they double-crossed the double-crosser? They had someone's money — maybe even the shipment's contents — and, not content with screwing over The Widow and The Viper, had they gone for the hat-trick and stabbed Alshahari in the back too?

'Let's find a fuckin' watering hole. Ask Sinbad, or Ali, or whatever the fuck he's called,' Mick said, jerking a thumb at the driver. 'Maybe even get old Stinky there a shower,' he added, laughing at Robbie.

Mohammed — the driver — knew just the place and led them to a dimly lit hovel in the arsehole of nowhere, beside an abandoned train station.

The bar stank of stale beer and sweat. The air was thick with smoke, making it impossible to see much, but the roaring voices, the clinking glasses, and the occasional burst of laughter told Robbie this was a busy spot — the kind of place where anything goes, and no one asks too many questions.

Robbie, Mick, Finn, and the rest of the boys settled into a dark corner, leaving Mohammed to sort the drinks. They didn't belong here. Everyone knew it. But they'd learned to live with that over the years.

Auld Davie's words came back to Robbie — *say nothing to no one, and keep saying it*. He nearly shed a tear for the poor auld creature.

Robbie leaned in, eyes darting like a paranoid fuckwit. 'We need to find out where Rej and Har are. Someone here's got to know something.'

Finn looked like he could drop dead of a stroke at any moment. Mick was eyeballing a pair of stinking locals sitting at the bar.

'Those cunts'll know. They're no better than the smelly Indians under the trees. For the price of a couple of beers, they'll talk. They always do. These fuckers must know that eejit, Rej, if he's been fannying around here for years. He's not the sharpest tool in the box.'

Robbie ran through the possibilities, each one worse than the last. Rej and Har, in bed with Alshahari? The whole thing was tangled, fucked up.

He nudged Mick. 'Who? Those old fucks? They don't look like they'd know their own name, never mind Rej Khan. Probably love that Imran Khan though. Don't they all? The corrupt fuck.'

Mick raised an eyebrow but didn't bother answering. Plod was getting on his tits. 'You got a better idea, ya fuckin' clown?'

They stood to approach the men.

The bar stopped.

It was fine for strangers to sit quietly, drinking, but it was a mistake to think they were entitled to anything more than that. This wasn't their bar, and the locals were making that crystal fucking clear.

The old man looked up slowly, his tiny eyes — like piss holes in the snow — sharp despite the years etched into his face. 'Wha u wan?'

Robbie produced one of Har's fake passports, and slapped it down on the bunker, jabbing a finger at the photo. 'You see him?'

The old man's eyes flickered for just a moment, but he said nothing, taking another sip of his hooch.

Mick pulled a wad of filthy notes from his pocket and slipped them into the old man's grubby little paw.

Robbie leaned in, his eyes narrowing just enough for the old man to notice. 'You see or no see?'

The old man shifted in his seat, clearly uncomfortable. He lowered his voice, as if speaking of something forbidden, and whispered in Robbie's ear. 'They here. He and more man. Local man. Many people look these men. Bad people. Police. Snake lady. Death lady. Too much people.'

Robbie's pulse quickened. *Fuck*. It had to be Alshahari, The Widow and The Viper. 'Where?'

The old man looked over his shoulder, making sure no one was listening. 'Market. Karkhano.'

Robbie nodded, trying to keep his expression neutral, but inside his mind was racing. Could this whole nightmare be coming to an end?

As he turned to leave, the old man grabbed him by the arm and muttered, 'Bad market. Danger.'

Mick motioned to the barman to line up another seven beers, and they retreated to their table. 'What do you know about this market, Top Shelf?' Robbie asked.

'Which one? The Storytellers'?'

'No, Karko… or something.'

Top Shelf let out a gasp. 'Karkhano? Please don't tell me it's fuckin' Karkhano Market?'

Top Shelf explained that Karkhano was an infamous black market, near the Khyber Pass. Guns, electronics, drugs… all kinds of counterfeit goods. He really had no desire to go anywhere near the place.

Chapter 46

Karkhano Market

Karkhano Market wasn't the kind of place you found on tourist maps. It sprawled along the western edge of Peshawar like a scar — disorderly, chaotic, and reeking of simmering violence. The market was a maze of makeshift shops, hawkers yelling over one another, and alleyways so narrow they felt like traps.

Smuggled electronics, bootleg DVDs, knock-off trainers, Kalashnikovs — you could buy anything here, if you knew who to ask and weren't afraid of the answer. Armed men loitered on street corners — some in uniform, some not — and it was impossible to tell which were worse. Young boys with missing teeth peddled single cigarettes.

Power lines sagged like dead snakes overhead. The air was thick with the choking stench of burnt plastic, open sewage, and roasted meat hung out for days in the stinking heat. Stray dogs slinked around piles of rubbish.

If the two boys were hiding here, they were either very brave or very desperate.

And then they spotted them — Har de Luc and

Rej Khan, seated at a plastic table outside a dusty electronics shop, sipping chai like locals, looking like they hadn't a care in the world.

Robbie signalled to Mick and Dick to flank left, while he and Big Finn approached from the front. Har saw them coming. He didn't flinch. He even smiled.

'For fuck's sake. What took you so long?' Har said casually.

Robbie ignored the little quip and slapped one of Har's fake passports onto the table. 'Have you got any fuckin' idea the shite we've crawled through to get here.'

'Simmer the fuck down, Plod.'

'How the fuck did you know I was police?'

'It's written all over your red face — stress, isolation, blatant disregard for personal appearance, unshaven, beer-belly... do you want me to go on?'

'For fuck's sake,' muttered a visibly insulted Robbie.

Rej stood, tense. 'We can explain.'

'Start talking ya slimy Paki fuck,' Mick said. 'Fast.'

Har let out a little smirk and leaned back. 'You remember those six calls, Robbie? I couldn't risk calling any of these guys. If someone had checked their call logs, they might've been dragged into this. And as much as I love them, you've seen what these clowns are capable of — fuck all. I knew you wouldn't answer an unknown number — who does these days? — but I also knew you wouldn't stop until you found out who they were from. So I thought you were probably the only one who might be able to piece it all together.'

This time, Mick was the offended party, and he lunged violently at Har — only for Big Finn's quick reflexes to stop his fist landing square in Har's face. 'Fuck you, you cunt.'

'Piece what together? The fight? The empty container? The dead body? Jesus, man, start fuckin' explaining, would you?' Robbie barked.

'Oh, the fight was real alright,' Har said, casting a dirty look at Rej. 'He's a fuckin' arsehole. Who grasses you up over a fuckin' mince pie? We'd agreed to take the cash, but the lily-livered chicken-shit shat himself at the last minute and wanted to stick to Alshahari's plan. Then he tried to grab the cash. I wasn't about to let either of those things happen. I've been planning this too long.'

Rej muttered something incomprehensible, yet somehow Har understood.

'Says the cunt who's been trying to fuck me over for years,' Har shot back.

'What was supposed to be in that container?' Mick asked.

'Drugs,' Har replied. 'High-purity. Enough to start a war.'

Dick whistled. 'So why was it empty when Alshahari opened it?'

'It was never loaded,' Har said. 'Alshahari thought he was playing The Widow and The Viper by sending an empty container. He knew they couldn't blame Rej — because Rej was dead. The eejit was supposed to fake my death too, but he couldn't even get that right.'

'And the money?' Robbie asked.

'Long gone,' Har said, spitting a disgusting blob of green phlegm on the ground in disgust. 'We bought the consignment — just never loaded it. Do you know how much of a cut that weaselly little sand-crawler gives us? Fuck all! We're out here getting shot at, living in squaller, while he's wandering around with that stupid fuckin' beret on, eating dates and biryani. Well, no more. Fuck that for a game of soldiers.'

'So what now?' Dick asked.

Har looked around the market. 'Now we sell the drugs and disappear.'

'So why the fuck drag us all into your shite?' Mick roared. 'Eugene's fuckin' dead, Auld Davie's tied up in a warehouse covered in piss and petrol. We've spent four days in a floating coffin, Plod shat himself on a bus fit for pigs. Start talking, de Luc, or I'll rip your fuckin' tongue clean out of your head and eat the thing myself.'

'You should be thanking me, you Paddy cunt. You always wanted out, didn't you? Well, this is it. Final payout. After this, we all disappear. No more jobs. No more Al Hamra. No more fucking Arabs. Just sun, sea, golf, beer… and cheese. Fuckin' Stilton. Mmm.'

'And before you think I've gone all Mother Teresa on you, do you really think I'm gonna hang out with that eejit'— he jabbed a finger at Rej — 'in my retirement? After we cut and sell all this gear, there'll more than enough cash for all of us to vanish. That's why I wanted you here. I can't go back, and I doubt you lot can either. We're not out of the woods yet though. It's only a matter of time before Alshahari and those two bitches catch up with us.'

'They're already here, you daft twat,' Finn cut in.

Finn had barely closed his mouth when the first shot rang out.

A crack. Then screaming.

Then chaos.

Robbie dropped like a sack of meat — hit in the thigh, howling. Dick spun round, too slow — his shoulder exploded in a red mist.

'DOWN!' Tappie shouted, dragging Mick behind a rusted container.

The Widow's Meatheads charged through the market, firing like lunatics — no plan, just noise and death. One had an AK. Another, a sawn-off. Locals scurried like rats deserting a sinking ship.

From the other direction came a pack of *Lashkars* — thick-necked men with broken noses and prison muscles, scars curling from shirt collars, knuckles like bricks. They swarmed in behind Alshahari, who strolled like he owned the place — sunglasses still on, a revolver in hand, that faint, smug smile playing on his lips.

Rej — producing a pistol from God-knows-where — returned fire, wild and panicked — two shots cracked off, one hitting metal, the other possibly finding flesh. Then he screamed.

'FUCK!' he went down hard, clutching his gut. Blood pooled thick and fast.

Har — having often boasted of his splendid marksmanship — calmly produced a Glock 17, raised it like he'd been doing it all his life, and fired three rounds. One of The Widow's thugs dropped, head split open like a melon. Har didn't flinch.

'Get Rej,' he barked at Finn. 'Drag him!'

Finn grabbed Rej under the arms, and heaved.

Rej was moaning — still breathing — but choking, blood bubbling from his mouth. His eyes were wide with something like fear… or maybe regret.

Har fired again — two shots this time — before he turned and bolted, weaving through the chaos. 'Move! Move now!' he shouted.

Mick helped Robbie limp behind a shuttered stall, blood soaking through his shorts. 'It's gone clean through,' Mick said, grimacing. 'You're lucky today, Plod.'

'Doesn't feel very fuckin' lucky,' Robbie groaned, clenching his teeth against the pain.

Gunfire still cracked from both ends of the market. Shouts in Urdu and Pashto. A woman screamed. Somewhere, a generator caught fire and belched thick black smoke into the air.

'We're fucked,' Dick barked, crouching behind a rusted tuk-tuk. Wincing as he tried to tie an oily rag around his bloody shoulder, he bleated, 'We need to get out of here, or we're all fucked.'

Har reappeared, dragging a young local boy by the scruff of his neck. 'This wee cunt knows a back route. Old smugglers' alley. C'mon!'

The boy—glaikit, barefoot, barely out of puberty — nodded rapidly and beckoned with a skinny arm.

A life lived in fear had made these wee bastards tough, and he didn't give two fucks who was doing the shooting.

He darted — like a rat up a drainpipe — through a curtain behind a carpet shop, and the others followed, half-carrying Robbie and Rej.

They plunged into darkness: a cramped corridor of crumbling brick, cockroaches as big as your thumb, and piss-soaked concrete. The air was thick, the floor slick. Fat and unhealthy as they were, the motley crew ran for their petty little lives.

Behind them, the gunfire dimmed — then roared again, closer.

'They're following,' Dick panted. 'They're fucking following.'

Rej was fading fast. His breath came in wet, shallow rattles, and his grip on Finn's shirt weakened with each step. 'He's not gonna make it,' Finn warned.

'Fuck him,' Har snapped. 'We don't need him.'

'Fuck's sake,' muttered Mick. 'We can't just fuckin' leave him?'

'Why the fuck not?' Har shot back.

'Firstly, because those cunts will execute him — but more importantly, they'll torture him first, until he gives up everything he knows. Those wee Pakis aren't built for pain. He'll sing like a canary. And what's that going to do for your plan? We need him with us, or you need to put a bullet in his skull right now.'

If Mick had thought there was anything rhetorical about his statement, he couldn't have been more wrong.

Har stopped abruptly and turned to the men, his face serious yet at ease with his own mind. He walked over to Rej, whispered something in his ear, pulled his hand softly over the poor lad's face, and drew his eyes shut.

*"Into your hands, O Lord, I commend this soul.
The Lord giveth, and the Lord taketh away.
May God have mercy on your soul."*

Chapter 47

I hope they like barbeque

The boys burst into a dead-end alley, hemmed in by razor wire and cinderblocks.

'You've got to be fuckin' shitting me,' Mick spat.

The boy's skinny arm jabbed upward — there, a ladder... or rather, scraps of rotten wood, barely held together by ancient, rusty nails, clawing their way up to a low rooftop.

'Go!' Har ordered. 'Up, all of you.'

Dick went first, clawing at the rungs with his one good arm. Tappie followed, pushing him up by his arse.

'You better not drop one, ya smelly bastard.'

Robbie went next, propelled forward and upwards by Big Finn. Mick and Top Shelf followed, then Har. The boy vanished into thin air.

As they looked around at one another, trying to take in what had just happened, Top Shelf suddenly clocked it.

'Where the hell is Rudolph?'

One by one, they edged to the lip of the rooftop — peered over. There he was, flailing like a broken spider, utterly incapable of getting his spindly legs over the rungs.

'Oh sweet Jesus. Look at the fucking idiot,' Tappie roared. 'He's a fuckin' liability, always has been. Finn, go down and drag the cunt up.'

Big Finn groaned but didn't argue. He lumbered back down the ladder, threw the red-faced eejit over his shoulder like a sack of spuds, and hauled him back up to safety.

From the rooftop, the market burned. Smoke black as soot rose into the bone-white sky. Sirens in the distance — wailing, closing.

They huddled together, lungs raw, bodies scraped and shaking. Bloodied and bruised. Every last one of them looked to Har de Luc.

They'd seen Eugene crucified at the hands of Alshahari. Auld Davie left twitching in a pool of his own piss. But there'd been reasons for those actions — twisted, dubious, paper-thin ones—but reasons all the same.

But Rej?

Yes, he'd grassed Har up over a mince pie. Yes, he'd threatened to call the police over the "bad" word.

All pretty petty stuff. Childish shite. And Har had dropped him without blinking. Cold and clean.

It didn't sit easy. Not even with 'Mild' Mick — himself responsible for wanting to set the eighty-year-old Davie on fire.

Mick stepped forward.

'What the fuck, Har?'

Har just shrugged.

'Fuck him. Who's going to miss him? Princess?'

Princess. The word hit Robbie like a train. She felt a million miles away now — like a dream dissolving at dawn. A life forgotten. A sweeter life. A softer world.

If he survived this bloody nightmare, he swore to return to that world and never look over his shoulder again. No more Guards. No more cases. No more graves.

Below, through the heat haze and rising smoke, The Widow and The Viper's Meatheads stormed through the burning market like madmen let loose. Shouting and screaming.

And when The Widow stepped over Rej's lifeless body — without breaking stride — she drove her stiletto heel into his eye socket with a wet crunch, like stepping on a dead rat, its skull caving in with a splash of pus. She twisted her heel slowly, watching the pulp ooze.

'This cunt Alshahari's sold us out,' she hissed, her voice like nails on a blackboard — grating, cold, and full of hate.

The Viper spun on her heels, now face to face with The Red Widow — spit flying, rage boiling over, eyes wild and bloodshot, veins bulging in her neck. 'Don't you pin this on me, you bitch,' she hissed. 'That bastard's playing both sides — fed us straight to the fuckin' wolves.'

'Where the fuck is he *now*?' The Widow snarled, jerking her pistol free. Twitching. Flicking her gaze — left, right, back again. Every shadow moved. Every silence pressed in. 'He's here. Somewhere. Watching.'

The Viper's hand struck like a cobra — gun up, eyes cold as ice.

They circled each other like rabid dogs, teeth bared, twitching.

From their rooftop perch, Robbie and the others, crouched low, had their eyes locked on the carnage below.

Then they saw him.

Alshahari. Calm. Composed.

He strolled straight toward The Widow and The Viper like Christ across the water — unbothered — flanked by his Lashkar brutes, his loyal beasts, the revolver swinging low at his side.

He walked not like a man not going into battle, but like a prophet come to deliver ruin, with the smug certainty of someone who believed bullets couldn't touch him.

'They're after each other,' Robbie muttered. 'They're not after us.'

'Are you a fuckin' imbecile or what, Plod?' Mick snapped, irritated. 'They're after him. He's after them. And guess what? They're all after us. Fuckin' spastic.'

Below, The Viper's eyes caught the glint of Alshahari's ridiculous sunglasses. She shifted her aim from The Widow to his forehead and tightened her finger on the trigger.

'You sold us out!' she howled.

Alshahari didn't flinch. He strode straight towards her, raising a hand as if addressing peasants, his voice dripping with arrogance and disdain.

'Calm yourselves, ladies. We all play our parts.'

The Viper didn't answer with words.

Cold as ice, she fired. One, two, three.

All hell broke loose again.

Alshahari's Lashkars returned fire, but The Viper had already slipped away. The Widow — hysterical now — emptied round after round into them like a woman possessed.

Alshahari ran, but a bullet caught him. He crumpled to the ground, blood painting the filthy street, flesh torn and exposed.

Leaderless, his Lashkars — those still able — scattered. They were mercenaries: men without conscience, soldiers of fortune. They fought for no cause but died for good pay — soldiers in search of a war. Loyalty meant nothing. The moment their leader fell, they vanished.

'She got him,' Dick whispered, almost reverent.

'No way he survived that,' said Mick. 'No fuckin' way.'

Below, silence settled — broken only by Alshahari's coughing and spluttering. Valentina — The Red Widow — her composure fully regained, strode towards her fallen prey. He lay defenseless, dying, the pompous swagger long gone from his broken body.

She stepped over his crumpled body, heels crunching in the dirt. Alshahari was barely conscious, bleeding out, lips twitching prayers through his perfect, ivory-white teeth.

She drew a long, gleaming knife — surgical steel — and knelt beside him.

That dead stare again. Icy. Unforgiving.

'What did I tell you, you arrogant, camel-fucking whore?'

His eyes fluttered open. Blood bubbled from his mouth.

'Please... wallah... mercy... for Allah... my family —'

She leaned in close. Her voice a whisper.

'This *is* for your fucking family, pig.'

He moaned. Weakly turned his face away.

'Ya Allah... la... please... anything...'

She grabbed the edge of his blood-soaked kandura and hiked it up with disgust, then lifted his limp cock like it was a used tissue.

She scoffed. 'Is *that* all you've got?'

Zip.

One clean slice.

He jerked once, then stilled. She held the severed testicles up like an offering.

Then came the petrol. Then the match.

Fwoom.

The stench of burnt flesh rolled through the market.

She watched them burn, face blank.

'I hope they like barbecue.'

استعد للموت

Chapter 48

Florence Nightingale?

Where was happy hour now?

The boys, bloodied and broken, sat in stunned silence. Alshahari and his Lashkars were gone — that much was something. But they'd just watched another cold-blooded execution — their second in less than an hour.

These were simple men: beer, women, smokes, golf... have a laugh, take the piss. But this? This wasn't them. And it sure as hell wasn't what they'd signed up for.

Not that they'd signed up for anything.

Meanwhile, Robbie was losing a lot of blood — and fast. Dick wasn't as bad, but it was clear: if something wasn't done soon, there would be more fatalities. Some retirement party this was turning out to be.

'Right. Fuck de Luc,' Mick snapped, one twitch away from flinging Har off the roof. 'What now? That fecker's going to bleed out, and those bitches'll either starve us out or pick us off one by one the second we try to leave this fuckin' roof.'

Robbie had yet to see Har de Luc in action, but despite his own condition, he found himself quietly amused by the man's reaction to his old nemesis, 'Mild' Mick's outburst.

'Pipe down, Mick, you daft eejit. Limerick's got you all bent out of shape, boyo. Chill your head—I'll have these two patched up, and we'll be knocking back cocktails before you can say "Shamrock."'

With that, he edged over the lip of the roof once more, cupped his hands, and called out in a singsong falsetto, "Ay bacha, ay!" — the same call the street kids used to flag down rickshaws. Everyone thought he had lost it.

But, within seconds, the same skinny local boy was on the rooftop. Har began speaking to him — Rudolph surmised it was Pashto — and pointed at Robbie and Dick. The boy nodded and scampered back down the ladder.

Five minutes later, he reappeared carrying some fishing line, a safety pin, a can of kerosene, some plastic tape, and a bottle of local hooch.

Micks eyes lit up.

'Anyone got a light?' Har asked, as he laid his makeshift operating table out on the rooftop.

Robbie went from white to transparent.

No one had ever really believed Har de Luc's tales of French lineage — let alone his claims of being a skilled marksman. But now, hearing him speak Pashto, having slain Rej and gunned down three of The Widow's Meatheads with uncanny precision, the boys were beginning to wonder if there was more truth to his bullshit than they'd thought. Maybe it was time to treat this drunken ex-IT teacher with a little more respect. Could his father — Oo de Luc — really have been Surgeon-in-Chief? And could Har actually be a talented stitcher? For Robbie and Dick's sake, they certainly hoped so.

Har ran the safety pin through the flame until it blackened, then held the fishing line over it just long enough for the heat to bite. He doused both in hooch, then his hands, then handed the bottle to Robbie.

'Drink. Fast.'

Robbie took a swig and gagged. Har poured the hooch straight into the wound. Robbie bucked and screamed, the sound tearing from his throat as Mick pinned him down.

Har didn't speak — just got to work, hands steady, punching the line through torn flesh with cold, methodical precision, like he'd done it a hundred times. His eyes never left the wound.

Mick wiped his mouth, eyeing the bottle, wondering if there'd be a drop left after Dick's operation. There wasn't.

'Well, what now, Florence Nightingale?' asked Mick, irritated, thirsty, and rapidly becoming hungover.

Har's face was serious. 'We wait till nightfall, get to the van, collect the cash, and drive west. There's a crossing near Torkham — bribes should get us through. After that, we vanish.'

'And until then? I'm fuckin' parched. Unless you send that wee scrote back down the ladder to fetch me some hooch, I'm going down myself. Fuck those bitches. I'll take the consequences rather than die of thirst up here with you lot.'

Har motioned to the young lad in a language anyone could have understood, and off he scampered.

'Wee Ali has just informed me that they're holed up in the Peshawar Serena Hotel, so you won't see those high-maintenance whores around here tonight — but better wait here until dark. They'll likely have their own runners sniffing around for us.'

The sun dipped low, bleeding orange and purple across the sky. On the cracked rooftop, the boys sat in a ragged circle, hooch in hand, the market's noise a constant hum beneath them. The events of the afternoon were hours behind them, but the memories — would they ever forget this? How could they?

They drank in silence, the harsh burn of the local hooch helping dull the pain in their battered bodies. Mick, hunched in an Asian squat, glanced at each of them — weathered, traumatised faces, futures full of uncertainty.

'Where'll we go?' Mick asked softly, the gravity of the situation finally sinking in.

There'd be no more happy hour, no more Bay, no more of anything he'd worked towards over the last forty-odd years.

Fuck Har de Luc.

He'd been happy in Al Hamra, no matter what Har thought he knew. He'd been happy — and right now, he longed for his old life.

'More importantly,' said Top Shelf, still thinking clearly, 'how will we go? None of us have passports. We just upped and left on that stinking boat.'

Robbie stared at the horizon, the weight of everything he'd lose — maybe had lost already — pressing heavy on his chest.

He wanted to go home too. Ached for his homeland — for his own people, the cold, the endless rain…

He didn't belong here, not with these men.

And he fucking hated Mick.

There was no way in hell he was going to live out the rest of his days in some exiled hellhole with this crowd.

They'd already fucked his holiday — they weren't going to fuck his entire life as well.

Har smiled faintly. 'We all vanish tonight,' he said. 'Collect the cash — nearly one million each — passports, new names. No one's coming after you Robbie. I'm who they want. Go where you want. No one will find us.'

The Widow and The Viper — they were still out there somewhere, watching, waiting. Har was right, this wasn't over, but for now, that was a story for another day.

The night dragged on — seemingly endlessly — as the boys polished off their drinks and braced themselves for the journey ahead — for some, into new lives; for Robbie, trying to piece together what remained of his old one.

Friday 27th June

Chapter 49

Ali happy, we happy

As the minute hand on Har's battered watch struck twelve, shutters clattered down over the last of the open restaurants. The market was emptying out, the night drawing to an end. The boys exchanged tired, worried — but hopeful — looks. Could they really be nearing the end of this ridiculous saga?

One by one, they lowered themselves down the rickety ladder and moved stealthily through the market — the soles of their shoes sticking to the heat-softened tarmac. Trash festered in the gutters, meat rotted on hooks, and flies buzzed in thick, irritating clouds.

The bleeding had been stopped, but Robbie was hurting badly, and he knew the longer he remained in this filthy environment, the greater the risk of infection. He had to get out.

Around the corner, behind a shuttered restaurant, the van waited. It had seen better days — probably white once, now a patchwork of rust and dents. But it would have to do. Har reached into the glovebox, pulled out an old Nokia mobile and a stubby flathead screwdriver, which he rammed into the ignition. The engine spluttered, coughed, and stalled — once, twice — before reluctantly stuttering to life.

Har squinted at the scratched screen of the phone.

'The cash's been dropped at the old spice warehouse near the edge of the market. Passports too. Quick in, quick out. No fuckin' around.'

The van snaked through the narrow streets before juddering to a halt outside the dilapidated warehouse, where two armed men in dark jackets stood watch, arms folded.

Big Finn shifted in his seat. 'Locals?'

'Security,' Har said. 'They know who we are. They're expecting us.'

Before anyone could respond, Har stepped out and strolled straight up to them. He raised one palm and spoke fluently in Pashto. The men listened, nodded, and one tapped twice on the corrugated gate.

It creaked open.

Har turned to the van. 'Finn, Tappie — with me.'

Neither argued.

Beyond the reach of the dim streetlights, the warehouse was pitch-black. Still, Har walked like he knew the place like the back of his hand — because he did.

Behind them, the gate clunked shut.

Inside, a single bare bulb cast weak light over two large bags sitting alone on the packed earth floor.

An old man shuffled forward from the shadows, flanked by his own broad-shouldered muscle. Tappie and Finn did their best to mimic their unreadable, stony faces.

Har stepped toward the bags, hand outstretched — but was stopped in his tracks as both guards levelled their guns at his chest, eyes locked and unblinking.

The old man's lips curled into a grim smile. 'We want our cut.'

Har's mind raced. *They'd already had their cut*, he thought — *more than their fair share.*

He glanced at the bags. Light. Far lighter than they should be. But he'd been expecting this. These slimy fucks had no honour; they were opportunists. They'd stab you in the back for a fiver and slit your throat for less. Har was more than ready for them.

'Of course, Ali. Business is business.'

Har bent down and removed a roll of dirty banknotes from one of the bags. Ali's eyes lit up like disco balls, but just as he stretched out his grubby little hand to grab the cash, Har spun him around and snapped a blade against his throat in a flash.

The goons sprang to alert.

Har pressed the blade a little harder, drawing just a trace of blood from the old man's throat. 'Tell them to drop their weapons.'

The old man nodded his reluctant approval, and Finn and Tappie needed no further invitation. The tables had turned.

'Look, you shower of stinking, retarded Kanglus. Don't try to fuck with me,' Har said with quiet authority. 'Finn, Tappie, escort these gentlemen to wherever they have the rest of our cash.'

Tappie jabbed one of the goons in the ribs with his pistol.

'Where is it?'

The man flinched, glanced toward the back of the warehouse.

'Move,' Finn said, voice low but sharp.

They marched them past dusty pallets and sacks, the odour of old spices and rat piss thick in the air. One of the goons crouched down and pulled aside a mouldy tarpaulin. Beneath it: a heavy duffel bag.

Tappie yanked it open — packed tight with cash. Dirty, used notes, bound in bundles.

They hauled the bag over, raising small clouds of dust as they returned to the centre of the warehouse — where Har still had the old man at knife-point.

Har didn't look at the cash. His eyes were locked on Ali.

'That all of it?'

Ali gave a single, slow nod. No tricks left in him.

Har smiled.

'Good.'

Then he slit his throat.

It wasn't theatrical — just a clean, hard pull. Blood sprayed down the front of Ali's tunic as he staggered, made a wet choking sound, then dropped.

'Shoot them,' Har said, pointing at the goons.

'Jesus, Har—' Tappie said, shocked.

'Do it.'

Finn's hands trembled. He couldn't do it either.

So Har did it for them.

Two sharp shots rang out. One goon spun and crashed into a stack of boxes. The other dropped like a sack of meat.

Silence.

Tappie stared at Har. Finn looked sick.

Har wiped the blade on Ali's sleeve and picked up the bag of cash.

'Next time, just fuckin' do it.'

As the boys walked back toward the bolted door, Tappie kept glancing over his shoulder, but Har walked steady, like nothing had happened. He rapped on the door twice — same as the guards had done when they entered — and it opened.

The two guards straightened up outside, clocking the bags in the boys hands.

'That it?' one asked.

'That's it,' Har said. 'Ali said go now.'

He reached into the bag and pulled out a roll of notes.

'This for you.'

The guards paused. One took the roll, gave it a quick count. It was more than they were expecting.

'Ali happy, we happy,' he muttered.

Har gave a tight smile.

'He's not complaining — anymore.'

Tappie slid the van door open. They climbed in and shut it behind them. The engine was still running.

'Go.'

By the time the guards realised Ali wasn't answering his phone, the van was already half a mile down the road.

As the van lumbered it's way towards Torkham, Har produced a briefcase.

'You'll be needing these.'

He proceeded to hand out passports, one by one.

Rick Dublet – *Richard 'Dick' Butler*

Matt Paine – *Thomas 'Tam' Pieman*

Liam Chenquin – *Michael 'Mick' Quinn*

Sam Tristuth – *Stuart 'Rudolph' Smith*

Fergin Ioniani – *Finian 'Finn' Gerino*

Cornel Westrode – *Terrence 'Top Shelf' Woods*

Bo Riley Malone – *Robert 'Robbie' O'Malley*

Was this guy taking the piss? Robbie knew nearly every immigration officer in Dublin Airport, and there was no way he was breezing through with a name like Bo Riley Malone.

Cornel wasn't best pleased either.

The border came sooner than expected — a coil of wire, two half-asleep guards, and a checkpoint that looked like it hadn't been maintained since the Soviet war.

The guard barely looked up. Har leaned out, speaking calmly in Pashto, slipping a roll of cash through the crack in the window like it was a toll booth.

The guard took it. Didn't count it. Waved them through.

That was it.

No dramatic search. No dogs. No hassle.

Just like that, they were over. Afghanistan.

Robbie didn't ask where they were going next. Har had a plan, he always did. Tappie stared out the window in a kind of numb trance, and Finn was rattling his knuckles off the seat in front. Nobody spoke.

They drove for hours through dust and dawn. The road wound through mountains baked to bone, and the engine coughed all the way. Robbie sat in the back, leg propped up awkwardly, the makeshift bandage soaked through and stinking. Every bump in the road sent a shock up his spine. He clenched his jaw and said nothing.

The sun rose, hard and red over the hills. Somewhere past Jalalabad, they stopped for fuel and warm bottled water. Har talked to the pump attendant — a skinny lad with mirrored sunglasses and two goats tethered to the back of a Toyota. He paid in crumpled Afghanis and nodded toward the road ahead.

They didn't speak much after that.

By late afternoon they reached a grim little guesthouse on the outskirts of Kabul — cement walls, a tin roof, no questions asked. They paid in cash. The man at the desk gave them one dorm room with four bunk beds and a single ceiling fan that didn't turn.

That night, while the others slept, Robbie sat in the dark on the edge of his bed. He had nothing to pack — just the fake passport and one million dollars.

He limped down the stairs and out the back, into the stillness of Kabul at night.

No note. No sound. Just gone.

Saturday 28th June

Chapter 50

Welcome to Ireland, Mr. Malone

The immigration queue was long and hot.

He'd done his best to scrub up in the airport bathroom, but it hadn't helped much. His nose was broken, his eyes still purple-black from Mick's headbutt and the butt of Alshahari's gun. He stank. Filthy clothes, dried sweat, dried blood. No matter how hard he scrubbed, the blood was still under his fingernails.

Finally, he stepped up.

The immigration officer took the passport, scanned it, looked up.

Paused.

Robbie's heart stopped.

The officer tilted his head, a flicker of recognition passing across his face. Then he winked—barely—and stamped the passport.

'Welcome to Ireland, Mr Malone.'

Sean was waiting just beyond the barriers, clutching a coffee and looking like he'd seen a ghost.

'Jesus Christ, Robbie.'

'I know.'

'What the fuck happened to you?'

'I fell,' Robbie said.

Sean didn't push it. He just grabbed Robbie's bag and steered him towards the car.

Halfway down the M1, they had to roll the windows down—the smell coming off Robbie was too much to bear.

It had been eighteen days since Robbie had set off for the Middle East in search of sun, sand, and a bit of relaxation.

He'd certainly found the sun. And plenty of sand.

As they turned off the M50 onto the M4, heading west for Galway and Sligo, Robbie started to tell Sean about the trip: how he'd broken his nose — twice — been given two shiners, taken a gunshot wound to the leg, burnt his face and feet to cinders, shat himself on the bus to Peshawar, puked all over a taxi driver, fallen in love with a waitress, slept with a —

He decided maybe he'd keep some of the details to himself.

He told him about the guns and knives shoved in his face, the cold-blooded executions, the drinking, the floating coffin, the drugs, the dealers, the prostitutes, the corrupt cops, the lack of personal hygiene, the slave trade, the hypocrisy, the racism, the rats, the stinking streets. And the fake passport. And the million dollars.

Sean stared at him wide-eyed.

'Jesus. I thought you went to Dubai, Robbie?'

Robbie shrugged.

'I did.'

Kinnegad came and went, and the M6 finally crossed the broad, majestic Shannon. Robbie knew he was home. The call of the west had never been stronger.

The tailbacks started just as they turned onto the Dublin Road. Bumper to bumper, crawling into the city like a funeral procession. Sean rolled his eyes and drummed the steering wheel.

'You won't have missed this, Robbie,' he muttered, as a bus zipped past in the bus lane.

'Nope.'

The clouds were grey and low, dragging their bellies over the bay. A curtain of drizzle hung in the air ahead, washing the colour from the world. It was as beautiful a sight as Robbie could remember.

'A grand soft day, Sean.'

'That it is, Robbie. Grand, so it is.'

Robbie was thirsty. Not just dry-mouth thirsty—thirsty. His tongue felt like old leather. His lips were cracked and peeling. He could almost taste the pint already: cold, clean. Cream on top, bitter underneath.

They inched through Eyre Square, past students, shoppers, and lads in tracksuits shouting into phones. Robbie felt at home watching a city that barely moved, yet never stood still. He belonged here. This was home.

Sean leaned over. 'Reckon you'll make it through one?'

Robbie sniffed, coughed, nodded. 'Maybe two.'

Sean grinned and flicked on the indicator. 'Let's find you a pint then.'

Aengus had two pints waiting on the bunker before they'd even found stools.

Two pints.

Three pints.

Four pints... Same pub as always.

The usual crowd were up the back, by the market entrance, nipping in and out for fags and spliffs. No one cared.

Eddie shouted over, half-cut, slurring, 'Any craic, Robbie?'

He thought about it.

The warehouse. The cash. Har's calm expression as he slit a man's throat. The long road through the mountains. The state he was in. Princess. Elle. Rej. Har de *fucking* Luc. The look on the guard's face at the airport. Bo Riley Malone. The silence.

He took a slug. Smiled faintly.

'Not really.'

Printed in Dunstable, United Kingdom